UNDER A
BRIGHTER
SKY

BOOKS BY DIANNE HALEY

DIANNE HALEY

UNDER A BRIGHTER SKY

Bookouture

Published by Bookouture in 2022

An imprint of Storyfire Ltd.
Carmelite House
50 Victoria Embankment
London EC4Y 0DZ

www.bookouture.com

ISBN: 978-1-80314-246-3
eBook ISBN: 978-1-80314-245-6

For Mum

Whoever commands a small lifeboat that is already quite full, of limited capacity, and with an equally limited amount of provisions, while thousands of victims of a sunken ship scream to be saved, must appear hard when he cannot take everyone.

Minister of Justice and Police, Eduard von Steiger: 30 August 1942
Switzerland's policy of turning away Jews at the Swiss border

PROLOGUE

ANNE-MARIE

Annemasse, France
March, 1943

The door of the wooden outhouse crashed open, shaking the rotten frame and throwing clouds of dust into the early evening air. Silhouetted in the door, there was a slender man wearing tattered old clothes and a dark beret.

'You must leave immediately; the Nazis are searching the houses for Jews. If you stay here, you'll never reach Switzerland,' he said.

The man's voice was tense and, as he stepped into the pale light, Anne-Marie saw his lined face and the dark shadows under his eyes. He wasn't a young man, but he was fit and athletic, clearly ready to take flight at a moment's notice. He looked hunted, his gaze darting all around.

Anne-Marie's husband Pierre took a few steps towards him, saying, 'But Monsieur, we were told someone would come and get us tonight, once it was dark. Isn't it too dangerous to cross the border in the daylight?'

'Not as dangerous as staying here. I'm sorry, but someone told the Germans you're here and they're looking for you.'

Anne-Marie pulled her little daughter, Madeleine, close, her bony frame evidence of their struggles to get food since they'd left their home in Lyons.

'Will you take us to the border?' she asked, her voice cracking. Living in a state of constant fear was their reality now, never knowing if each sunrise could be their last, but somehow at this final stage of their journey, so close to safety, it felt even harder to keep herself together. If it wasn't for her children, Madeleine and Jules, she felt certain she would barely have the strength left to move another inch.

The man nodded and she grasped Pierre's arm. 'We must go, Pierre. This could be our only chance.'

In the silence that followed, Anne-Marie reached out and smoothed Jules' dark hair, trying to take away his confused frown as he stood between his parents, glancing from one to the other. She felt a heady rush of anger flow through her body and clutched both her children close to her as if she'd never let them go. They were so young and innocent, and yet they were forced to run for their lives, with no comprehension of why their world was filled with so much hatred.

'It could be now or never,' she insisted. 'We'll just have to risk the daylight. This is the only way, Pierre.'

Pierre held her glance and his tense features softened as he ran his fingers down her face in a brief caress. Then he picked up their thin leather bag, now battered and worn but containing all they could carry with them, all they had left in the world, and he walked to the door, clutching Jules' hand. Anne-Marie and Madeleine followed them.

The man who had come to help them had his hand on the door, tapping his fingers impatiently on the splintering wood, until they all gathered next to him. 'We must walk normally. If we hear a patrol coming, you must all hide until they pass. I'll get you through the barbed wire on the French side and then you'll need to run like hell across no man's land to get to Switzerland. Someone will be waiting for you there. Keep running and don't look back, whatever you hear, even if you get separated.'

They nodded and followed him outside to a world that seemed normal and at peace. Birds were singing in the trees, the scent of mimosa flowers filled the warm air, and if it weren't for the gnawing hunger in their bellies and the terror in their hearts, it would have been a pleasant spring evening. But the distant rumble of a truck coming from the centre of town hastened their steps, and Anne-Marie's heart thudded heavily in her chest.

Their world had been far from normal since the fall of Vichy France the previous year when the Germans had occupied their town and Lyons became one of the Nazis' main centres in the south. Pierre couldn't get any work, even as a legal assistant, and the money that Anne-Marie earned as a schoolteacher was all they had to live on. And then one of Pierre's former colleagues, a fellow lawyer, told them the police were rounding up Jews and their names were high up on the list, as the Nazis knew Pierre had been producing false papers for other Jews among other illicit activities. The man also said he could give them the name of someone who could get them into Switzerland, but they had to leave everything behind and escape that same night.

They already had a bag packed and had been living on the edge of a precipice since the occupation when their home, once a place of happiness and security, had suddenly become unsafe, the risk of someone beating the door down and taking them away an ever-present threat. Neighbours who'd once smiled and chatted with them on the street now crossed the road to avoid them, stopping their whispered conversations when they came close. So, like everyone who was desperately trying to escape into neutral Switzerland, they ran into the unknown, praying that they would be among the lucky ones who made it across.

Beyond the outhouse, there was no sign of the kind elderly couple who had taken them in and given them bread and cheese, risking the wrath of the Nazis if they were discovered helping Jewish refugees. Anne-Marie hesitated, wanting to thank them for their compassion, but a sharp glance from their guide made her hurry to catch up with the rest of her family.

They started to walk out of town, skirting along fields of crops that stretched into the distance. There were a few stick-like figures working in the fields, which were punctuated here and there with low farm buildings. Feeling terribly exposed in the wide-open space, Anne-Marie kept looking round at the slightest noise, and she stumbled on the rough road. Nausea was rising in her throat, caused by a combination of fear and the tiny life growing in her belly, but she smiled down at Madeleine to try to stop her dread and discomfort from infecting her daughter. She was relieved to see that Madeleine was simply glad to be in the fresh air after days of hiding inside, her blonde hair bouncing as she skipped along like any normal six-year-old, pulling her mother ahead of the others.

Suddenly, the harsh noise of a car engine ripped through the peaceful scenery and she saw a large black Mercedes turning into the road ahead of them. Anne-Marie's heart leapt into her throat and Madeleine stopped skipping, casting a look of terror up at her mother. Anne-Marie whipped round to find Pierre and Jules, but they weren't there.

She saw their ankles disappear as they scrambled over the deep verge across the road after the guide. Anne-Marie went to follow them with Madeleine, but staggered and cried out when she twisted her ankle on the rough track. Her heart sinking, she stopped when the ankle wouldn't bear her weight.

'It's too late...They've seen us,' she gasped. She glanced across at the verge where Pierre and Jules were hiding. Pierre lifted his head and she saw horror flash across his face before the guide pulled him out of sight. Anne-Marie turned back to face the car that slowed down in front of her, and pulling Madeleine close to her, she swallowed the bile rising in her throat.

The men in the car were wearing Nazi uniforms.

'Don't say a word,' she managed to hiss quietly to her daughter, as the car glided to a halt beside them.

She'd walked right into the enemy, but the enemy was smiling, eyes crinkled in sympathy. One of the officers jumped out of the car. He was the younger of the two men and had open, pleasant features, his expression full of concern. He spoke French with only a hint of a German accent.

'Madame, I saw you trip. You have hurt your ankle?'

'Yes, Monsieur, but it's nothing...'

'No, no. I can take you to the hospital. You must get someone to check it.'

He wouldn't listen to her protests and guided them into the back of the car. The door closed like the clang of a prison cell, and she flinched as the car pulled away, forcing herself to stare forward and not look behind her to where Pierre and Jules had disappeared. Would she ever see them again?

She tucked Madeleine's wispy hair behind her ear with a shaking hand, trying to act normally, glancing at the older man who was smiling at her daughter. His heavy features were lightened by a smile and his German accent was strong.

'She looks about the same age as my girl.'

Taking a deep breath, Anne-Marie forced a smile on to her face, thankful that their blonde hair had protected them for now. With her heart beating wildly, she filled her mind with desperate plans about how to escape when they got to the hospital, before they were discovered.

She couldn't allow herself to think about Pierre and Jules or her resolve would fail. It was up to her now to protect Madeleine and ensure they could one day see the rest of their family again.

ONE

VALÉRIE

Geneva, Switzerland

Valérie skidded her bicycle to a stop in the Rue de Savoie, her way blocked by two men lounging against the door of the address she'd been given, their grey coats grubby and dishevelled. Catching her breath, she glanced back towards the Avenue de la Gare Des Eaux-Vives, but none of the early-morning Saturday commuters had followed her into the quiet street. The few figures she could see in the mist were all walking briskly towards the centre of town, staring straight ahead and minding their own business. No one looked at the narrow street with its closed-down shops and shuttered apartment windows.

'Mademoiselle, why are you in such a hurry?'

She looked beyond them for some means of escape, shivering in the chill despite her new coat, the tall buildings on either side keeping this part of town cold and dull even though the spring sun would soon come up over the city. The old garage Jean had chosen for their meeting place was only a few yards away but felt as unattainable as the stars. She swallowed hard and tried to keep her voice steady.

'Messieurs, I will be late for work.'

They didn't move out of the way when she pushed her bike in their direction and she stopped, her foot poised on the pedal. They were just having a bit of fun, she told herself, making fun of a silly young girl who'd been foolish enough to go out alone in this part of town. But the predatory look in the men's eyes belied their casual smiles. Her breath came in short gasps and her heart slammed against her chest.

'What have you got in there?' said the younger man, his Swiss-German accent echoing around the quiet street. He came closer and reached for the packages in her basket. He was only a teenager, but his beady eyes had a mean, avaricious look.

Valérie pulled her bicycle back a few inches.

'Just watch parts,' she said, trying to keep her voice from shaking.

The man's bony hand shot out and jerked the basket towards him so roughly that it almost pulled her off her feet. He leaned forward, his thin face close enough for her to smell his sour breath.

'Why are you so keen to get away? What are you hiding in there?'

The other man, older and heavier, was suddenly behind her and grasped her arm in an iron grip.

'Just show us what you have in the basket and we might let you go...'

She opened her mouth to scream, but his hand clamped roughly over her mouth so the only sound she could make was a strangled cry. Valérie felt a trickle of sweat run down her back. An image of her fiancé Philippe flashed into her mind, his presence and his love like a talisman. But Philippe wasn't here to help her now. She could hardly breathe and pushed down the wave of panic that dulled her instinct to fight back. In the months she had spent carrying messages for the Resistance among the watch part packages she delivered for her father, a local watchmaker, she had avoided trouble and deflected any awkward questions. And now this. Attacked by thugs who were only interested in what they could steal, who would take anything of value and throw her into the gutter. Or maybe they were Nazi sympathisers who knew what she was up to and would beat her up or worse; at the very least, they would add her name to the list of those helping the French Resistance, ready to be handed over to the Nazis when they invaded Switzerland. She was well aware of just how dangerous such men could be, having already lost more than one Resistance friend at their hands.

Valérie struggled against the man's iron grip, anger at the thought of her courageous murdered friends giving her a burst of extra strength. The letters hidden among her father's packages carried information about Jewish refugees escaping across the border, safe houses and meeting points. If these men got their hands on them, innocent lives could be lost and not just her own. She wasn't going to give those people up without putting up a fight. Not if she could help it.

The man's grip loosened as his younger compatriot leaned forward to pick up a package from her basket. Seizing her chance, she twisted round in his grasp. Her fingers groped for the knife stuck into her belt and closed over the hilt, her instinct to protect the refugees driving her to do something she never thought she would be capable of. She pulled the knife free and turned to plunge it into his body.

'Halt. What is going on here?'

They spun round to see a short, slim man standing at the end of the street. He was dressed in workmen's clothes, but his calm control of the situation was in stark contrast to the scruffy men he addressed. His cropped fair hair shone in the early morning light and his sharp grey eyes took in the scene.

'We didn't mean any harm,' said the older man deferentially, taking a step away from Valérie.

Her bike crashed to the ground, the contents of the basket scattering across the pavement. Coming to her senses, Valérie slid the knife back into her belt before they could see it, then bent down to gather the small packages and letters. By the time she'd put them safely back into the basket and picked up her bike, the two men had left the street and the fair-haired man was standing in front of her. He was only a few centimetres taller than her, but he made up for his lack of height by the intensity of his stare, his good looks hardly marred by the thin white scar below his left eye that stretched along his cheekbone. He bowed briefly, and when he lifted his head, he smiled and his eyes were warm and apologetic.

'I hope you're all right, Mademoiselle. I'm glad I was able to help.'

Her heart was beating so fast that she could only fix her gaze on his even features and mumble an inaudible reply, but he seemed satisfied.

'You are unharmed, I hope?'

'Yes, I'm all right. Thank you.'

'And you have all your belongings?'

She glanced at her basket. 'Yes, I think so.'

His smile widened. 'Maybe it would be better if you did not walk alone in this area of town.'

'Yes, I'll be more careful in future.'

He nodded again and swung around, disappearing at the end of the street as quickly as he'd appeared. She leaned on her bike and wiped her brow with a shaking hand. A few seconds later and she'd have stabbed one of them with Simone's knife. Simone would have been proud of her if she had. The brave French Resistance fighter she once knew wouldn't have hesitated to use it to protect the innocent people fleeing from the Nazis. Valérie felt suddenly sick and took a couple of deep breaths to try to conquer the nausea, tempted to leave the grimy, shadow-filled street and go straight back home. But she still had a job to do. The Jewish refugees she was helping didn't give up. They didn't have any choice.

When she felt steadier, Valérie pushed her bike into the alley running under the block and knocked twice on the door. It led into a disused car workshop and she glanced through to the courtyard at the back of the building, imagining what must once have been a busy place, full of cars waiting for attention and mechanics milling around in oil-stained overalls. She knocked more loudly and waited, holding her breath and straining to hear any noise inside, but there was no sound of footsteps or of the door being unlocked.

Where was Jean? The arrangement was for her to knock twice, and her Resistance contact would come to the door. Something must have gone wrong. Valérie turned the handle and pushed the heavy metal door with all her strength. Glancing behind her again to check the street was empty, she went inside, dragging the bike behind her and closing the door with a dull bang. She leaned her forehead against the metal of the door panel and waited for her breathing to get back to normal, trying to block out the thought of how close she'd come to her messages being discovered.

A heavy thud behind her shattered the calm and she spun around, staring blindly into the darkness.

'Who's there?'

Fearing another attack, her heart racing furiously again, she groped for her knife and pulled it out. But she couldn't make out anything moving in the darkness and blinked furiously to try to get her eyes used to the gloom. Slowly, an outline of cabinets appeared to her left, next to two cars in the middle of the shed perched on bricks instead of wheels, their bodywork dented and paintwork mottled with rust. A small table and a few chairs were set out in the space to her right in front of open shelves, which were now empty but must have once been full of spare car parts. She looked up and saw a metal walkway circling the building at first-floor height, with stairs leading down to the ground.

A torch beam snaked across the shadows at the back of the workshop and past the staircase before someone lit an oil lamp, the dull glow illuminating the table and chairs. Jean, the head of the Resistance cell Valérie worked for, walked briskly out of the darkness towards her and sat down at the table.

'I was getting worried about you, is everything okay? You look shaken.'

Valérie lowered her arm and put the knife away, then sat opposite him.

'I'm okay, sorry I'm late. Why didn't you open the door?'

'I wanted to check it was you. Someone was following me.'

Valérie took a brown envelope out of her pocket with shaking fingers and placed it on the table. Jean didn't look down but continued to stare at her, his even features expressionless, but his dark brown eyes full of sympathy. 'You're shaking, Valérie. What's going on?'

'It's nothing. I ran into some thugs in the street. They wanted to see what I was carrying, they probably just wanted to intimidate me. But they didn't see anything, it's all okay.'

'Did they follow you here?'

'No. They were scared away by another man.'

He frowned. 'What did he look like?'

'Not very tall, blond. The others seemed almost afraid of him. They were Swiss-German but he sounded like he was from here.'

Jean watched her thoughtfully for a few seconds, then sighed and picked up the envelope.

'It's all in there,' she told him. 'The cash you asked for.'

He was counting out the notes slowly, as he always did, and she bit her lip, holding back her exasperation. Why did he have to check it was all there? If Henry Grant trusted her, wasn't that good enough? Henry was the Special Operations Executive contact in Geneva, part of the British organisation funding the French Resistance and organising espionage and sabotage against the Axis powers. He had vouched for Valérie personally when she began working for the Resistance.

But then, she didn't fully trust Jean either, this PE instructor who came across the border under the nose of the German border guards. He seemed to be only ever truly comfortable with his French compatriots and she wondered what he really thought of her. She was Swiss, her country wasn't occupied, so how could she be a true comrade? She could almost hear him saying it.

Jean's voice cut through her thoughts. 'We need you to hide some refugees. It's a family, we tried to get all four of them across but only succeeded with two. We hid them overnight and will be taking them into the city later today.'

'Of course, whatever I can do. Where shall I meet them, and when?'

'Cathédrale St-Pierre at four.'

'The usual place?'

He nodded. 'Sébastien will take them there.'

Sébastien was a young railway worker who lived in the farm next to some land that had been owned for generations by the family of Valérie's friend Marianne. Tall, dark-haired and thick-set, his skin tanned from working outside, he took the refugees, frightened and exhausted, into Geneva and handed them over to Valérie, often in the cathedral at the centre of the old town. His dependable bulk and practical approach seemed to fill his charges with quiet confidence, and she had grown to rely on his calm good sense.

'Marianne said that the Germans are strengthening the security at the border. She heard them discussing it on a call,' Valérie told Jean as he continued to flick through the money.

He glanced up at her, his dark eyes bright in his weather-beaten face. 'Marianne's back at work in the telephone exchange?'

'Yes, she's feeling a little better now.'

Valérie fell silent, unable to express to this cool and abrupt man how worried she'd been about her friend, how worried they'd all been. The shock of losing Marianne's brother Emile a few months ago had hit Marianne so hard that Valérie had wondered whether she'd ever be able to go back to work on a regular basis. It was Emile who had first brought Valérie into the Resistance. He'd been like a brother to Valérie too and she missed his courage and his kindness, often imagining she had caught sight of his thin frame and loping gate in a crowd before she had to tell herself he was gone, and she'd never see his smile again.

After Emile's death, the SOE had been scouting round for a replacement for Marianne to ensure that the flow of intelligence from the telephone exchange was not interrupted, but finally she began to miss less days. She still avoided the Café de Paris, though, where Valérie and her friends all congregated, retreating home to her family farmhouse on the outskirts of the city at the end of the days she did get to work.

A knock on the door broke the uneasy silence and Jean jumped up to open it to a fresh-faced youth, hardly out of his teens but already stunningly good-looking. He walked confidently into the garage and nodded at Valérie. His clothes were old and faded, but he still managed to appear stylish, the worn leather jacket fitting his slim figure like a glove and a scarf jauntily tied round his neck.

'This is François. He'll be your contact from now on – I've been called away.'

No one had told her about her contact changing. Valérie smiled at him tentatively and then looked at Jean. 'Where are you going?'

She knew she shouldn't ask any questions but couldn't stop herself. To her surprise, he gave her an answer.

'I'm needed on the Glières Plateau. The Maquis operating in that area have lost too many fighters.'

The mountainous area in the Haute-Savoie area of France was difficult to access and therefore an important place for young people to escape the clutches of the French Milice, which was created to execute members of the Resistance.

'We shouldn't stay here for too long,' said Jean. 'I think this area is being watched. You two could meet in the Café de Paris on the Place du Bourg-de-Four. It's more public, so less suspicious.'

Valérie glanced over her shoulder, her skin prickling at the thought of someone lurking in the shadows outside, then gave her thick auburn curls a shake. She couldn't start imagining dangers, the real ones were bad enough.

Jean took a pistol out of his pocket and handed it to her. 'You should take this.'

She took the ugly-looking weapon from him and turned it over in her hand, checking whether it was loaded.

'I won't insult you by asking you whether you know how to use it.'

Jean had never acknowledged she was an expert shot. Like most Swiss, she still practised regularly, ready like the rest of the population to take up arms in the event of a German invasion. Valérie pulled a handkerchief out of her pocket and wrapped the pistol in the clean linen, before hiding it beneath the packages in her basket.

Jean turned to François. 'You should go now. Once I've assessed the situation on the plateau, I'll be in touch to tell you what I need.'

They hesitated briefly and then the two men embraced.

'A bientôt, mon petit,' Jean murmured.

Valérie had never seen Jean display so much emotion

before. He pulled away from François with an effort, shook her hand briefly, then walked away from them, avoiding her gaze. She picked up her bike and followed François outside.

As she followed him, Valérie's mind went to the refugees she had been instructed to meet. Jean said they were a family of four, and only two of them had made it across. What had happened to the others? Had they been captured by the Nazis or were they still being hunted in France? How desperate and afraid they must be feeling, torn between two countries. Crossing the border was incredibly dangerous, and so many did not make it over.

Her nerves still frayed from her encounter with the men in the street, Valérie forced herself to think about the much greater danger those people were in. She knew she had to keep going for them. No matter what.

TWO
VALÉRIE

They walked back to Geneva's old town in silence, past the wood-panelled Eaux-Vives station building and across the main boulevards, waiting for the trams to pass before climbing up the cobbled street to the Place du Bourg-de-Four. As she climbed the steep hill, Valérie lifted her face towards the sunshine, filling her lungs with the sweet air. François sauntered along next to her, hands in his pockets and beret perched on the back of his head, as if he hadn't a care in the world. He seemed even younger outside in the daylight than he had in the dingy work-shop and grinned at her when she looked across at him. She smiled in response, his charm catching her unawares.

'How old are you?' she asked.

'Nineteen.' His grin widened. 'Well, almost nineteen.'

'How long have you known Jean?'

'All my life, he's my cousin. He's changed a lot since the war. He's always been the responsible one, but he used to be light-hearted too, always joking around. He's seen some awful stuff in these last few years, lost people I know he cared a lot about. So, he keeps his feelings hidden away now most of the time. But he's the best man I know.' He nodded his head. 'And me, I can fix anything. If you have a machine that's broken, I'm your man.'

She felt a weight lift from her shoulders. Jean had been the head of the Resistance unit since she'd first started working for them and had always been a taciturn and suspicious character to deal with. It seemed that it wasn't just her who thought that, and his young cousin seemed an altogether more straightforward prospect. She liked him immediately, and she knew Philippe would too.

They emerged on to the Place du Bourg-de-Four, one of the oldest squares in Geneva, and ahead of them Valérie saw her friend Geraldine wiping the tables outside the Café de Paris, her blonde wavy hair glinting in the sunlight. Her yellow dress created a splash of brilliant colour as she sashayed between the tables. Geraldine always seemed like sunshine breaking through the clouds.

On the other side of the square, Bernard was unloading grocery supplies from his father's old van in front of the shop, lifting heavy boxes as if they hardly weighed anything, his stocky frame hardly straining. She'd known Bernard from when they were small, but he usually kept himself apart and through the war had traded with all sorts, including giving information to the SOE. He stopped to wipe his brow and watched Geraldine flirting with a burly delivery man, before shaking his head and stalking into the shop. Poor Bernard. Valérie was sure he'd never said anything to Geraldine, but he clearly had feelings for her.

They stopped across the square from the café, and François' dark eyes glanced around at the row of shops along the street at the side of the open space, and the women queuing outside the food shops with their empty baskets.

'We'll meet in there?' he asked, pointing at the café.

'Yes. I pass by here most days around five o'clock. If there's a problem, just leave me a message with the woman in the yellow dress. That's Geraldine, she's my friend and her father owns the café. You can trust her, she means well, but she can be a little careless so don't tell her too much.

'I'm looking forward to meeting her.'

He flashed another grin and Valérie suppressed a sigh. Geraldine wouldn't be able to resist that smile, despite all her other admirers. She kept them apart with a skill that was both instinctive and effective. Valérie knew that it was her way of taking her mind off the war in Europe and she also knew that while Geraldine could appear flighty, if Valérie ever needed something, she would be the first to offer it.

Suddenly, a harsh shout ripped through the air. Valérie and François turned to the noise and saw a man career around the corner into the square and swerve to avoid crashing into Bernard, who dropped the box he was carrying in the middle of the pavement.

The man jumped over the box and landed clumsily in the road, scrabbling to keep his balance on the uneven cobbles. He looked behind him as three pursuers erupted into the square behind him, then turned down the hill again, picking up speed to get away.

He was heading straight towards Valérie and she stared at his bearded face as if frozen in time. She felt François hesitate for a split second beside her, then he pulled her out of the way at the last moment. The sudden movement arrested the man's flight and he stopped in front of her, chest heaving below his faded shirt and jacket, the staring eyes darting around to see his best route of escape. Then he was gone, hurtling down the cobbled street towards the lake, still chased by the other men.

She recognised him. He was the man who had hurried swiftly away from the platform after her old friend and Resistance comrade Emile had fallen on to the tramlines, a hand pushing him over the edge. She'd seen it all.

'Are you all right? You look like you've seen a ghost.'

François' concerned face hovered a few inches away and Valérie clutched his arm. 'Have you seen him before? The man they were chasing?'

'No, I've never seen him before.'

Around them, everyone went back to their business, forgetting in an instant the drama they'd witnessed.

'Another thief, I expect,' grumbled an old woman standing near Valérie, shaking her head, arms crossed over her chest. 'Coming across the border and stealing our food... as if we didn't need it to feed our own children.'

'Well, if they catch him, he'll be sent right back,' replied her friend in a softer voice. 'He was terrified, poor soul.'

On the other side of the square, two Swiss police officers came out of the station down from the Café de Paris, looking curiously around to see what the commotion was about. The fair-haired man who'd rescued her that morning strolled up to them and engaged them in conversation, gesturing down the hill, hands casually in the pockets of his worn trousers. She couldn't hear what they were saying, but it was obvious from their conversation that he was asking what was going on. Surprised to see him again so soon, she wondered who he was and what he was doing in Geneva.

Valérie felt her fingernails digging into her palms. She had been searching for that bearded man ever since she'd seen Emile die, scanning every face she saw in case he appeared, desperate to find out the truth about who had killed her friend. Emile knew someone in the Resistance was betraying them and after several refugee children in his care were shot dead at the border, he was determined to find the traitor. But whoever it was had got to him first, through that man. And Valérie knew that that same traitor was continuing to endanger the lives of countless refugees, thwarting the efforts of the Resistance at every turn. With every fibre of her being, she hated collaborators for what they did to her friend and to those poor people, and what they would do to so many more if they had the chance.

After her testimony, the police said they had tried to find the man, but they had failed. The case was still open, but she knew they'd stopped searching and had never really seemed to believe her story that Emile was pushed. She had to act fast, before she lost him again.

'Where are you going? I thought you were going to introduce me to your friend.' François let go of her arm as she reached for her bike.

'There's someone I have to see.'

She saw Geraldine hurrying to them, and she shouted across at her. 'Sorry, I must go. I'll come over later.'

François was forgotten, and Valérie's heart was thumping with excitement as she pedalled through the streets. Not only was that man Emile's killer, but she felt sure he could also unlock the identity of the traitor in the Resistance. For Emile's sake, and for the sake of every innocent person trying to escape across the border and trusting the Resistance to keep them safe, she had to find him.

THREE

VALÉRIE

Valérie cycled down from the old town to the Place de Bel-Air and crossed the wide junction before the Rue des Moulins, passing people going purposefully about their business, official cars and trams converging on to the square from all directions, engines growling through the broad boulevards. She crossed to the north bank of the river and went into the Rue des Etuves, leading to the Place De-Grenus, a peaceful residential square with grand town houses split into stylish apartments.

She rang one of the bells next to a familiar wooden double door and waited, staring through the thick glass panels and absentmindedly playing with her engagement ring that she wore on a gold chain round her neck. It was slightly too large for her, so she'd decided to wear it like that to keep it safe until it was fixed, and she grasped it tightly, relieved that the men who had confronted her that morning hadn't seen it. She missed Philippe so badly. They'd agreed to wait a little while to get married, because they would have to be apart anyway with him being away in the army, and she wasn't sure she could feel truly happy with so much misery around them. But she wished sometimes they'd just gone ahead. Getting married to him would have been a beacon of joy in such dark times, for them and for their families.

She stood a few steps back and looked up at the first-floor window to see if Henry was moving around behind the curtain. Tapping her foot impatiently on the ground, she glanced up and down the street. He might not even be here. He could be in the manor house at the side of Lac Léman, which was also used by the SOE. But lately, since she'd agreed to provide information from the Resistance for the SOE and find out who was betraying them, they usually met here.

Sighing with frustration, she hauled her bike away from the wall and headed up the street, oblivious of the people she passed along the way.

'Valérie... wait.'

She turned to see Henry run the last few steps towards her, his long raincoat billowing out behind him in the warm breeze and his dark hair flopping over his brow. He caught the handlebar of her bicycle as it lurched to the side and steadied her.

'Watch out, you're going to topple over.'

He clasped her in his other arm and held her for a moment until her feet were firmly on the ground.

'I'm all right now,' she muttered into the air between them. 'Henry, I need to speak to you.'

He frowned and she saw the lines deepen on his face as he pushed the hair back from his brow. 'I have news for you too. You'd better come inside.'

She followed him into the grand marble hall and waited as he picked up some letters from the table just inside the door. He walked past the ornate brass lift nestled in the curve of the grand stairway and pointed to the alcove on the other side of the hall. 'You can leave your bike there.'

Then he ran up the stairs two at a time, and she leaned her

bike against the wall and followed him, arriving on the first-floor landing as he pushed open the front door.

She pulled off her coat and sat in the lounge while he made tea. There were no photographs, no personal belongings left on shelves or tables, and the doors to the other rooms were firmly closed. She wrinkled her nose. As usual, the place smelt dusty and stale, as if it had been unoccupied or uncleaned for months.

Henry came back with a tray and poured the tea, handing her a cup. He seemed thinner than before, the deeper lines on his forehead making him more haunted than the man she'd first met. They'd all been worn down by the grim news coming from across Europe, and from what was happening only a few kilometres away in France where Jewish families were being rounded up and transported to concentration camps. The newspapers were full of it and news spread fast across the border. It seemed that however hardened he was, even Henry wasn't immune to what was happening around them.

She put the cup down, unable to keep silent any longer. 'I saw the man who pushed Emile in front of the tram. Today... in the Place du Bourg-de-Four. Some men were chasing him.'

His hand paused in mid-air, cup poised. 'Today? Are you sure?'

'Yes, I'm sure. I'd know him anywhere. It was definitely the man I saw that day.'

'Did he see you?'

'He looked right at me... actually he almost knocked me over. I had to tell you right away; you said you'd help me find him.'

'Valérie, I told you the last time you asked me that the police tried to identify the man you saw, but they had too little to go on.'

'Well, they can search again. I can give them a better description now and other people saw him.'

'The police have closed the case. They don't have the manpower to start looking again.'

'But the last time I saw Emile he said he knew who the traitor was, and he was going to confront them. I'm certain the traitor got this man to kill him to protect their identity.' Her voice was loud in the quiet space.

He shook his head. 'We don't know that for sure.'

She blinked back tears, unable to forget Emile's expression of terror, the hand pressed against his jacket and his mouth opening in a final scream. She even dreamed about it, reliving the horror repeatedly when she sought the oblivion of sleep. 'Look, I know now that the man who did it is still in Geneva. I'm sure he knows who the traitor is, the person who is endangering every refugee we try to help.' She knew she sounded emotional, and she was perilously close to tears, but she didn't care any longer.

Henry continued to drink his tea and didn't reply.

'I thought you would do something, that you would help me,' she insisted, her voice raising slightly.

She looked for any sign of him unbending, but there was none. He hardly seemed to hear her, his mind brooding on something else.

Had he just been manipulating her all this time? When she took Emile's place, helping the refugees get to safe houses in Switzerland, Henry had led her to believe he would help her find who killed Emile, in return for her investigating the traitor in the Resistance and reporting back to him. Philippe had always warned her not to trust him, and perhaps he'd been right. She'd been flattered at the thought that a real English spy might want her help, and Henry always seemed so charming and trustworthy. But he clearly thought what happened with Emile had nothing to do with the traitor, so he wasn't interested in investigating his death.

She took a sip of her tea and grimaced, the perfumed earl grey tasting bitter.

'Valérie, I'm concerned that this whole thing about Emile could be distracting you from what I've asked you to do. Someone is still passing information to the Germans on Resistance operations and we're losing more refugees and resistance fighters than ever before. The police have already investigated Emile's death and can't afford to spend any more time on it. You need to let it go.' He paused and then carried on. 'Three Resistance fighters were seized by the Nazis two nights ago in Annemasse. Their bodies were found this morning, dumped on waste ground outside the town.'

She couldn't drag her eyes from his face, the horror of his words filling her mind.

'They were beaten to death. The Germans used anything they could find... spades, wooden clubs, whatever they could get their hands on. They tossed the weapons to the side when they'd finished and left the bodies to rot.'

She caught her breath and clutched the arm of the sofa, feeling sick, wishing he would stop.

'One woman and two men. Someone had informed on them, told the authorities they were meeting a group of refugees. Someone connected with the Resistance. All the refugees were shot. I know I said I would find out who killed Emile that day, but you must understand that my priority is to identify the traitor in the Resistance before we lose even more people. I honestly think searching for this man you think you saw that day is just a wild goose chase.'

'How do you know someone gave the information to the Germans?'

'Because they were waiting for them. It was a new meeting place, only agreed a few hours beforehand, and the Resistance were ambushed as they arrived. One of our agents was on his way there and saw everything – he was lucky to escape in time.

It's why all our meeting places are being changed. We think the Germans are picking them off, one by one. They seem to be ahead of us all the time. We're going to lose more refugees if we can't find out who's behind it. And it's not just the Resistance and the refugees at risk, but my agents too.'

He bent his head down and ran his fingers through his dark, wavy hair. Valérie had never seen him like this before. She was about to speak when he raised his hand and lifted his head.

'I appreciate that you think you've seen the man who pushed Emile. I'll look into it and speak to the police again. But it could be like searching for a needle in a haystack, and my priority right now is to find out who Emile suspected and do it quickly. I have to find out if he confided in anyone before he died, and I need you to help me with that.'

Valérie nodded, and they sat in silence for a little while. Sipping her tea, she thought again about the events of the day. 'I saw a short fair-haired man twice today. I'd never seen him before, but he got me out of a difficult situation when two men were bothering me. He was...' She paused as she remembered the presence of the man, trying to convey the strong impression he'd made. 'He appeared ordinary, wasn't very tall, but he seemed so intense and in control of the situation, as if he was used to being in charge. He had a magnetic quality; when he focused on you, he captured your complete attention. He had a scar under his left eye.'

Henry leaned forward, immediately alert. 'That sounds to me like a German called Schneider. I know all about him.'

'He spoke French without an accent.'

'He speaks French like a native. We think he's been operating undercover in France for years, infiltrating Resistance networks. He's now squeezing his contacts hard, and we think he may be behind the recent spate of attacks in Annemasse.'

'He was wandering round Geneva like he belonged here.'

'That's the way he operates, on the margins, picking up

information from everyone he speaks to. He knows the French Resistance have powerful contacts here in Geneva. Anyway, if it's him, you need to keep out of his way.'

'Fine. But Henry, what can I do to find the traitor? I'm at a loss. I've been trying to find out information, I'm keeping an eye out for anything suspicious. But the problem is I don't even know everyone involved in our network myself.'

Her fingers were twisting the strap of her satchel and he reached out and stopped them. 'Find out who else Emile worked with, who else gave him information. I have people in France asking the same questions of their contacts. Between us, we'll have to get to the truth.' His hand tightened on her fingers. 'We have to try.'

Valérie held his gaze, her frustration ebbing away at the raw emotion in his voice. 'Did you know Jean was leaving, that he's going to help the Maquis?'

He took away his hand and shrugged. 'No one told me formally, but I'm not surprised. The Maquis in the Haute-Savoie have lost some of their most experienced fighters in the last few months. We can provide funding and weapons, but they need reinforcements first.'

'I know he'll do anything for the Resistance, but I'm not sure Jean trusts me.'

'If it helps at all, I don't think Jean trusts any Swiss, neither you nor Emile, none of the passeurs he works with. And remember, the traitor might not be someone in France. The leak could come from Switzerland, from someone working with the French Resistance or who has dealings with them.' Henry sighed. 'Anyway, my immediate priority is to get an English agent safely away once he crosses the border, before the Gestapo agents in Geneva find him. He had a narrow escape the other night. They knew he was directing drops of supplies into central France and helping to arm the Resistance. They even knew his code name.'

Henry bent down, pulled out an envelope from his raincoat pocket and handed it over to her. 'More orders for your father.'

The watch mechanisms Albert Hallez supplied to Henry's business concealed a supply of jewel bearings used in Allied weapon sighting systems.

The humour glinted in his eyes. 'We need to justify our investment in his new watch workshop.'

She managed a weak smile in return. 'It's fully equipped now. He's already planning the grand reopening reception.'

He nodded. 'That's important. Your father needs to demonstrate that he still supplies watch mechanisms to all his old customers and even favours his German contacts. If the authorities ever suspected how much he does for us, they'd close him down.'

'Too scared of annoying their Nazi friends,' she spat.

The rumours of a possible German invasion were still circulating more strongly than ever, and everyone knew that any firm evidence of the Swiss assisting the Allies could tip the fragile balance and change Hitler's irritation at Swiss independence to a desire for revenge.

Valérie put the envelope at the bottom of her satchel.

'Tell Albert that there are different instructions for the parts once they're ready,' said Henry. 'All the details are in there. This is an important assignment, and we don't want it to be intercepted on the way.'

She glanced up at him. 'Do you think someone suspects he's supplying more than simple watch mechanisms?'

'Possibly. We haven't forgotten that the German consulate was keeping a close eye on him last year. They might still be doing so.' Henry stood up. 'It's just our usual precautions. Keeps everyone safe.'

Valérie picked up her satchel and followed him to the door. It was vital to keep her father's real work for the SOE hidden and if their neighbours believed he favoured his German customers, so much the better. Not so long ago, she had been furious at her father's willingness to work with Germans and supply them with watch parts even while the war raged all around them and they could be invaded at any point. But at least she knew the truth now and understood where his allegiance truly lay. She could help protect him.

'When my agent gets across the border, I'm going to take him here, and I may need you to bring him some food until I can get him out of Geneva. He's called Tom.'

Soon afterwards, Valérie left Henry's apartment and pushed her bike in the direction of the Rue du Mont-Blanc, brooding on their conversation, hardly aware of the queues of morning shoppers.

Despite the warmth of the March sunshine, she felt cold to her bones when she thought about the murdered refugees and Resistance fighters, the fear they must have felt in their final moments. She could not comprehend the hatred the Germans harboured towards them, how they could treat human beings with such abject cruelty.

Since she'd started working for the Resistance, Valérie had learned that Gestapo operatives were everywhere, and there were many Swiss people who despised people in the Resistance too, for helping more refugees to come into their country. Her work seemed to grow more dangerous by the day, but every time she ferried a frightened refugee child into a safe house, she knew it was worth it. It wasn't so long ago that all her fears had been about Philippe, worrying about his safety in the army with an invasion looming, afraid she'd never see him again. She carried a heavy fear for them both now, but she knew neither of them would have it any other way. They would do anything for their country, and anything to protect more people from ending up in the concentration camps everyone knew existed.

And she'd learned another thing from her meeting with Henry. No one was going to get justice for Emile unless she did, and nobody was going to investigate the lead she had found, that she was sure could take her straight to the traitor. She didn't trust Henry at all when he said he'd look into it, he'd been so dismissive. He had made her feel ashamed about pushing him to investigate one person's death when he had such important work to do for the war effort. But Valérie was certain that if she could find and talk to that man, she would know who was betraying them all.

FOUR

VALÉRIE

Just before four o'clock, Valérie walked towards the cathedral, clutching her basket and breathing deeply to calm her racing heart. It wasn't unusual for her to meet refugees during daylight; indeed, it could be safer, but she always felt nervous without the cover of darkness. She told herself that they would melt into the crowd visiting the church, pretending to be friends greeting one another.

When she emerged into the square her confident step faltered as she saw the bulky figure of a local policeman speaking to one of the cathedral clerics on the steps leading to the main door. The cleric was an older man, short and round with snowy white hair, someone she'd known from childhood. She stopped and sat on the low wall at the edge of the square, then breathed a sigh of relief when she saw the policeman shake the cleric's hand and leave in the opposite direction.

Nicolas Cherix, Philippe's father, was second in command at the police station for the old town and often turned a blind eye to his fellow citizens' attempts to help desperate refugees escape from France, despite his public stance of refusing to take sides. But there were many Swiss police officers who saw it as their duty to adhere strictly to the law forbidding citizens to get involved in the war raging around them.

Cascading notes from the bell at the top of the cathedral swept over the square as she walked quickly to the pillars lining the main entrance and up the flight of steps. The cleric smiled at her, his whole face lighting up.

'Valérie, my dear. How are you? And how is your father?'

'We're well, Monsieur. Thank you.'

He studied her expression. 'Is anything the matter?'

'No, no. I just wanted to come in for a few minutes.'

'Of course. God's house is always open to his children.'

She heard a commotion from the other side of the square and saw the policeman come back, accompanied by two other men. They stopped and surveyed the square, standing between her and the safe house. Had someone tipped them off about the escaped Jews?

'I'm sorry Monsieur, I'm in a hurry.'

The old man bowed and opened the door for her to enter and she went inside the cathedral and looked at the last pew. A young man and a small boy were sitting on the bench, their backs rigid. A movement at the end of the pew caught her eye and Sébastien stood up and turned towards her. She walked quickly to him.

'This is Pierre and his son, Jules,' he whispered, then shook her hand and walked past her to the door. Valérie took his seat, watching as he drew back to let a group of worshippers enter before he disappeared. She felt the man next to her shudder at the loss of Sébastien's familiar presence and she placed her hand on his arm to try to reassure him. He was so tense and thin, his other arm wrapped around his son's shoulders.

More people were coming in as the afternoon service was about to start. Valérie looked around to see if the policeman was there but couldn't see him. She didn't want to let Pierre and

Jules know how much danger they could be in, but if they didn't get out quickly, they'd be trapped.

There was a door at the side of the cathedral. It was their best hope.

Before she could move, a soft voice whispered in her ear from behind her. 'You need to follow me now. Don't worry, you can trust me.'

She grasped Pierre's arm and twisted out of her seat to follow the cleric, walking along the pews and up the aisle at the side of the cathedral. Pierre stuck close behind her, only pausing to lift Jules up into his arms. The little boy must have been about seven years old, but he was thin and pale, and Pierre swung him up easily. Jules hid his face in his father's shoulder, his small hand clutching on to his collar.

They turned left towards the door, and she breathed a sigh of relief, knowing they were out of sight of the main entrance. The cleric carefully unlocked the bolts, making no noise, and opened the door a few inches so they could squeeze through.

'Turn right up the passage and go through the gate at the end. You'll avoid the police if you go that way.'

'Thank you, Monsieur,' she whispered.

'Go carefully, my child.'

He closed the door silently behind them.

To her great relief, the narrow lane running along the side of the cathedral was empty and Valérie spoke gently to Pierre and Jules. 'Don't worry, we should be safe now. Just follow me and walk slowly. We aren't far from the safe house.'

At the end of the lane, they emerged into the light of the late afternoon, and she led them towards the old bookshop she now used as a safe house, which was just a few streets away.

Valérie glanced at them, a wave of pity washing over her when she saw the fear in Pierre's face. Jules was gazing at her from his father's arms, his eyes shining with curiosity under the dark locks of hair falling over his forehead. She took Pierre's arm. 'We should pretend to be a family. No one will look twice at us.'

Pierre nodded and gave her a small smile, but his narrow face was pale, his brown eyes wide above the shadows that betrayed his exhaustion.

They turned into the street and Valérie saw a group of youths standing in front of the narrow alley next to the book-shop. Their way into the safe house was blocked and her heart sank. They would never get past without making a scene, which was the last thing they needed right now.

But thankfully, as they walked slowly towards them, the young people began to move away and soon their way was clear.

'Don't be afraid. I just need you to go into the passage next to this bookshop. Watch you don't bang your elbows on the wall, it's very narrow. Wait for me when you get through. I'll be right behind you.'

Looking up and down the street to check no one was watching, she smiled encouragingly, directed Pierre into the alley and then bent down to follow him. She heard Jules whimper softly at the darkness, but Pierre didn't stop. They emerged into the lane that ran behind the bookshop, and she took out the key, unlocked the door and hustled them inside. 'You're safe now. Just go up the stairs and I'll follow you.'

The lane running behind the shops was empty, so she went inside the bookshop and exhaled heavily when she finally closed the door behind her.

She paused for a moment at the bottom of the stairs to take in the shop where her late mother had worked, a place once so familiar to her. It was cold and dark now, with old boxes piled up to the side in front of one of the original carved wooden bookshelves, which were empty and broken. She wrinkled her nose as the strong dank odour filled her nostrils, the sweet smell of books and coffee a fond but distant memory. Through the gloom she could still see how the shop used to be, her mother smiling at her across the space, the owner Monsieur Steinberg greeting some new arrivals, the ghost of the customers still hovering around the room, their chatter a potpourri of German, French and English.

Valérie followed Pierre and Jules up the stairs to Monsieur Steinberg's apartment, clutching the wooden rail in the gloom and touching the familiar patterned wallpaper with her fingers, her memories of the place stronger than ever. It was fitting that the apartment Monsieur Steinberg had occupied after fleeing from Germany was now being used to protect others escaping from the Nazis. He would have approved of what she was doing, and she was certain that her mother would have done the same, if she was still alive. Valérie knew the apartment above the shop like the back of her hand. The stairs opened out on to a small landing, with doors leading to all the rooms. There used to be a small table on the landing, but the space was now empty.

Pierre had put his son down now, but Jules clung on to him, his only anchor in this strange and frightening new world. They looked so alike, but Jules' face was more rounded, while Pierre had narrow features and a well-defined moustache, a handsome man despite his scruffy clothes and worn shoes.

'The bedrooms are through there, next to a bathroom, and the parlour is in here.' She led them into the parlour and placed her basket on the table, taking out the bread and cheese and lighting a candle. There was nothing left here to link the apartment to its previous owner. The furniture was old and stained. The dark carpet was torn around the legs of the sofa where someone had dragged it across the room and the flowery wallpaper was faded and yellow. The wooden shutters were closed against prying eyes from the lane below.

Before she began using it to hide refugees, the SOE had been using the old bookshop as a safe house for their agents ever since Monsieur Steinberg, the owner of the bookshop, had left. Henry said he'd never met her mother there, because he'd arrived in Geneva after the road accident that had caused her death. She did wonder how his organisation were first drawn to the place.

Pierre and Jules sat on the sofa, their expressions full of relief. As they relaxed, Pierre roughly wiping away a tear and hugging Jules to his side, she felt suddenly very young and wished that her mother was here to help her. 'I hope you'll like it here,' she said shyly. 'At least it's warm and dry.'

She made sure the shutters were firmly closed and saw little Jules move shyly towards the basket on the table. He had more colour in his cheeks now that his fear had ebbed away, his brown eyes shining as he bent down to gaze closer into the basket. He looked back up to her. 'It's like a feast.'

Her heart went out to him, and her eyes filled with tears. He must be so hungry. She picked up an apple and handed to him, and he grabbed it greedily with a wide grin and bit immediately into the red skin.

'I'll come for you at eight tomorrow morning,' she said to Pierre. 'We'll meet someone who will take you out of Geneva.'

Pierre shook his head. 'No. I'm sorry, I know you're going to great risks to help us. But we can't leave yet. We must stay here until my wife and daughter join us.'

His voice cracked and he broke into choked tears, his hands covering his face.

Valérie sank down on to one of the wooden chairs next to the table. 'I heard that they didn't make it across, I'm so sorry. But the sooner you leave here the safer both of you will be. I can't guarantee that you won't be found here by the Swiss police who will hand you back to the Nazis in France, or even by Gestapo spies.'

She glanced at Jules, who was watching them silently. She didn't want to frighten him, but this close to the border they were still in terrible danger.

'I know you're right,' said Pierre, raising his head. 'But I can't go any further without them... without knowing what's happened to them.'

The pain in his eyes pierced her heart. Something about his earnest gaze reminded her of the man she loved, and she knew that if Philippe was in the same position, he too would never leave without her. He would be here, desperately pleading for her life. Valérie couldn't begin to know the pain and trauma the family had been through, but she had once felt a very real terror that she might lose Philippe forever. And as she looked into the young man's eyes, she saw that terror reflected at her. This young family was going through a nightmare, and with absolute clarity, she knew she would do anything to end their suffering.

'I know it must be painful to talk about, but can you tell me what happened at the border? How did you get split up?'

Pierre dragged his hands through his hair, as if he couldn't keep them still. He was like a coiled spring and took a few deep breaths to try to calm himself before he could continue. 'We were crossing the road when a car came round the corner. I grabbed Jules' hand and ran after our guide. But my wife Anne-Marie tripped, she must have hurt her ankle and couldn't follow us. I wanted to go to her so badly, but I had to stay with Jules... I saw her climb into the car with our daughter Madeleine.' He made a strangled noise, holding back tears. 'There were Nazi officers in the car, and they drove away.'

Valérie didn't know what to say. They all knew what happened to Jewish refugees caught trying to escape to Switzerland. If they survived their capture, they were destined for the concentration camps. There was no doubt any longer about what the Nazis did to Jewish people, and if this poor man's wife and daughter were in their clutches then if they weren't already dead, they probably soon would be.

'I'm sorry,' he continued, 'I should introduce myself. My name is Pierre Weil. I was a lawyer in Lyons until I could no longer practise. My wife Anne-Marie is a teacher. She was still able to work in a local convent, where they were helping children escaping from the Nazis and we were producing false papers for them and their families. I was doing some work for the Resistance too, anything I could to stop the Nazis from destroying our country. Then one of my old colleagues told us we were on the Germans' list not only because we are Jews but because they'd found out what we were doing, what I was doing, and we had to flee immediately. He had contacts in the Resistance who told us where we could stay in Annemasse. We thought we'd been so lucky to get to the border and then everything changed in a second.' He shook his head, his shoulders drooping and his eyes full of despair. 'If the Nazis have got them, if they know who they are or that they're Jewish, I don't know what I'm going to do. I can't bear it; I can't think about it. She's expecting another child...'

Valérie swallowed, feeling a hot tear running down her cheek. She brushed it away, looked up and held his gaze. 'I'm so sorry, Pierre. I'll do my best to help you, to find them and get them across here to safety.'

'Can you really help us?' He looked into her eyes, seeking strength, afraid to hope.

'I promise I'll do all I can.'

'And we can stay here for a bit longer?'

'Yes, if you must. You'll be safe here for a little while, so long as no one sees you. Everyone thinks this place is deserted, so you'll need to keep the shutters closed. If the police find you, you know they'll send you both back to France.'

He nodded. 'I'll do anything... anything. I'll get you money, somehow. Whatever you need.'

'No, please. You don't need to do anything at all, I want to help. I'll try to find out where they are, and I'll bring you food. You just need to stay here and keep safe.'

'Thank you. Thank you so much, Valérie.'

He looked down at Jules, who was already asleep on the

sofa next to him, large dark lashes fluttering on his smooth cheeks, still clutching the half-eaten apple.

'I need to get him to bed. He's exhausted.'

Valérie stood up. 'Of course, you both must be. I know you're terribly worried, but please try to get some rest. I'll come back tomorrow.'

She closed the door behind her and pushed her bike through the alley and towards home, still seeing the agony on Pierre's face rather than the cobbled streets and familiar old buildings.

She'd promised to find Anne-Marie and Madeleine, but the truth was that she had no idea how she would do it. All she knew was that she had to try.

FIVE

ANNE-MARIE

Annemasse, France

Anne-Marie held her daughter close in the dark, praying that she wouldn't make a sound. She was trying to get them to the other address they'd been given, but there were too many German soldiers patrolling the streets. To escape the last unit, they had run into a deserted outhouse next to some bombed-out houses.

'Where are we going, Maman?' whispered Madeleine. 'Why couldn't we stay in the hospital with the nurse? It was warm there and I had a comfortable bed.'

Anne-Marie shuddered when she remembered the German soldiers in the hospital corridors, searching through the wards and coming closer to them. If it hadn't been for one of the other patients fleeing from the Nazis, they wouldn't have escaped. She could still hear the sound of the shot.

'It wasn't safe, mon trésor. We have to get to the next step in our game.' Anne-Marie cuddled her daughter close into her and tickled her gently, and Madeleine choked down a giggle. In this hell they were living through she could still laugh, and Anne-

Marie felt a burst of love and gratitude that her daughter, just a six-year-old girl, wouldn't let their situation damage her spirits. Jules was a quieter and more reflective boy, more likely to be affected by their flight than his light-hearted, fun-loving sister. Jules would be asking questions that Pierre would struggle to answer, rather than treating everything as a game like Madeleine. But at least he was safe, she told herself, picturing him and his father safely across the border in Switzerland, cared for by some kind souls. Now she just had to make sure that Madeleine could join him.

They huddled in the corner of the outhouse and Anne-Marie listened carefully for anyone outside, knowing that it was more likely to be someone who would hand them over to the Nazis than to risk their own life to help them. Most French citizens would choose their own families over Jewish fugitives trying to escape the country.

She got to her feet quietly and looked out of the smashed window, but couldn't see anybody, and she averted her eyes from the destroyed houses, trying not to think about the people who may have been caught in the bombing. Sitting back down, she pulled Madeleine towards her.

'I'm going to get us to another house, ma chérie. It's just all part of our adventure! And once we're there, we won't need to run anymore, and we can take a little break from our game.'

'And then we can go and join Papa and Jules? I miss them. I have no one to play other games with.'

'I know. I want to see them too and I promise we will, very soon.'

Anne-Marie held her daughter close, breathing in the scent of her hair. She just had to make sure that Madeleine thought they were playing, that it was all a fun adventure. She didn't know how long she could pretend that she wasn't terrified for their lives, but so long as she sounded in control, the happier Madeleine would be; if Madeleine were frightened and panicking, she didn't know how she would be able to cope and get them through this. For both their sakes she had to keep the act going, and pray that they would make it to safety long before Madeleine ever realised how much danger they had been in.

Her hand crept down to her stomach, and she felt the roundness that had only recently developed. All this running, the hunger, the sleepless nights and the fear, it couldn't be good for the baby.

But it was the only way if they were to have a chance of survival.

They couldn't stop, not until they were safe across the border.

SIX

VALÉRIE

Geneva, Switzerland

Valérie left her bike outside the Café de Paris and went to look for Geraldine. The tables outside were busy in the late afternoon and a hum of conversation followed her as she walked below the green canopy and into the wood-panelled bar. It was quieter inside, with a group of men in smart suits staking their claim in front of the open fire to fend off the evening chill and a few regulars lounging over the polished wooden bar. They looked up curiously as she came in.

'She's fetching something from the cellar,' said Geraldine's father from behind the bar, a bottle poised in mid-air as he topped up the glasses ranged in front of him. 'Have a seat outside and I'll tell her you're here.'

Thanking him, she sat down at an empty table outside beside the door and pulled the collar of her coat more tightly round her neck, grateful for a moment of quietness. Bernard came out of the grocer's shop across the square and closed the shutters with a snap that echoed across the Place du Bourg-de-Four. Geraldine soon burst out of the café and perched on the chair opposite Valérie. 'Is everything all right?' she asked. 'Why did you go off so quickly this morning? One minute you were there and the next you'd disappeared.'

'I'm sorry I rushed off. I wanted to see you, but I needed to speak to someone, that's all. Everything's fine, honestly.'

Glancing round the tables, Geraldine seemed satisfied that she wasn't needed, and she wiped the surface between them with a flourish. 'So, where did you meet François?' She patted her golden curls. 'He's a dish. Very handsome. And he's offered to come and mend our wireless. I was trying to get it to work today but it wouldn't come on. We need it for our customers, some of our regulars are already complaining that it's not working.' She was looking over Valérie's shoulder. 'Well, well... someone's a lucky girl. Guess who's here.'

Valérie felt hands go over her eyes from behind and heard a familiar chuckle. She grasped the fingers and twisted round to see Philippe grinning down at her. 'Philippe! You're home.'

Her heart leapt with joy, and she stood up and moved into his arms. As he crushed her against him, she lifted her face up instinctively, feeling a quiver of excitement ripple through her body. He kissed her fiercely and then moved a fraction to the side, keeping her in the circle of his arms.

His closest friend, Christophe, was standing behind him. They were both soldiers in the Swiss army, preparing to fight back a German invasion and stationed at a military fort high up in the Alps, near a small town called Saint-Maurice.

'You didn't say in your letter you'd be coming home,' said Valérie, grinning.

Philippe looked brown from the days spent skiing in the mountains and his hazel eyes shone. 'It's so good to see you my love, you look as beautiful as ever. We didn't know we were getting leave until yesterday. We only have twenty-four hours but it's better than nothing.'

Christophe came forward and gave her a brief hug, his

blond hair ruffling in the wind and his deep blue eyes sparkling down at her. 'We arrived half an hour ago and had to see you first, Philippe insisted. He said you might be here.' He stretched out his hand to a small blonde woman in a smart black dress who was standing at a distance and looking at them shyly. She came quickly to his side, stepping neatly round some chairs, and when she smiled at Valérie, her face came alive, and she looked even prettier.

'This is my girlfriend, Nathalie.' Christophe put his arm round the woman's shoulders. 'She's just finished work. We thought the four of us could go out tonight, maybe to the movies and then have a meal. It's Saturday night after all and Philippe and I can celebrate our promotion.'

Infected by his enthusiasm, Valérie nodded, her eyes sparkling.

'Let's order a drink.' Christophe looked around for Geraldine and waved at her.

'We can't wait for long, I need to go to see my grandfather before we go out.' said Philippe, pulling Valérie down to sit next to him, keeping hold of her hands in his warm grasp.

She turned eagerly towards him. 'I met your mother in town last week and she said he was back home with them. I couldn't believe it after such a bad heart attack.'

'I'm not sure I quite believe it either, but it's true. The doctors didn't think he'd recover before Christmas and here he is now, demanding to go back to his own house.'

'Will he be able to go back home? Live in the old farmhouse alone?'

'You know my grandfather. He certainly thinks so. He's complaining already about living in the city and he's only been with my parents for a couple of months. They're trying to persuade him to stay, there's plenty of space in their apartment for him, but the first chance he gets he'll be off back home.'

Philippe's grandfather never stopped complaining that his

son had joined the canton police rather than taking on the family farm in the commune of Vessy to the south of the city. The fact that the neighbouring farmer had been glad to manage the farm didn't improve his temper, even though it came as a relief to everyone else.

She studied Philippe's tanned features, drinking in his presence, revelling in the feeling of his arms around her, and touched the new stripe on his arm. 'How smart you both look.'

'We both have our own units now.' His pride shone through, and she felt her own heart lift at his happiness.

Geraldine came back to their table and Christophe ordered for everyone as Philippe leaned closer to Valérie and lowered his voice. 'I'm so sorry I couldn't come back for Emile's funeral, that you had to go through that alone.'

She gripped his hand more tightly and felt her eyes fill with tears. 'I knew you would have been there if you could. It was awful for everyone. Marianne is only now properly back at work, and it's been months. I still miss him all the time. You know I've taken on his work helping refugees, because the authorities are still determined to send them all back. It's no better than it was last year.' She shook her head. 'And the police couldn't find the man I saw push him, I'm not sure they even believed me. But I saw him today, Philippe. I'm going to find him.'

'But how can you do that, if the police couldn't find him?'

She shrugged. 'I don't know, but I'm going to try.'

'What are you two whispering about?' said Christophe, looking from one to the other.

She squeezed Philippe's hand. 'Let's not talk about it. You're only here for one evening.' Valérie smiled at Nathalie. 'It's lovely to meet you. How long have you known Christophe?'

The young woman cast a shy glance at Christophe, who grasped her hand and held it to his lips. 'Since last summer.'

'Do you live in Geneva?'

'I live with my aunt in Nyon during the week and come into work at one of the jewellers on the Rue du Rhône in Geneva. Saint-Maurice is my real home.'

'That's where we met,' added Christophe. 'I got to know Nathalie's brothers and they introduced us. Her brothers work at the train station at Saint-Maurice in the goods yard, helping to move the supplies arriving at the station. All different kinds of supplies, you'd be surprised what you can find there.'

'Christophe... not here.' Nathalie grasped his arm, and he covered her hand with his.

'Don't worry about Valérie. You can trust her.'

Valérie glanced at Philippe, who was shaking his head. 'Keep your voice down,' he muttered to Christophe.

She stood up. 'We should go inside and sit at the table at the back, it's quieter in there.'

'Do we have to go inside? It's still so nice out here.' Christophe protested before Nathalie stood up and grasped his arm, her shoulder-length hair rippling in the light as she pulled him up.

'Come on. Valérie's right.'

He muttered in protest but let Nathalie lead him into the café, and Valérie and Philippe followed with their drinks. Once they were sitting in a corner away from curious ears, Christophe leaned across the wooden table and his blue eyes flashed in the glow of the table lamp. 'We're taking German stolen goods from under their noses, and they have no idea we're even there.'

Valérie looked at Philippe, who sat back in his chair out of the lamplight and watched his friend, smiling at his enthusiasm.

'How exactly are you managing that?' she asked Christophe.

'We found a secret tunnel where they hide trains carrying stolen jewellery and works of art bound for the auction houses in Bern and Zurich.'

Christophe paused to take a gulp of his beer, and Nathalie

chimed in: 'One night when they were working at the station, my brothers found a disused siding under the rock face along from Saint-Maurice with two train carriages. When they looked inside the carriages, they found paintings by Picasso, Gauguin and others. They were all going to art dealers in Switzerland. There were also boxes full of jewellery and silver. But the next night the carriages had gone. We think the valuables were stolen from Jewish families, probably in France over the last few months.'

Christophe continued, 'When they told me what they'd found and the names of the dealers on the pictures, I knew who they were. My father was an art dealer before the war, and these were some of the people he used to deal with.' He looked grim now, all trace of laughter erased from his face. 'Dealers who've decided they can make a fortune in a booming art market by collaborating with the Germans, buying and selling their stolen goods and ignoring what happened to the poor souls who originally owned them.'

He fell silent, as two men came into the café and started flirting with Geraldine, before he lowered his voice again.

'So, we picked off the best pieces and sold them ourselves, making sure that the money never got back to the Germans. There are still a few honest art dealers who knew my father, and I can trust them to sell the pictures without giving away how they got them. They're happy to give me the money if they know it's going to the French Resistance. And if they know who the original owner was, they'll keep them safe until the war is over and give them back to them then. If they're still alive.' He shook his head. 'There aren't many pieces where we can identify the original owner, so I figure that if we can't return the stuff, at least we stop it staying in German hands and we use it to defeat them.'

'I'm taking the jewellery back to Geneva and selling it to dealers here, then giving money from the art and jewellery to the Resistance.' Nathalie spoke quietly but her voice was determined.

Before Valérie could react, Philippe interrupted. 'I'm afraid he won't let me help him. I keep offering but he won't hear of it.'

Christophe sighed. 'Philippe's responsible for the specialist marksmen unit in the Fort and they're out most days on exercises. Not only that, but he's still working on the maps of our mountain defences. It's vital work, I can't let him get mixed up in anything that could risk that.'

'I understand, and I know the Resistance desperately need that money. But I'd watch your back too,' cautioned Valérie. 'You could get caught, or even shot by the German thieves guarding the train.'

'It's not that dangerous. There aren't any proper guards, because they're so confident no one knows the stuff is there. Nathalie's brothers tell me when the train comes in and I help them take away as much as we can carry. Then I hide the valuables in the regular supply runs up to the Fort.'

'He really does have the perfect cover,' added Philippe. 'They've put him in charge of the unit managing provisions and supplies, so nobody asks questions when he's late coming back after a trip down the mountain collecting deliveries.'

'Works like a dream,' said Christophe, and he nudged Philippe. 'I promise you'll come with me one day. You'll love it. Better than exercises and drills.'

After they'd finished their drinks and talked about everything from the stolen art to the looming invasion, Philippe walked Valérie through the streets they knew so well. They could have been returning from the shooting range or from their old school, so many times had they made the same journey through the cobbled back streets, talking about the events of the day and sharing their thoughts.

Valérie glanced up at him as he waved to Bernard, who was making deliveries from the grocer's shop. Although Philippe looked the same and sounded the same, she could tell that he had changed. She'd always been the one who would take risks and persuade him to take part in her adventures, but now he was bursting to take the lead. She could see he was itching to play a full role in Christophe's operation and, from the sound of it, he wouldn't be content to stand back for much longer.

Reluctant to end the precious few moments they had alone together, Valérie sat on the stone wall opposite the Cathédrale St-Pierre and pulled Philippe down beside her. He held her close, dropping a kiss on her hair. 'You smell nice.'

She nuzzled into his neck, and they sat in silence for a few moments. He still seemed tense. 'I'm sure Christophe will ask you to help before long,' she said gently.

'Maybe. But you haven't heard some of his stories. It's as if he wants to get as close to being caught as possible. He loves the adrenaline rush, and it's making him reckless. I could protect him, if he'd let me.'

He tightened his arm round her shoulders and sighed. 'Do I sound like an old man? It's just that I never thought anything would happen to Emile, even though I knew he was working for the Resistance. I still can't believe he's dead and that I'll never see him again. I just couldn't bear to lose Christophe as well.'

Valérie knew what was coming next.

'And you too... I worry about you all the time, what you could be doing, the risks you might be taking. I can't get it out of my mind.' He tightened his hold. 'I'm not going to ask you to stop helping the Resistance, I know now how important it is to you. Christophe was right when he said you're fighting for our country just as much as we are. But it doesn't mean I don't still worry about you.'

'I know you do, but I can't give it up, particularly now.'

'Why particularly now?'

She sat back in his arms to look at him. 'I want to reunite a family who were split up when they were coming across the border. They're broken, Philippe, and in so much pain. I desperately want to help put them together again. If you'd heard what the father said...'

Philippe's brow was furrowed. 'You aren't going into France to look for them, are you?'

'If I have to.'

'Valérie, you can't,' he gasped, his eyes widening. 'The Nazis will kill you if they find out what you're doing. I could lose you.'

She stroked his hand, trying to find the words to explain the strength of her feelings. 'I know, Philippe. But... they could be us. You and me, a few years from now, with children of our own, and in desperate danger. And if it was us, I'd like to think someone would help us, when everything seemed impossible.'

He pulled her tightly against him. 'Just promise me you won't go into France. Please, Valérie.'

She took a deep breath, unsure what to say, not wanting to spoil their time together when he was only home for such a short time. 'Okay, Philippe. I'll do everything I can to stay safe.'

He looked as if he was going to say something else but it seemed one glance at her face changed his mind. 'I won't say anything more about it. Let's forget it tonight. I love you, Valérie.'

Valérie kissed him, but even as she sank into their embrace her mind went to Anne-Marie and Madeleine, somewhere across the border in Nazi-occupied France.

Were they still alive? Were they safe? And if so, for how long?

SEVEN

VALÉRIE

'Valérie, Philippe is here for you.'

She heard her father open the front door and then the sound of voices drifted upstairs. She paused, hairbrush in her hand as her engagement ring sparkled in the glow from the lamp, then started brushing her hair more quickly, tugging the tough bristles hard through her thick auburn curls, and making her eyes water.

'Are you coming down?'

One last look in the mirror and she pulled a few stray wisps of hair into place. The pleated skirt of her favourite green dress swished around her knees, and she smiled at her reflection. Fine leather shoes replaced her sturdy boots and she felt as excited as if she was going to her first date. It had been so long since she'd had something to look forward to and Philippe's surprise arrival and the promise of a night out was like a flash of colour in a dark painting.

As she walked into the parlour, Philippe whistled, tall and smart in his uniform, and her father beamed.

'Don't you both look handsome!' She smiled at them as Philippe came across and helped her into her coat.

'Have fun, ma chérie,' said her father.

She kissed his cheeks, glancing behind him into the dining room, the lamp on the table still on. 'Don't work all evening, Papa. You don't have to do everything yourself any longer.'

He shook his head, his short hair now more grey than black, with specks of white at the temples. 'I have a few things to prepare for tomorrow.'

'Okay, well, don't wait up for me.'

She took Philippe's outstretched hand. They'd agreed to meet Christophe and Nathalie at the Carouge Cinema, west of the old town.

'Could we walk?' said Valérie. 'It's a lovely evening.'

'Fine by me. The more I'm outside the better, I spend most of my life underground in an airless mountain fort after all.'

Valérie looked up at him gratefully. 'Thank you. I prefer to be outside too. Since Emile's accident, I don't like going on the trams. They remind me too much of his accident.'

He squeezed her hand. 'You don't need to explain. Look, I know we said we'd go out with Christophe and Nathalie tonight, but honestly I wish I could have you all to myself. It's been months since I last saw you, and I miss you every day.'

He frowned and she tried to lighten his mood. 'Well, I can't remember the last time we went to the cinema, or out for dinner. It's going to be perfect.'

She tucked her hand in his arm and they walked through the university district, passing other couples and groups all intent on having a good time. Valérie felt pulled along by the atmosphere around them, the high spirits and laughter. People still seemed determined to go out and enjoy themselves when they had the chance, knowing that any day the invasion could come, and all their freedoms would be taken away.

'This war can't go on for ever,' she continued. 'Then you'll be back in Geneva at the university, I can pick up my English studies and we'll have all the time in the world together.'

'I know. But peace seems so far away sometimes. What's happening in France... it just seems to get worse and worse every week. We're still on high alert at the Fort, expecting an invasion at any point. And there are even more German spies nosing around than there were last year. We've all been warned not to talk about our work.'

She squeezed his arm. 'Don't think about it all just now, Philippe. Let's have some fun.'

They crossed over the Arve river that flowed up from France and paused on the bridge to watch the fast flowing water, which would join the Rhône further north in the city. After a few moments they walked briskly towards the cinema near the Place du Marché, passing restaurants full of diners.

'Hi there! We're over here.' Christophe waved at them from the crowd of people standing at the main door and thrust their tickets towards them. 'We were early so I bought the tickets. They're playing Gilberte de Courgenay. Come on, the newsreel is just about to start.'

They emerged a couple of hours later into the cool evening air and Christophe's voice rung through the air above the hubbub of the dispersing crowd.

'Time to eat. I don't know about the rest of you, but I'm famished. You know this city, where can we eat?'

'We could go back to the Café de Paris,' suggested Valérie. 'Give them some business.'

But Christophe waved away the suggestion. 'Where we had drinks today? No, let's go somewhere new. This is a special occasion; it's going to be months before we'll have the chance to do this again. What's the best place in town? Nathalie, where would you go for a smart dinner?'

'Oh, let's go to the Hotel d'Angleterre. It's just across the lake from where I work and it used to look so magical in the evenings, like a fairy palace.' Nathalie shrugged. 'The blackouts have spoiled that recently, but I still remember it.'

The blackouts were another way the Swiss authorities pandered to the Germans, putting out the lights that would have guided Allied planes crossing Europe to bomb Italy or drop supplies to arm the French Resistance. It didn't stop the planes, you heard them most nights, but it made their work even more dangerous.

They wandered back to the old town, past the Cathédrale St-Pierre and through the cobbled streets down towards the Rhône. Between the old city and the lake, Nathalie paused in front of a smart jewellery shop on the Rue du Rhône.

'Look, this is where I work.'

Valérie stared into the large shop window, with its mass of deep red velvet cushions empty of expensive rings and neck-laces, and then through to the polished wooden counters inside the shop. This wasn't a small, local business, dealing in everyday items, but a sleek and luxurious emporium. Valérie glanced up at the name above the door, where ornate gold lettering spelled out *Savarin*.

Nathalie followed her gaze. 'Monsieur Savarin inherited the business from his father and his grandfather before him. And his son will take over from him.' She fell silent as she seemed to contemplate the prospect. 'But that won't be for a while yet. He doesn't want to retire, even though his son wants to take over the business.'

'I'll bet he does,' added Christophe, lighting up a cigarette and stamping out the match with his boot. 'To make money out of all of his new German friends.'

Nathalie sighed. 'Monsieur Savarin says he must do busi-ness with everyone. He can't refuse to sell to anyone, if they have the money to pay.'

'That's all well and good,' said Christophe. 'It's one thing being even-handed, but quite another keeping your best pieces for your Nazi friends.'

Nathalie shook her head. 'Well, I have to stay on their good side. I can't risk Monsieur Savarin or his son finding out that I'm selling the jewellery. In a way it's helpful that his son only cares about the Germans and the big companies. Part of my job is to deal with the smaller dealers, so I just add a few things into the orders. It's the safest way.'

Valérie knew more than anyone the difficulties businesses faced in trying to keep going by selling to the Allies as well as to their powerful German neighbour. It was exactly the dilemma her father had faced with his watchmaking business, continuing to sell to the Nazis, although he was also using the business as a front while he was carrying out crucial work for the Allied war effort. She changed the subject, to try to inject some cheer into the sombre mood.

'I often come this way home, maybe I could call in and see you sometime?'

Nathalie nodded enthusiastically. 'I'd like that...' She hesitated and then carried on in her quiet way. 'I don't have many friends in Geneva. Most of my friends are still in Saint-Maurice, so I go back home most weekends.'

Valérie took Nathalie's arm and they continued down the street together, leaving Philippe and Christophe to follow them.

'You should come and meet Geraldine properly, the blonde woman from the café. And I can introduce you to Marianne. She works over there in the telephone exchange.' She pointed over at the top of the PTT building, just visible above the tall blocks at the end of the street. 'You'll like them – we've been friends since we were very small. Philippe too, and Marianne's brother, Emile.' Valérie felt quietly proud of herself that she'd managed to say his name as part of a normal conversation. Progress indeed. But then Nathalie's next words shot through her fragile defences.

'Christophe told me about Emile. He said Philippe was terribly shocked when he heard. He'd never seen him like that before, so angry. I know it's why Philippe gets so worried about what we're doing in Saint-Maurice, he supports us of course, but Christophe does get so careless sometimes.'

They carried on towards the lakeside and walked across the Pont du Mont-Blanc, to the Hotel d'Angleterre entrance on Rue de Monthoux. At the main door to the grand old building, several limousines were drawing up and disgorging smartly dressed couples on to the narrow pavement. They crowded at the bottom of the stairs into the foyer where a doorman was trying to restore some order into the excitable crowd. 'Wait for a few moments please, ladies and gentlemen.'

The men wore dinner suits and the women's jewels glittered and sparkled under the chandeliers inside, their long dresses a patchwork of colour as they took off their fur coats.

'It's very busy tonight... and everyone looks so smart.' Nathalie hesitated and looked across at Christophe uncertainly. 'Maybe we should go somewhere quieter instead.'

'It's just some stuffy dinner, they're all dressed up for that. The main restaurant will be fine.' Christophe grabbed Nathalie's arm and pushed his way through the crowd, followed by Philippe who clutched Valérie's hand and set off after Christophe. At the door, the doorman bowed to a smartly dressed couple who were trying to leave, fighting against the crowds streaming inside. The man was in evening dress and the blonde woman wore a long fur coat over a silk white dress that shimmered as she moved. Pulled along behind Philippe, Valérie almost walked right into the gentleman.

'Hello Valérie,' said Henry.

She stopped in her tracks, her hand slipping out of Philippe's grasp, buffeted by the moving crowd. 'Hello...'

The people behind Valérie pushed her forward and she grasped Henry's arm before she was swept off her feet. He

caught it and pulled her towards him, clamping her to his side
and looking over the heads of the crowd. 'Come on, we have to
get out of here.'

He steered both women outside the hotel to the side, out of
the main rush. Valérie pulled back and took a deep breath.
'Thanks.'

Henry turned to his companion, who was grasping the
collar of her fur coat tighter round her neck and looking down
her nose at the crowd flocking into the hotel.

'You haven't met my friend Elsa Bauer.'

'Pleased to meet you, Mademoiselle...?' said the blonde
woman, her blue eyes sharp as ice.

'Hallez, Valérie Hallez. It's a pleasure to meet you.'

Elsa looked her up and down, then spoke in heavily
accented French. 'I am pleased to meet you, Valérie.'

She clutched Henry's arm. 'I can't stand these awful
crowds. Let's leave.'

He took her elbow and looked back at Valérie, a smile in his
eyes. 'I think your friends are looking for you.'

The other three were waiting for her at the top of the stairs,
gesticulating at her to come inside. Valérie watched as Henry
and Elsa walked away, her blonde hair against his dark shoulder. Then she smoothed down her skirt and took advantage of a
lull in the guests arriving to run up the stairs.

'Who was that?' asked Philippe while Christophe looked
faintly amused.

'That was Henry Grant. He's the SOE contact in Geneva.'

'I've seen that woman in our shop now and then,' said
Nathalie. 'She's Austrian and came here before the war. I think
she's very beautiful.'

Christophe gave her a squeeze. 'In an ice maiden kind of
way. That cold type never appealed to me. Anyway, we need to
eat. Come on.'

·   ·   ·

The meal was wonderful, as good as the food they'd had before the war, though the portions were smaller than they used to be. They ate perch fished that morning from Lac Léman, accompanied by local Vaudois white wine from the Lavaux vineyard terraces, which rose steeply up above the lake.

It wasn't until much later, when he was walking her home through the deserted streets, that Philippe raised the subject again. 'I don't want to interfere, but my father talked to me about Henry Grant. He said he's a dangerous man, that he has connections everywhere. I know the SOE fund the Resistance, but please don't go into France even if he asks you to.'

Soothed by the good food and wine, Valérie moved closer to him and leaned her face against his shoulder. 'He hasn't asked me to. Did your father say anything else?'

'Not really. Only that he would use the Swiss to do his dirty work if he had the chance.' He hesitated and then carried on. 'I asked him what he meant, but he wouldn't tell me. Just said that he was very persuasive when he wanted to be. I know you don't always agree with my father, but he's very fond of you.'

Finally they were at the corner of her street and Valérie buried herself in Philippe's arms. 'When am I going to see you again?'

'Probably months, again. I'm sorry, Valérie. I'll write, and I'll be thinking of you every day.'

She pulled his head down and he kissed her, holding her body tightly against his, as if he would never let her go. After a few minutes he lifted his head. 'I should be on my way.' But he didn't relax his hold.

She raised her hand to stroke his face and he kissed her palm.

'Take care,' said Philippe. 'Write to me and tell me what you're doing, it makes me feel closer to you.'

'Of course, I will. Stay safe.'

She let herself inside and when she went to close the door

he waved and then walked away. After locking the door behind her, she leaned against the wall, feeling more alone than ever. Every time he left, and she knew she wouldn't see him for months, it felt even more painful than before.

But then she reminded herself of Pierre, Anne-Marie and their children, torn brutally apart by the Nazis, not knowing if they would *ever* see one another again.

She could hardly imagine their pain and their fear.

Whatever it took, she was determined to reunite them.

EIGHT

PHILIPPE

Saint-Maurice, Valais, Switzerland

'Wake up – I need to speak to you.'

Philippe felt a hand shake his shoulder and pushed it away. It seemed like only a few hours since he'd fallen into his bunk and into a dreamless sleep.

'Come on Philippe, it's morning. Get up,' hissed Christophe in his ear, like an insect buzzing round his head.

'Leave me alone,' he groaned. 'It's still the middle of the night.'

'No, it's almost six o'clock. If you don't get up now, we'll lose our chance. I need your help.'

His plea finally got through and Philippe sat up, rubbing his eyes and yawning. Christophe thrust his jacket towards him. 'Get dressed. I'll be in the officers' dining room. There'll be coffee waiting for you.'

Philippe slowly got dressed, looking enviously at the sleeping figures around him. They had a quiet day in front of them today and then an evening pass to go into town. What was Christophe so excited about? Why couldn't he wait for another hour? He trudged wearily along the corridor, breathing in the smell of coffee as he approached the dining room. Christophe was sitting alone at one of the tables and gestured at him to come over and sit down.

Philippe sat down opposite his friend and picked up the cup of coffee, avoiding his avid stare as he took a couple of gulps of the strong liquid. He knew the signs: his friend fidgeting in his chair, his leg jiggling, ready to burst at any moment.

'Are you awake yet? Talk about the sleep of the dead... I thought I'd never get you to move.'

Philippe grinned at him, never able to resist Christophe's smile.

'What's so important that you had to drag me out of my warm bed? I'd only just got to sleep.'

'Rubbish. You've been asleep for hours. I looked in last night and decided not to wake you.' Christophe glanced around the room.

'Relax, you've got me on my own. We're the only people I can see...' grumbled Philippe.

'Okay, look. We have a job tonight at the train station but one of Nathalie's brothers can't make it.' Christophe cast his eyes to the ceiling. 'Bloody fool broke his leg last night, fell off a ladder at work in one of the station storerooms. He'll be in hospital for weeks.'

'So you want me to come? Finally?'

'I heard your unit has the evening off. You'll be down in Saint-Maurice anyway, so you can take his place. I'm scheduled to pick up supplies at the station so I can take you back up to the Fort afterwards. It all fits.'

'About time.'

Christophe was shaking his head. 'I'm not asking you to come inside the carriage. I just need you to be waiting outside, making sure the coast is clear, and then help me with the stuff and drive us away. There are so many trains going through the station and people working in the station at night, no one will ask us what we're doing.'

'But aren't the carriages being watched all the time?'

He shrugged. 'There are guards, but they always finish at midnight. The train usually leaves around one or two in the morning, so there's a gap of about an hour.' Christophe leaned forward, his blue eyes flashing in excitement. 'Also, I've figured something else out. We already know that the jewellery is all stolen from French Jewish families who have been taken to concentration camps, and the art from private collections.'

He lowered his voice, as if there was someone listening, though they were still totally alone in the room. 'That isn't the whole story though. I don't think the Swiss or German authorities know anything about these trains. They don't appear on any timetables or have any paperwork. Nathalie's brother Yves alerts me when they arrive, usually in the middle of the night, but other than that there's no pattern we can determine. We think they wait there because once they're in the siding, they don't interfere with the trains going through the station and can't be seen by anyone else. Someone is stealing treasures and selling them off, or even keeping them for themselves, all under the noses of the Nazi authorities.'

Christophe frowned before he continued. 'None of it smacks of the usual German efficiency, though the men we see there are definitely German. One gives the orders and it's always the same man, short with glasses. The two guards don't change either and they don't always follow his orders, as if they have some kind of hold over him.'

'Haven't you tried reporting them to the authorities?' asked Philippe.

'What do you think would happen? All they'd do is tell the Germans across the border, and while the people stealing from them might get caught, the theft of art treasures and jewellery won't stop. Paintings from occupied countries will keep on appearing in German art galleries. Jews forced to accept artificially low prices for pictures that are then sold at market price by the dealer who keeps the profit. Jewellery and valuables stripped away from people before they are sent to their deaths. It's wrong, Philippe, it's all wrong. This is our chance to do something to reduce the thousands of Swiss francs the Germans are making from people who are desperate. It isn't much, but it's at least something.'

Philippe looked at his friend's urgent expression and felt his spark of excitement grow. He'd heard the stories of stolen treasures, of people forced to sell their belongings for centimes, their houses stripped of valuables. He was the son of a policeman, had been brought up to respect the rule of law. It could hardly be a crime to steal from thieves. They'd never manage to return most of the goods to their original owners, even if they could identify them. But at least they could take away some of their profits and give the money back to the people in the French Resistance fighting to liberate their country. He'd wanted to help ever since Christophe had told him about it, and now was his chance. 'Of course, I'm in. You can't keep me away.'

Christophe punched the air. 'Yes.' He stood up. 'I've got to go to work now, I'll see you this evening.'

When darkness had fallen, Philippe sat hunched up in the cramped van, growing colder and colder as he waited for Christophe to come back at the agreed time. He was wearing Nathalie's brother's work clothes so he could blend into his surroundings. Christophe had failed to mention that Mathieu was several centimetres shorter than Philippe, so he might fit in while he was sitting down, but the moment he stood up he looked like a schoolboy who had grown out of his uniform.

It had been more difficult than he'd expected to leave his men without them wondering what was so important that he had to miss their first night out in months. It had certainly been noisy enough in the bar. They'd joined up with one of the artillery units and the place was full. He'd left once everyone had had a few drinks and managed to slip away without attracting attention.

At least the station was busy – Christophe had been right about that. Passenger and goods trains were arriving and leaving all evening and even now, just before midnight, when there were few passengers left, goods trains swept through the station on a regular basis, some stopping and unloading supplies and others speeding through to their destination.

'Park next to the other vans,' Christophe had instructed. 'Hide in plain sight, no one will notice you're even there. Then at a quarter past twelve, move to the barrier where the railway line runs under the cliff face. I should be back by then. We'll need to store the stuff nearby, and then we can get back to the truck and pick up the provisions for the Fort.'

'Won't someone see you coming out?'

'It hasn't happened yet, there's usually no one at that end of the station. We have a window of about half an hour for me to get into the carriage and take away as much as I can carry with me. I need to get clear of the siding before the German officer comes back. I also have to watch out for trains coming through the main tunnel before I go in or out because the through draught could pull me off my feet.'

'Doesn't anyone else use the siding?'

He shook his head. 'Not as far as Yves knows. It was built years ago but everyone thought it had been blocked off when the railway got busier. No one has used it for years, very few people even knew it existed.'

Now that Philippe was here, he could see the barrier was only a few hundred metres from the tunnel entrance. It looked like the platform stopped at the entrance to the tunnel, but Christophe had said there was a narrow strip that disappeared into the blackness, just wide enough to squeeze past.

Philippe looked intently into the mouth of the tunnel. It seemed unbelievable that only a few metres away, paintings and jewellery worth millions of Swiss francs were lying undiscovered in the dark space. A small part of the huge theft of property perpetrated by the Nazis to fund their war machine that stretched all across Europe.

He stared at the entrance to the siding for a while, then checked his watch. Christophe was late, it was way past the agreed time. Philippe craned his neck but couldn't see Christophe anywhere.

Where was he? He should be out by now. Something must have gone wrong.

Philippe pulled his coat up over his ears and frowned. Should he wait, or get out and go and look for him? He flinched as a train thundered through the tunnel into the station. You certainly didn't want to be stuck at that opening when a train came through. At the other end of the station, a train going the opposite way snaked along the platform. He saw the station guard exchange a few words with the driver, then blow his whistle. The train slowly moved off, coming towards the cliff face. He caught a glimpse of the driver in his cab for a few seconds before it thundered past and disappeared into the tunnel.

Still no sign of Christophe. Philippe looked in the other direction, to the station, and instinctively sank further down in his seat when he saw a figure walking along the platform towards the tunnel. It wasn't someone in railway overalls, but in an army coat. It must be the German Christophe had told him about, the one in charge who Christophe thought was stealing from his own side. The man was looking all around him, constantly checking to see no one was watching him, his small round glasses glinting in the station lamp above him as he turned his head one way and then the other, before he slipped round the corner and disappeared into the tunnel.

Philippe's heart was thumping in his chest. He looked around frantically to see if anyone else was there, but the platform was empty, the station guard safely back in his warm office. But more trains were due to come in through the night and they would be trapped. The other men would come back soon, and Christophe would be stuck in the train. He had to do something, he couldn't just sit there and wait.

Taking a deep breath, he slid out of the van and crouched down low before running along the platform. He didn't look behind him but went to the edge of the tunnel, waiting for a split second to make sure there were no trains coming and slipped round the wall. The platform of the siding hewn out of the rock face widened out in front of him, exactly as Christophe had said. He clutched on to the cold, damp wall of rock to steady himself, his eyes growing accustomed to the darkness, the siding lit only by a few makeshift lamps strung along the wall. A few metres in front of him, the back of a carriage loomed high in the space. There was no sound apart from the dripping of water running down the side of the cliff wall, the melting snow descending from the icy slopes down to the valley below.

He took a few steps forward, looking out for the German, but could see no one. There were two carriages in front of him, with a faint light coming out of the front of the first one. He must be in there, waiting for his men to join him. Philippe glanced behind him uncertainly. That was all he needed, to be caught between them.

There was no sign of Christophe as he crept along the side of the tunnel. After what seemed like an age, his fingers clasped the door handle at the end of the carriage and he tried to open it, but it was locked. He made his way to the next carriage, looking ahead to check that the man hadn't come out of the cab. He tried the next handle, but it didn't open. This was useless, he was too close to the front of the train to keep out of sight. Then a low knocking noise came from the carriage. He pressed his face closer to the door and whispered, 'Christophe?'

'Hey, Philippe! I'm in here.'

'What happened?'

'I stayed too long, and the head man came back. He caught me, and he's tied up. You're going to have to get me out before he comes back.'

'But all the doors are locked. I can't open them.' He rattled the handle again, but the door didn't budge.

'Don't make so much noise. You'll have to come in through the cab. Knock him out from behind, and don't let him see you.'

Philippe looked back towards the entrance to the tunnel, trying to think of another way out, but there was only one way to rescue Christophe.

'All right. I'm coming in.'

He crept forward to the front of the cab and stopped at the edge of the door. The light from inside the cab was brighter here and he waited for a few seconds, listening for any noises. He could hear nothing so slowly leaned round to look inside. The man was facing away from him, bending over some papers. Philippe ducked back out of sight when he stood up, holding his breath in case he decided to come and investigate. He pressed himself back against the carriage when he heard footsteps, but the steps went behind his head. He must have gone to question Christophe. This was his chance to attack when he wasn't expecting it.

Philippe took a deep breath, looked around to check the cab was empty, then jumped up the steps inside as lightly as he could. He could hear voices from inside and looked round to see the man facing away from him and bending over his friend.

He saw him strike Christophe with the back of his hand, blood spraying from his nose. This was his chance.

He ran through the carriage and caught the man as he

turned, with a punch that sent him crashing to the floor with an enormous noise that echoed around the enclosed space. Philippe stood over him, breathing heavily, and saw that he was unconscious. Christophe was grinning widely although his face was streaked with blood.

'Good punch,' said Christophe, twisting round to show his bound hands. 'Now get these ropes off me so we can leave before the others come back.'

Philippe untied him and helped him up. The German was still out cold and he leaned down and took his pistol.

'I don't want him waking up and coming after us with this.'

They ran through the carriage and to the door of the cab.

'Be careful... the others might be out there. And remember, no guns, the noise would alert everyone.' Philippe put his finger to his lips to warn Christophe, who nodded. He leaned round to look out of the door up the platform. It was deserted.

'Come on.'

He jumped down from the cab and Christophe followed him. They ran back along the platform, trying to stop their heavy boots crunching on the dirty surface. Philippe glanced back towards the light at the front of the carriage, fervently hoping that the German was still unconscious and wouldn't try to stop them.

Christophe was panting behind him and suddenly clutched his arm.

'What's the matter?' Philippe hissed.

'It's my bad leg. If I run too fast, it'll give way. It should be all right. I just need a minute,' he stammered, teeth chattering from the cold.

He grabbed Philippe's shoulder, testing his weight on the weak leg, his knapsack banging on his back.

'I think it's all right now.'

Philippe grabbed the knapsack.

'I'll take that. You focus on getting out of here.'

Philippe swung the heavy knapsack over his shoulder, and they carried on to the tunnel entrance, trying to make as little sound as possible. He was aware of Christophe limping behind him and winced each time his foot dragged across the ground.

They were almost at the entrance. Philippe put his hand out to hold Christophe still, and they listened for the sound of any trains. To his horror, it wasn't the noise of a train he heard but the unmistakeable sound of voices ahead of them, coming from the platform. It must be the other Germans, their voices low but distinct. Christophe took a sharp breath in, and Philippe braced himself. There was no other way out, only the open platform ahead. He clenched his fists, ready to strike. He had the advantage of surprise, but it would be two against one. He would have to make the first blow count before their eyes could grow accustomed to the darkness. He pushed Christophe further back against the wall and turned to the opening, fists raised.

Suddenly the voices stopped, and Philippe held his breath, waiting to see a figure appear at the mouth of the tunnel. Then he heard footsteps walk away, growing fainter as they walked back along the platform. Philippe bent his head and let out a deep breath, wiping the sweat from his brow. He had no idea what was going on outside, but for some reason they had decided not to come into the siding. He jerked his head up again when he heard a low voice whisper harshly from the mouth of the tunnel.

'It's clear... Get out now while you have the chance.'

He hesitated, reluctant to emerge from the protection of the darkness.

'What are you waiting for? That's Yves.' Christophe tried to push past him, but Philippe clutched his arm, causing them both to sway perilously close to the edge of the platform.

'Are you sure it's him?'

'Yes, it's him all right.'

He didn't need to be told twice. Philippe bent low and ran out of the tunnel, focusing on the van ahead of him, not looking up or to either side. He felt painfully exposed, expecting at any moment to hear a shot.

He checked that Christophe was behind him and caught his friend as he staggered the last few paces to the vehicle, his knee finally giving up.

Philippe grabbed the door handle and threw the knapsack across the front seat, then bundled Christophe inside. He clambered in and slammed the door behind him, turned the key he'd left in the ignition and started up the van. He took a deep breath, thankful they'd managed to escape with at least some treasures they could sell to fund the resistance, but it had been close.

His heart pounding, Philippe drove out into the deserted streets of Saint-Maurice, checking in the mirror to make sure they weren't being followed.

NINE

PHILIPPE

'Where do you want me to go?' Philippe's voice broke the silence. They had stopped at a crossroads in the middle of town, and he looked enquiringly at Christophe, who was wiping his face with a cloth, trying to get the worst of the blood off.

'Which direction?'

'Straight on. Over the bridge and turn right.' Christophe grinned. 'You should guess where we're going.'

Philippe went over in his mind the various houses and farms between Saint-Maurice and the road up to the Fort at Lavey-les-Bains. He shook his head. 'Tell me, Christophe. I'm too tired for riddles. I know you have friends all around Saint-Maurice. Is it someone else in Nathalie's family?'

'It's someone you know very well. You're the one who introduced me to him.' Christophe nudged his elbow. 'You aren't usually this slow. It's your old friend Max... Max Reynauld. He hides the stuff for me at the shooting range. It's perfect, lots of space and nobody asks any questions.'

Philippe gazed at Christophe. 'I didn't know Max was involved.'

Max had taught Valérie and Philippe to shoot when they

spent summers at Valérie's Aunt Paulette's farm in Gryon. Philippe still took his unit to the shooting range for practice. He felt a pang of guilt when he realised he hadn't seen his old friend for months.

They were silent for a few minutes before Christophe spoke again, his voice quiet. 'They were going to kill me. They were going to take me away in the train and throw my body out. No one would have ever found me. I heard them discussing it.'

'Don't think about what might have happened.' Philippe reached out to Christophe's shoulder. 'I'm just glad I was there, and that you're okay. You can't leave me behind anymore, Christophe.'

Philippe drove in silence to the shooting range and turned into the rough ground next to the familiar low building. It was in complete darkness. He glanced over at Max and Sofia's house a few hundred yards further along the rough track among the fields and saw that it too was dark. He felt his skin prickling, as he looked out at the velvety darkness and jumped when Christophe spoke. 'Drive round the side where the deliveries get dropped. It's the door at the end of the building, hidden from the main road.'

Philippe did as he was told, then stopped the van and switched off the engine. He looked at the door and saw it open slowly, the beam of a torch moving around as a dark shape walked towards them. The car door opened, and Max's face was reflected in the torchlight, his familiar growl loud in the confined space. 'Where have you been? You're late.' He shone the torch on to Christophe's face. 'What happened to you?'

'Help us get the stuff inside and we'll tell you.' Christophe thrust the knapsack at Max, and they trooped inside, Philippe bringing up the rear. Before closing the door, Philippe took a last look around the silent countryside, relieved that he could hear no sounds in the cold night air, then went into the warmth of the building's main storeroom. The familiar smell made him blink a few times, as he realised how long it had been since he was last here and how much he'd missed it. He sank down on to one of the chairs and watched Max light the oil lamp in the corner of the room, then sit down at the small table he used to check the deliveries. He'd obviously been waiting for them there, some paperwork cast to the side, the room warmed by the low fire in the hearth.

Max glanced at Philippe from under his thick bushy eyebrows, which were now almost totally grey. 'Haven't seen you here for months, not since before Christmas. Sofia is always asking where you are, when we might see you again.'

Philippe felt a stab of guilt. He knew that he'd been Sofia's favourite. He should have visited her more often, and he cursed himself for his thoughtlessness. 'I've been busy getting to know my new unit. Now the weather's better, we'll come down more often. A few of them could do with better instruction than I can give them. You'd do a much better job.'

'Well, if they're anything like the lot you had with you the last time you came to the range, I'm not surprised.'

They smiled at one another, and Philippe felt time ebb away, seeing only the guide and mentor he'd known for years. 'How is Sofia? I'm sorry I haven't been down to see her. Valérie said she hasn't been well.'

A flicker of emotion crossed Max's face and he sighed heavily before giving an answer. 'No. She's had a hard time. The doctors say they've done all they can.' His brow furrowed. 'I've taken her to all the best people, here and in Martigny. They can't do anything else, just keep her comfortable.'

'I'm sorry.'

He carried on, as if Philippe hadn't spoken. 'The doctors say it's only a matter of time. She's a fighter, always was, but this is one fight she isn't going to win.'

Philippe flinched when a loud thud echoed around the room. He jumped up and took a step towards the door, but it was still firmly closed. He glanced at Christophe, who had been quietly emptying the knapsack and storing the rolled-up paintings in an empty gun cabinet, then relaxed again as his friend bent down to roll up the painting he'd dropped.

Coming over to look, Philippe looked down and saw a photograph of a family that must have been slipped inside the painting. The grandparents looked proudly out at the camera, their grandchildren held next to them. The picture was taken in a garden on a bright summer's day, the sea in the background.

Where were the family now, he wondered. Were they still alive? He handed the photo to Christophe. 'This needs to be kept with the picture,' said Philippe. 'This must be the owner.'

Christophe turned over the photo and nodded. 'These impressionist paintings come from a well-known private collection in Nice. They belonged to this man. We'll keep them safe and hope that the family survives the war.'

He closed the door to the cabinet and handed Max a leather bag, which he locked in one of the ammunition drawers. Philippe could see they had done this many times before, the paintings and jewellery stowed away in a matter of minutes.

Christophe picked up the empty knapsack. 'I'll be back next week to arrange for the pictures to be sent to the dealers.'

Max nodded and they stood up, Christophe leading the way to the door. Max held Philippe's arm to slow him down and whispered in his ear. 'I'm glad I saw you – I wanted to talk to you. I've been told that the Germans have a specialist unit working in the area trying to get information about the Swiss defences, how many troops you've got up there, the artillery positions, everything. They're asking where the maps are kept, who works on them, what they contain. They're based in Saint-Gingolph but they're operating right up the valley past Martigny.'

Philippe nodded, not trusting himself to say anything.

'You know that Sofia comes from the Swiss side of the town and still has family there.'

The town of Saint-Gingolph was split by the border, half in occupied France and half in neutral Switzerland.

'I didn't know.'

'She saw one of her nephews recently, he runs a garage and gets all the border traffic coming through, and he told her there's a group of Germans offering a lot of money for information. They seem confident they'll find someone to talk.'

'Who's in charge?'

He shook his head. 'I don't know, but it doesn't sound like the usual Wehrmacht. Sofia's nephew said the one giving the orders strides around in civilian clothes, acts like he owns the place, straight out of Berlin. He's a big, powerful guy, mean around the eyes. Her nephew said you wouldn't want to get in a fight with him. I think one of his men was in here one day, trying to find out what I knew, but I didn't see anyone like that.'

'Could you find out for me?'

'I'll ask him, but I wanted you to be on your guard. You know as well as I do that these types don't just use money to get what they want.'

The rumours of a German invasion were surging through the Fort, redoubling efforts to protect the Swiss National Redoubt, the major defence against invasion over the Alps. Discussions in the officers' mess rarely moved away from dissection of the German losses on the Eastern Front. The radio and newspapers were full of it, and speculation that the Germans would defeat Switzerland was rife. Most of the officers believed that an invasion across the Alps was the only remaining strategic option left for the Nazis, which meant that they were Switzerland's last defence against attack.

Max gestured towards Christophe, who was waiting impatiently in the van, door wide open. 'I didn't know you were involved in this caper. More the kind of thing Valérie would get herself mixed up in. I thought you had some sense.'

He sounded just like the old Max and Philippe suppressed a grin. 'It's important, Max. We're funding the French Resistance. And nobody saw us.'

But the truth was, Philippe's plan of getting Christophe out of the station without leaving any trace behind them had spectacularly failed. He wondered what they would encounter when they returned to the station.

'I hope not.'

Philippe put his arm round Max's shoulder as they walked outside. 'Thanks for the information. I'll make sure I come down to the shooting range very soon. Please tell Sofia I'll come over to the house to see her.'

He stuck out his hand and Max gripped it. 'I'll tell her. Make sure you keep an eye on your friend here.' He nodded his head towards Christophe. 'If he wasn't up to this mischief, he'd be doing something else. And taking everyone else along with him.'

'Are you coming or are you going to chat all night?' Christophe had got out and was holding the door open for Philippe.

'I'm coming now. We're done.'

Max disappeared back inside, and they drove off. They didn't see a soul on the road on the short drive back to Saint-Maurice and neither Philippe nor Christophe seemed inclined to talk. Philippe was too busy thinking about Max's warning. He had no doubt that given his level and the military secrets he knew, he was a target and the Germans would find their way to him before long. And then there were the dangers Valérie was facing. The photo he'd seen had filled him with emotion, and it had given him a tiny glimpse of how she felt, with her determination to reunite the French family. It made him fearful of the risks she might take.

As they got closer to the station, Philippe's thoughts went to what they might find there. Christophe was obviously thinking the same thing. 'I think we should park the van round the corner from the station, change into our army clothes and act like we were just arriving.'

'Have you got our uniforms in here?' asked Philippe.

Christophe pointed into the back seat with a smile.

'Right,' said Philippe. 'And remember the German knows what you look like, so you'd better be careful.'

Although it was the middle of the night, the goods yard was busy with people picking up their deliveries from the train that had just arrived. Everything from farm machinery to animal feed was being loaded on to battered carts and trucks by young and old before being driven away into the night.

Yves came round the back of the truck, and Christophe shook his hand warmly. 'We owe you for getting us out safely.' He grinned at Philippe. 'You need to be properly introduced. This is Yves, Nathalie's older brother.'

Philippe could see the resemblance in the stocky young man standing in front of him, the cropped blond hair and shy smile the same as his sister. He was looking serious and glanced over his shoulder before starting to speak in a low voice. 'I can't stay for long. I don't know what happened to you tonight but if I hadn't managed to distract the guards away from the tunnel, it would have been all over. They raised an almighty rumpus when they found the man you knocked out. Of course, they couldn't report it. They know the authorities would be very interested in what they're doing.'

'I'm sorry. It was my fault.' Christophe looked crestfallen, but the mood only lasted for a moment before the glint returned to his eye. 'We got out though. It all worked in the end.'

Yves shook his head. 'It was too close, they suspected something was going on. You could have been killed in there. And Philippe, some of the station workers were asking me about you.

One of them saw you in the van.' Yves frowned. 'And I bet the Germans will be paying that station worker to keep quiet about what they're up to. I don't think they'll get away with it for much longer. They're getting jumpy for a reason and it's because they're worried about being caught by their own side. Some official is going to realise that part of their hoard is going missing en route. We saw tonight how unpredictable they're becoming, the usual timings all changed.' Christophe tried to interrupt but Yves raised his hand to silence him. 'And that makes it too dangerous for us to carry on. We can't risk doing this again, we have to stop before someone else gets hurt.'

They heard a shout from the other side of the goods yard and they turned round to see that everyone else had left, the last truck disappearing up the street through the town.

'Someone needs me,' said Yves. He shook their hands in turn. 'I'm sorry but I can't help you anymore. We can't risk doing this again.' He slapped Christophe's shoulder and his face broke into a grin. 'Nathalie would never forgive me if I let anything happen to you. You haven't seen my little sister lose her temper. It doesn't happen often, but when it does, you need to take cover.'

He walked briskly back into the station, leaving Philippe and Christophe staring at one another.

'He doesn't mean it,' said Christophe. 'He'll change his mind.'

'It sounded like he meant it to me.'

'No. He just got a fright tonight, that's all. It's the first time things have gone wrong. He'll get over it.' Christophe closed the tailgate on the back of the truck with a flourish. 'We need to get back.'

They got into the cab and Christophe started up the engine. 'Thanks for helping me.'

'You're welcome. Felt good to punch a Nazi. I told you I should have come before.'

They didn't speak until they were passing the Grand Hotel and turned into the road leading up to the Fort.

'How's Stefano getting on?' asked Christophe finally. Stefano was a young soldier from Ticino, the Italian-speaking part of Switzerland. 'You know I was surprised when Stefano volunteered to join your sniper unit. He'd never shown any interest in shooting before, so it seemed to come out of nowhere.'

'What are you getting at?'

Christophe didn't answer and Philippe looked at him. 'Come on. Out with it.'

'I spoke to a couple of my men about him. One of them said he knew Stefano, they come from the same town, Locarno, on Lake Maggiore.'

'And what did he say?'

Christophe didn't reply until he'd negotiated one of the sharp turns on the mountain road. 'He's a friend of his younger brother. Didn't know Stefano so well but I got the impression that the family is pretty well known in the area. One of his uncles in Italy is high up in the Fascist party. I guess that isn't exactly something Stefano would want to broadcast.'

'So, is Stefano a Fascist? Is that what the man said?'

Christophe shrugged. 'He didn't say that in so many words, but that's what worried me. He almost seemed scared of saying anything. He was very keen that Stefano didn't know we were talking about him. Asked me why I wanted to know, made me promise you would be the only person I told.'

Philippe thought about the quiet young man he'd known since coming to the Fort. Stefano had never hinted at having political views of any kind and carefully avoided expressing any opinions on the Axis powers when they were roundly criticised by the other soldiers in his unit. 'I'll keep an eye on him, but it sounds a lot like hearsay to me, Christophe. He doesn't neces-sarily share the same views as his family.'

Christophe looked unusually grim as he turned into the gate of the Fort and switched off the engine. 'I know, but I don't like the sound of it. Why was he so keen to be in your unit? If there are German spies nosing around the valley, you don't want them getting too close. Just make sure you have other people around you when you're out on exercises with him, that's all I'm saying.'

Philippe climbed down from the truck, deep in thought. That was twice tonight he'd been warned about German spies.

As the door clanged shut behind him and he walked towards the fort through the bracing mountain air, Philippe couldn't shake the feeling that something was coming at him at a breath-taking pace, a danger he could do nothing about.

Whether it was coming for him, Christophe or Valérie, he did not know.

TEN

VALÉRIE

Geneva, Switzerland

A few days later, Valérie slipped into the bookshop and went up the stairs to the apartment. As she walked upstairs, it got darker, the shop windows replaced by the closed shutters in the apartment. By the time she got to the parlour, the shutters made it feel like night-time, the room only dimly lit with a few flickering candles.

'Valérie! I'm so glad you're here.' Pierre jumped up from the sofa and Jules looked at her eagerly. 'I'll make some tea.' He walked to the kitchen and Valérie took his place next to the little boy, who looked pale and wan this morning.

She put her arm around him and squeezed. 'I thought I'd see how you were settling in. I'm doing the deliveries for my father, but I've got a little time spare.'

Jules looked up at her seriously. No smiles today. 'I was asking Papa some questions and I want to ask you too.'

'You can ask me anything you like.' She felt her heart contract, she would do anything to give him back his smile.

'Why are the Germans chasing us? Why do they hate us so much?' He waited for an answer expectantly.

She swallowed, knowing that he might be a child, but it wasn't a child's question. He deserved a proper answer. 'You know that the Germans have invaded all of Europe, everywhere apart from Switzerland?'

He nodded. 'At home, we would listen to the radio, and we heard what they were doing.'

'I think the best way to explain it is that they want everybody to be like them. It's very sad, and of course it's wrong, but they don't want people of a different race, religion or political opinion. And they've decided they want to remove all those people, including Jewish people like you. That explains why they're imprisoning people in France, and why even before the war they forced people to leave Germany.' She thought of Jacob Steinberg, forced to leave Frankfurt, lucky that he could take enough money with him to start a new life.

She looked down at his wide brown eyes. 'Does that make sense?'

He thought for a moment, then nodded again. 'But how can they do things that are so wrong, and they think they're right?'

'I don't know, Jules. But lots of people don't agree with them. And that's why I'm helping you, why so many of us are fighting to beat them.'

Pierre came back into the parlour carrying two steaming cups, smiling when he saw the lighter expression on his son's face. 'Did Valérie answer your question better than me?'

'Not really better, just differently. I want to understand what's happening, why it's happening. It makes me less frightened.'

Pierre handed Valérie a cup. 'Jules needs to know why these things are happening to us. He's always been like that, full of questions and never satisfied with easy answers.'

'He's quite right,' replied Valérie. 'Too many people don't

want to know the answers or face the truth, because it makes life difficult.'

'I don't like it here,' said Jules. 'It's always dark and I can't go outside. I want to see the sky.'

'I'm sorry.' Pierre smiled sadly. 'We are very grateful, and I know we must keep the shutters closed for our own safety, but he's missing the sunlight. We need to stay here, though, I don't want to go out of Geneva. I'd feel like I was leaving Anne-Marie and Madeleine behind.'

They talked for a while, and Valérie listened with a heavy heart as Pierre told her all about his beautiful wife and their darling daughter, who was always so full of laughter and smiles, even in these dark days of war.

Reluctantly she took her leave, but as she walked slowly down the stairs, she felt seriously troubled about Pierre and Jules. Pierre was worried about Anne-Marie and Madeleine's safety, but every day they stayed in Geneva the risk they would be discovered grew and grew. What if all four members of this precious family were soon to be lost to the Nazis?

Valérie had been calling in to the post office to try to speak to Marianne, hoping she would have heard news of Anne-Marie and Madeleine through her Resistance contacts or from any of the phone calls she'd put through, but she had missed her each time. Today she would go directly to Marianne's home. There was no more time to waste.

ELEVEN

VALÉRIE

Valérie cycled along the Route de Florrisant, one of the main
roads out of Geneva, passing by small gardens and then larger
fields, all being cultivated for food. Every spare piece of land in
Switzerland had been taken over for food production. There
were many more people working the land than before the war,
when she'd cycled the familiar route to the farm across the
border from Annemasse where Marianne and Emile lived.
Now there were older men, women and children dotted around
the fields bent over their tasks, as well as a few younger men,
demobilised from the army now that the Swiss forces were
concentrated on protecting the Alps.

She turned off the main road just before the Swiss-French
border at Chêne-Thônex and paused at the junction to watch a
convoy of German lorries beyond the border post. More
German soldiers to police the French countryside and flush out
refugees trying to escape. Marianne's family's farm had been
searched many times over the years by the Swiss police sympa-
thetic to the Germans, even before the fall of Vichy France.

It was during one search that Marianne's father had been

shot at the start of the war, after coming back to the farm late one night, when he was caught in a fight between the Resistance and an undercover German unit working in Vichy France. An unfortunate accident, the Swiss police had said, with the hint of a suggestion that it had been one of the French Resistance fighters who had been responsible.

None of them believed it. Emile said that even before the fall of Vichy France, the French authorities had identified the safe houses on the border and had been waiting for the chance to block another escape route. From the start of the war, the Nazis wanted to destroy the Jewish people and obliterate them from Europe.

Their actions only resulted in Marianne and Emile agreeing to work for the Resistance. Since that day, they led families and children across the border to safety in Switzerland and refused to take any payment. And now Emile was dead too, taken from his family just like his father before him.

The family's stone farmhouse was in the municipality of Presinge, standing proudly above the low barns where they kept the cattle in winter. There weren't many cows left now and the house looked shabby and neglected, with little money spare to spend on buildings when people were short of food and few men were around to do the work.

She leaned her bike against the wall of the farmhouse and heard a familiar voice. 'Valérie, how lovely to see you.'

Marianne's mother came round the corner, two farm dogs prancing around her ankles. She wiped her hands on her apron and hugged Valérie tightly. When she drew back, Valérie felt a stab of sorrow when she saw the familiar face so lined and worn. Marianne's mother was an older version of her friend, tall and strong from years of hard work on the farm, but she was thinner now and seemed to stoop as she led the way into the house.

'Is Marianne at home?'

A shadow passed over the older woman's face. 'She's upstairs in her room. She couldn't face going out today, so she'll be pleased to see you.'

Valérie followed the older woman up the wooden staircase.

'How are you both? We've been so worried about Marianne.'

Marianne's mother stopped with her hand on the banister and looked at Valérie, eyes moist with tears. 'It's been hard, and some days are worse than others. Marianne always looked after Emile and feels that she let him down, that she wasn't there when he needed her most.'

Valérie looked down at the hand gripping the rail and took a step forward. 'Madame, you need to sit down.'

She looked as if she would collapse if she wasn't holding on to something. But she didn't hear Valérie. 'It was such a shock. We didn't know he was planning to go into town that day, he never told us.' She shook her head and opened the door, unable to carry on. 'Marianne, look who's come to see you,' she said gently before leaving them alone and closing the door quietly behind her.

Valérie crossed the room swiftly and hugged her friend, keeping hold of her hands as they sat down on the bed. Marianne used to be tall and buxom, bronzed and healthy from hours spent outside, but she was thinner now, her rosy cheeks pale against her black hair, and there were dark rings under her eyes.

'I've been worried about you, we all are. You haven't been in the café for months.'

'I know. I've wanted to come back, but the thought of laughing and joking, after what's happened... I just couldn't face it.' She clutched Valérie's hands, the words tumbling out. 'I thought I was getting over it, but when the police told me they couldn't find the man who you said had pushed him that day, it felt worse than ever. Work was bad enough, going into the same building where Emile met me and walked me home. But going into the café, I wasn't strong enough to deal with everyone. Can you understand?'

'Of course.'

The sound of dogs barking floated in through the open window and Valérie stood up and looked out at the green fields stretching in front of the farm, trying to suppress her questions, their urgency threatening to overwhelm her. She took a couple of deep breaths. It was a tranquil place, far away from the bustle of the city. Valérie could understand why Marianne found solace there, but she would have to crash into her friend's sanctuary to ask about Anne-Marie and Madeleine.

'What's the matter? Has anything happened?'

She hadn't forgotten Marianne's uncanny ability to sense what others were feeling. It seemed as strong as ever.

Valérie sat down next to Marianne. 'Did you hear what happened to the French woman and her daughter, Anne-Marie and Madeleine, who didn't get across the border at the weekend with the rest of the family? The husband saw them being picked up by a German car and thought they'd been arrested. He's refusing to move from Geneva until he knows. Have you heard anything?'

'Yes, I have. They weren't arrested. We have someone in the hospital there who saw them arrive.'

Valérie felt relief flow through her body. 'So, they're still in the hospital? We could get them out from there?'

But Marianne was shaking her head. 'They were there, but the Germans started checking papers, so they disappeared. Our contact doesn't know where they went.'

'But they haven't been captured?'

'Not as far as we know, but the Germans are looking for them. That family are on the Nazis' most wanted list, so we think if they were captured, the Germans would make quite a big thing out of their execution. Not just because the family helped too many Jews escape, but the father was involved in sabotage operations that killed some high-profile Nazis. Their spies in Geneva will be searching for him and will get him sent back to France before long. They'll kill them all. You must persuade him and his son to get away from the border. I didn't realise they were still here.'

'I've tried, Marianne, but he won't budge. If there is still hope his wife and daughter haven't been taken and that they could be joining them soon, he won't leave.'

Her eyes moved down to the chest of drawers next to the window. Photographs crowded on the top and she went closer to look at them. They were of Marianne and her family, some of Marianne and Emile as children and, to one side, a recent photograph of a group of what appeared to be farm workers at harvest time, laughing at the camera. She picked it up and came back to sit next to her friend.

'I haven't seen this one before. I recognise Emile and Jean, but who are the others?'

'People from the area, mostly friends of Emile. They helped us last year with the harvest. We had such fun together.'

She looked from one figure to another and smiled. 'They all look like farm workers, but they aren't.' She pointed at the figures. 'He's one of the teachers at the local school across in France. The woman next to him is called Geneviève. She volunteers for the Swiss Red Cross and works at a children's home near Lyons. Her parents still live near here and she came back for a few weeks to stay with them. The two at the side of the group work on the railway. They're train drivers and will stop the train at unscheduled stops to let the children get off. You know Sébastien who lives in the farm next to us. The man with the moustache runs the local hotel, the small one a couple of streets away... you know the one, serves the best fondue round here.'

She touched another figure. 'This good-looking one, he's François.'

'I know him. I met him yesterday. He's my main contact now in the Resistance.'

Marianne nodded. 'Jean came to see us to tell us he was going away.'

She smiled at Valérie's look of surprise. 'We've known Jean for years. He was a friend of my father's when they were young, he always came to visit us when he worked at the local schools. When Emile was so angry after father died, so desperate to do something to fight the Germans, it was Jean who suggested he help the Resistance by collecting children and families and leading them into Switzerland. He didn't want my mother to know, but I'm sure she suspected, even though she never said anything about it.'

Marianne pointed to an older man at the edge of the group. 'Monsieur Colbert runs a small engineering business, repairing all kinds of machinery. Typewriters and that kind of thing. François works for him, delivers parts and machinery right across the whole area.'

'François is very good-looking, isn't he?'

Marianne chuckled, sounding much more like her old self. 'Believe me, he's so charming that all the girls are half in love with him. I've seen him in action. When he turns on the charm, he makes you feel like you're the most important person in the world.'

'They're all your Resistance contacts, aren't they?'

Her smile faded and she looked at Valérie. 'Yes. And before you ask, I don't believe that any of these people could be the traitor.'

Valérie didn't respond, so many questions rushing through her mind that she didn't know where to start. She never normally had to deliberate before speaking to Marianne, they knew one another so well and had no secrets from one another. But for the first time, Valérie felt unsure. Someone was betraying them, endangering all the people they were trying to help, and it could be anyone in that photograph. Staring at it, she wondered how many of those smiling faces would make it through the war, particularly now the Resistance were in so much danger.

Marianne's pale face was flushed now. 'So, is that why you came to see me today, to get information about that family and the Resistance?'

Valérie shook her head, trying to make her understand. 'No, I wanted to see you anyway because I was worried about you. I miss you. We all do.'

No longer able to hide her urgency, Valérie sat down again on the bed and grasped her friend's hands again, looking up into her face, pleading with her. 'But it's true that I need your help. Someone is still leaking information about the Resistance to the Germans. Three fighters were killed because of it, just a few days ago, and I'm terrified that whoever it is will find out where Jules and Pierre are. Did Emile ever mention anyone he suspected of being the traitor?'

Marianne gazed at the photograph, shaking her head.

'Emile said to me before he died that he was going to meet someone who knew who it was,' insisted Valérie. 'Please, Marianne. Who would he have spoken to? You must help me, or more people will die. I can't bear to think about what could happen to Pierre and Jules if the Germans find out where they are.'

'All right, I'll tell you what I know, but it's not much more than I've said.'

Marianne pointed at the figures in the photo. 'Emile didn't talk about his work for the Resistance, but he often told me who he was meeting when he went out late at night. It was usually the teacher Patrice or Anaïs from the Swiss Red Cross. Some-times it was Jean. They led the groups of children from the school and handed them over to Emile to take across the border. Monsieur Colbert prints false identity papers, passports and other documents for the children coming across the border, and François helps him.'

Marianne looked back down at the photograph. 'I know Emile suspected someone. And that person didn't just leak secrets to the Germans but also caused trouble among the Swiss working with the Resistance, lost passeurs their money, made them mistrust one another. Both things would damage the French Resistance and affect their ability to fight back, of course.'

The passeurs, people who took refugees into Switzerland, sometimes took money to guide people to safety. There were many who saved lives and refused to accept payment, but there were others who stole the money and left the refugees to their fate.

Marianne continued. 'It might have been a member of another unit in the Jura Mountains. They take people through the Risoux Forest into Switzerland, north of Geneva. It's the other route across the border that the smugglers use too. I hear the Germans talking about it all the time on the phone at the telephone exchange. The border goes in a straight line north of Nyon and the police are forever patrolling that section, trying to catch as many refugees as they can and send them back. '

'Do you know anyone in the unit?'

'No. They operate in the Jura Mountains, they all live up there.'

Valérie stood up and hugged her friend, holding onto the photograph. 'Can I keep this for a while? I promise I'll give it back.'

Marianne nodded and Valérie stretched out her hand. 'Come back with me to the café, please Marianne. I've got someone I'd like you to meet. She's called Nathalie, she works in a jeweller's shop in Geneva, the smart one on the Rue du Rhône. She's a friend of Christophe and Philippe from Saint-Maurice and I don't think she knows many people in Geneva. I promised to introduce her to you and to Geraldine.'

Marianne looked uncertain. 'I'm sorry, I'm not sure I'm ready yet. Maybe tomorrow, I could come into town and meet you after work.'

Valérie took her hand gently. 'Why wait? Come back with me now.' She looked out of the window at the trees swaying gently in the warm breeze. 'It'll only be for an hour or so. I need to go back to have supper with my father anyway, so I won't be able to stay for long.' She smiled. 'Come with me, Marianne?'

But Marianne shook her head. 'Not yet. I promise I'll come to the café in a few days.'

They came downstairs together, and Valérie picked up her bike. 'You're going into work tomorrow? I've missed you every time I've tried to see you.'

'Yes. I've taken too many days off as it is, and they'll give my job to someone else if I don't turn up more regularly. I'm sure a few of the other girls would jump at the chance.'

As they kissed each other's cheeks to say goodbye, a tall, thick-set young man walked round the corner of the house, two large dogs at his heels. It was Sébastien, and he nodded to Valérie and spoke to Marianne. 'I'm glad to see you're out in the fresh air.'

Marianne blushed. The dogs ran towards her, and she bent down to make a fuss of them.

'I was coming to see if you wanted to take a walk with me. The dogs need some exercise.'

Valérie left them and headed back to the city. She glanced back once and saw them walk down the side of the field next to the farmhouse, Marianne laughing at something Sébastien had said. Her stomach tightened anxiously.

Could he be the person betraying them?

Frustrated, she shook her head to clear her mind of its swirling suspicions. Without any real leads or evidence, they were meaningless. And finally, she had some news about Anne-Marie and Madeleine. She was so relieved to hear they had escaped from the Nazis' clutches at the hospital.

But where were they now?

TWELVE

ANNE-MARIE

Annemasse, France

Anne-Marie pulled the old blanket round Madeleine's shoulders.

'I'm cold, Maman. Why do we have to stay outside in this horrible shed? It smells bad. Why won't that lady let us stay in her house?'

Anne-Marie didn't know how she could answer without making things worse. As if they could be worse than they already were. She tried to make her voice light and tinged with laughter, determined not to allow the worry and fear to over-power them.

'It isn't that cold Madeleine. It's March, not the middle of winter. Anyway, the lady said it was better if we stayed out here. She's been so kind, so I didn't want to be difficult. Remember, this is our special adventure. It's like hide and seek, and we'll be harder to find in here. And then we can tell Papa and Jules all about it later.'

'But it's so dark. There isn't a light we can put on, not even a candle.'

'The light will come in the morning, mon petit chou. It's late. You need to go to sleep.'

But despite her quiet breathing for the next few minutes, she knew Madeleine wasn't asleep. Her daughter wouldn't give up so easily. She was like Pierre, tenacious to the point of stubbornness.

'Maman, do you think Papa and Jules really managed to get to Switzerland? They couldn't still be in France, could they? Hiding like we are?'

Anne-Marie's fears for Pierre and Jules burst into life. She missed them so much. Despair at her small family being split apart and terror that they might never be reunited filled her mind, and she struggled to find the words to comfort a frightened six-year-old.

'You heard what the lady said. They got across the border to Switzerland and they'll be waiting for us there.'

'Is that man coming back for us? The one that tried to get us across before?'

'I don't know, Madeleine, it might be someone else. We'll just have to wait and see.'

The whispered warning of the scared Frenchwoman came back to her. 'The Nazis are looking for you everywhere. Someone has told them your husband managed to escape and they've redoubled their efforts to find you and your daughter. I don't know what you did to them but, whatever it was, it's made them determined to catch you. And they'll kill anyone that gets in their way.'

Anne-Marie could have told her exactly why the Nazis were so determined to catch them and why they were so angry they'd failed to get Pierre. It wasn't just that they prepared false papers for the Jewish children they helped escape, or that she coached them for hours in their new identities. It was Pierre's late-night sabotage missions they really hated. The night he came back from blowing up a German armament depot, saying that a Nazi officer had been killed, was the beginning of the end. First the Germans had shot ten innocent civilians to show the Lyonnais the price for killing German officers. Then they had hunted down everyone who could have taken part that night. If Pierre hadn't been warned, they'd have been pulled out of their beds in the middle of the night and shot too.

Madeleine shifted in her arms and, kissing her hair softly, Anne-Marie knew she was finally asleep. She leaned against the wooden side of the shed and watched the door, alert to the sounds outside. She was exhausted, but her mind was too active to sleep, and she flinched at the slightest sound. Even the breeze in the trees and the sound of an owl made her jump and tense her muscles.

How much longer could she keep going? She lay down, clutching Madeleine tightly, and closed her eyes, unwilling to think about the future, trying to ignore the pains in her belly.

THIRTEEN

VALÉRIE

Geneva, Switzerland

The road back to Geneva was busy with people going home from work at the end of the afternoon and others leaving the fields after a long day. Valérie had just enough time to swing round to meet Nathalie before the jeweller's shop closed, and then she would be on her way to the bookshop. She was desperate to tell Pierre that Anne-Marie and Madeleine weren't being held in a Nazi prison, and that so far as the Resistance knew, they were still alive.

Valérie cycled as fast as she could down the Rue de Rhône, worried that Nathalie may have already left. But when she reached the jeweller's, she saw Nathalie reaching into the corner of the shop window, facing away from her, carefully removing the rings and necklaces from the display to store them safely for the night. Her blonde hair was gathered into a ribbon at the nape of her neck, a few strands escaping and lying against the ruby velvet cushions as she stretched across to gather the last few items.

The noise of the busy street was sucked away as Valérie went inside and the heavy door swung shut behind her. She stood in the haven of quietness, blinking at the glass cases holding silver and gold ornaments, sharp edges glinting as they were struck by the golden shards of the late afternoon sun streaming through the window.

'Mademoiselle, can I help you?'

A very old man came out of the door concealed in one of the polished wooden panels at the back of the shop, dressed all in black, his hair completely white. His head was bowed, and he held on to the counter as he made his way towards her, as if his thin legs couldn't support him. When he stopped and raised his head, she looked into a pair of very sharp eyes.

'Thank you, Monsieur, but I've come to see Nathalie.'

Hearing her voice, Nathalie twisted round, her hands over-flowing with sparkling gems. She smiled at Valérie. 'Valérie! I didn't see you come in – I won't be long. I just have to close up the shop.'

The old man smiled at her excitement. 'My dear, I can finish everything. I'm pleased to meet your friend?' He paused, his voice ending on a question.

'Valérie Hallez. My father is—'

'Ah, Albert Hallez, one of our most skilled watchmakers. Please give my regards to your father, Mademoiselle.'

'Are you sure, Monsieur Savarin?' Nathalie looked at the old man, concern curbing her pleasure.

He nodded and Nathalie smiled as she carefully put the jewels she was holding into a strongbox on the counter. 'Thank you! I'll get my coat.'

The shop door opened again, the sound of the street intruding into their quiet oasis, and Valérie moved out of the way of the new customer, catching sight of a dark coat at the corner of her vision. Monsieur Savarin raised his thin voice.

'I am sorry Monsieur, but we are closed.'

A younger man had come in behind him and shut the door with a bang. He was tall and dark-haired, dressed in a smart grey suit that was marginally too tight, his face flushed with irritation.

'It's me, Father... we can't close yet. Herr Fuchs is looking for something special. I promised we would keep the shop open a bit longer.' He looked at Valérie almost accusingly, as if to ask what she was doing in their way, when Nathalie came running out of the back and stopped when she saw him.

'Hello Maurice.'

He didn't hesitate. 'You're leaving early, are you?'

'I have said that Nathalie can go with her friend,' his father intervened, the calm voice settling over his son's abrupt tone. He turned to his young assistant.

'Enjoy yourself my dear. I will see you tomorrow morning at the usual time.'

'Thank you, Monsieur.' Nathalie and Valérie hustled themselves outside before Maurice could think of another reason to delay them. Valérie picked up her bike and they walked briskly along the street and towards the old town. Apart from one glance they were quiet until they'd turned the corner and then, finally out of sight, burst out laughing.

'I thought we weren't going to get away,' said Nathalie after a few minutes. 'Monsieur Savarin never likes arguing with Maurice, especially if there are customers in the shop.'

'It isn't difficult to see why Christophe doesn't like him,' said Valérie. 'And that German, looking down his nose at me. I had as much right to be there as he did.'

'Maurice is always bringing in people after hours to look around on their own. He says that's why he gets such good sales from businessmen buying things for their wives and sweethearts. That's when I met the blonde woman who was with your friend the other night, she came in with Maurice at the end of the day.'

Valérie caught sight of a necklace that had fallen out of the neck of Nathalie's formal black dress and caught the light.

'Your pendant is lovely. What is it?'

Nathalie's hand went up to her neck and she blushed.

'It's an edelweiss flower, silver with mother of pearl leaves and a diamond in the centre. Christophe gave it to me.' She slid it back beneath the neck of her dress. 'It's my favourite flower, I gather bunches of it when I'm up in the mountains above Saint-Maurice. Christophe gave me it to remind me of home.'

'Why do you keep it hidden?'

Nathalie pulled out the silver chain and looked again at the flower shape, fingers fluttering over the fine tendrils stretching out from the glittering diamond in the centre. Her features clouded over. 'Christophe had it made for me in a local jeweller's in Martigny. I know that the edelweiss is important to the Germans as well as to the Swiss, but I loved it so much. Christophe made me promise to keep it hidden. We wouldn't want anyone to think I sympathise with the Nazis or with what they're doing.'

Nathalie sighed. 'Someone came into the shop who wanted an edelweiss necklace for his wife, and he went away without buying anything when I said we didn't sell anything like that. But I always wear it under my clothes. I never go out without it.'

By this time they had emerged on to the Place du Bourg-de-Four and Nathalie stopped to look around her at the ancient square, the tall buildings with wooden shutters stretching away on either side and the bustling chatter of people sitting at the outside café tables spilling onto the pavements under colourful canopies.

'It's so pretty here,' said Nathalie.

Geraldine was speaking to Bernard outside the front door of

the café and neither noticed them cross the square, too busy having their argument to be aware of anyone else.

'That's my friend Geraldine, and Bernard works at the grocer's shop opposite,' Valérie said to Nathalie as they came closer. 'They're either arguing or the best of friends. You never know which it's going to be from one day to the next.'

Valérie raised her voice. 'Hey, what's the matter? What are you arguing about?'

She didn't really expect an answer, but they both turned on her.

'Where have you been?' said Geraldine.

'Why won't she answer a simple question?' snapped Bernard, frustration boiling over in his voice. 'I only asked when you would be back and all I got was a lecture about how it was none of my business and why did I want to know anyway.'

'You can't be too careful these days,' flashed back Geraldine. 'You don't know how people could use the information you give them.'

He stuck his hands into the pockets on his apron and hunched his powerful shoulders. 'People? I'm "people" now, am I? You've known me for years, Geraldine. Have you just decided I'm not to be trusted? You'd better not ask me for any more chocolate or cigarettes. You might not know what I'm giving you.'

Geraldine had tired of the argument and was smiling at Nathalie. 'Ignore us. We don't mean it really. We haven't met, have we?'

'Nathalie is a friend of Christophe, she works in one of the jewellery shops in town. I can't stay long, but I wanted you to meet her.'

Turning her back on Bernard, Geraldine took Nathalie's arm and led her past the tables into the cafe. 'I'll show you round. It's lovely to meet someone new, especially a friend of Christophe's.'

Valérie watched them go and then shook her head at Bernard. 'Don't be so hard on Geraldine. She was only trying to look out for her friends. Everyone has been more on edge since Emile died.'

He sighed and dragged his fingers through his dark hair. 'I know I shouldn't rise to it, but I can't stop myself. I only asked when you'd be back, and she started haranguing me about asking too many questions. Honestly, I know these are strange times but how can she not trust me by now?'

Valérie watched Geraldine point Nathalie towards their usual table at the back of the café, introducing her to her father at the doorway.

'She's just trying to be a good friend, in her own way,' she said finally.

All she got was a grunt from Bernard. She looked at his glum expression and felt sorry for him, remembering a time when he and Geraldine were the best of friends. 'Why did you want to see me?'

'I've got a message for you from Henry,' he muttered in a low voice. 'He wants to see you tonight. His friend Tom arrived, and he'd like you to meet him.'

She paused as Geraldine's father looked out of the door of the café to check no one needed to be served outside and waited until he'd gone back in. 'Where?'

'In the apartment on the Place De-Grenus. Come to the shop first and I'll give you the key Henry left with me. He said he'll probably be late.'

She nodded and went into the café. Geraldine was sitting next to Nathalie at their favourite table with a clear view of the front door, and furthest away from the other tables. Even low-voiced conversations couldn't be overheard; Valérie had checked.

'Has he gone?' Geraldine glanced out of the door.

'Yes, he's gone. I know you were trying to protect me, but

why were you so harsh with him? It's just Bernard, he's our friend. You're always asking him to fetch some delivery or other when you run out. One of these days he'll turn round and refuse. Then where will you be?'

Geraldine's eyes filled with tears, and she tossed her blonde head as if she could brush away Valérie's words, but her voice was unsteady. 'I thought he liked me, but he's always criticising me these days, he says I'm too friendly with the Italian soldiers now. What does he expect me to do? Be rude to them, when soldiers are the only people who have any money to spend? They keep this café going.'

'I don't think anyone expects you to be rude to them, Geraldine. But you don't have to be quite so friendly either.' Valérie couldn't resist adding that, though she knew it was a waste of breath.

'Excuse me, I have to work.'

They watched her glide to the door and delight the group of soldiers who had just come into the café by greeting them in fluent Italian, then lead them to a table outside and take their order, flirting with each in turn.

'She's incorrigible,' said Valérie, torn between amusement and exasperation. 'I think she's fonder of Bernard than she's prepared to admit. His disapproval just makes her worse. I wouldn't be surprised if they end up together.'

Nathalie giggled. 'She's fun. And she was very kind to me, said we could go out for the afternoon one day when she's off work. I think she really means it.'

'Yes, I'm sure she does. And she won't forget either.'

Valérie frowned and took a deep breath. She was well aware of all the times Geraldine had provided support when she'd needed it, showing an extremely practical and resourceful side to her character. But Marianne's conviction that Geraldine let slip more information than she knew to her customers and admirers gave her no choice but to warn Nathalie.

'I know Geraldine can be kind, and I think you should meet up with her if you can, but...' She sighed, not able to find a way of softening the warning. 'I think you should be cautious about what you say. She means well and I'm sure she would never intend to let slip information she's been told in confidence, but she loves to be spoiled. I worry that she forgets everything else when she craves that attention.'

She watched her friend laughing with the group of soldiers outside. 'I just wouldn't confide in Geraldine or tell her anything you don't want repeated to anyone else. Then you won't risk that information being passed on.' She felt like a traitor as Nathalie followed her gaze with a worried look, her innocent pleasure in making a new friend deflated. 'I'm sorry, but it's better you know now.'

'I suppose so, but it makes it hard, doesn't it? This war is making it so difficult for everyone.' Nathalie touched the edelweiss pendant round her neck, as if it were a rosary, protecting her from harm. 'Christophe said I could trust you, that you are helping Jewish people escape from France. '

Valérie sighed. 'I'm doing my best, but right now I feel like I'm failing. The family I need to get out of Geneva have been split up and I can't do anything until they're all here.' She shook her head. 'The father and son are in my care, but we don't know where his wife and daughter are. He won't hear of leaving until we find them, and I just don't know what to do.' She looked down, her voice unsteady.

Nathalie grasped Valérie's hand, stilling her restless fingers. 'Let me help. We could try and get them to come with me. They could stay at my aunt's house in Nyon. It's not that far into Switzerland, so they wouldn't feel too far away from the border, but it's a small town and no one would be looking for refugees there.'

Valérie's spirits lifted a little at the offer. Maybe this could work. 'It's worth a try, they're only a few minutes away. I need to speak to them now anyway.'

She looked at Nathalie, wondering if she should really take her new friend to the safe house and show her everything. But instinctively, she knew Nathalie was trustworthy. She was already risking so much to help the Resistance.

'Come on, let's go. I'll ask them.'

FOURTEEN
VALÉRIE

They crossed the Place du Bourg-de-Four and strolled along the cobbled streets towards the old bookshop, enjoying the cool of the early evening and the smells of ragout and roasted meats wafting from the open windows along the way. Valérie caught Nathalie's arm. 'It's through this lane. Just follow me and watch your head.'

She looked around to check no one was watching them and then they ducked into the alley. They emerged into the lane at the back of the bookshop, Nathalie brushing the cobwebs from her hair. She looked around her with curiosity. Old Geneva was a rabbit warren of alleys and back streets hidden from sight and only used by the locals. 'You'd never know there was a lane running down the hill behind the shops. Where does it lead?'

'It drops right down and curves round the side of the city wall. Comes out at the bottom of the hill. You could go to the station that way. I often use it as a shortcut.'

'I never knew it was here.'

'No one does. It was closed up for years.' Valérie kicked an old broken pipe to the side of the lane. 'You have to watch your step, it's still full of rubbish along here.'

'Handy if you want to get in and out without being seen.'

Valérie nodded and took out the key for the bookshop. As they entered, she lifted her face to look upstairs, the sound of beautiful, haunting piano music unmistakeable in the small space. They went quietly up the stairs before turning to the smallest bedroom at the back of the apartment. Pierre was playing the piano, his dark head swaying as he was caught up in the music, unaware of his audience until Jules saw Valérie coming through the door and jumped up in excitement.

'Hello, Jules.' She smiled. 'This is my friend, Nathalie.'

'Valérie, come and see.'

On a cushion next to him on the floor, in a patch of light coming through a crack in the wooden shutter, a long-legged grey cat stretched his paws out. She came across to stroke the cat, who leaned into her hand and purred. 'How on earth did he find a way in here?'

Before Jules could reply, Pierre came over and shook Nathalie's hand. 'I'm pleased to meet you. I wasn't playing too loudly, was I? You couldn't hear me outside, I hope.'

Valérie shook her head. 'Not at all. I didn't know you played the piano. That was lovely, you must play for me sometime.' She looked round the room and saw an old blanket, which must have hidden it from sight, carefully folded in the corner. 'I didn't even realise the piano was still here.'

'Look what else I found in the cupboard over there,' cried Jules, holding up a chess set proudly.

Pierre was staring at Valérie anxiously. 'You've got news, haven't you?'

'Yes. My contacts said Anne-Marie and Madeleine were taken to the hospital, but the Germans you saw just left them there. They didn't suspect them.'

Pierre let his breath out in a long sigh and closed his eyes. 'Thank God they're safe.' He paused and then asked, 'Are they still there, in the hospital?'

'I'm sorry, no. They fled when there were rumours of a Nazi search of the hospital. My contacts don't know where they are, all they know is that they haven't been taken. They got away before the Germans reached them.'

Valérie could think of no way to soften the news and felt a stab of pity as she watched the emotions flit across his face, from joy and relief to fear. Jules clasped her hand, his large eyes tearful. 'So, you don't know where Maman is? Or my sister?'

She crouched down to speak to him. 'No, but I promise I'm doing all I can to find them.' She scratched the cat's ears. 'He's beautiful. I wonder how he got in. And what he's surviving on? Most of the cats around here are thin and hungry, not healthy like this handsome fellow.'

Some of the tension in Pierre's face melted away as he looked across at the cat and smiled. 'That's because he's feasting on the mice downstairs. He keeps bringing us examples of his hunting prowess and then disappears under Jules' bed to eat them.'

'Disgusting animal.'

'But I like him, Valérie. Don't you like him?' Jules looked up at her uncertainly and she hugged him close.

'Of course, I do. He's a sweetheart.'

Pierre ran his hands through his dark hair. 'I think I know where they might have gone.'

He reached into a pocket on the inside of his jacket and took out a tiny piece of paper, which he handed to her. 'The first address is where we stayed before we tried to cross the border. We got away before it was searched. She might have tried the second one. I know she memorised it.'

Valérie looked down at the scrap of paper. 'I know this area, south of the centre. I can ask if they're still there.' She put it into her satchel and swallowed, her determination solidifying in her stomach as she looked at his distraught face and then down at Jules, who was still holding onto her hand.

'But listen, Pierre. I still think you should leave. That's why my friend is here. She can take you out of Geneva, not far from the border but to somewhere safer than here. It will give us more time to find them.'

Pierre immediately shook his head, but she spoke over his objections. 'It's really not far, only a few kilometres away, and you won't have to live in darkness. It will be better for you and Jules.'

Nathalie spoke for the first time. 'I come in and out of Geneva every day for work, so I'll have the information about your wife and daughter as soon as we know. You can stay at my aunt's house for as long as you need to.'

But Pierre was still shaking his head. 'I'm sorry, you're being very kind. I can't explain it, but if we go away from here, I feel I'll lose them forever. We always said that if we were separated, we would meet again in Geneva.' He looked from one to the other. 'Please. Don't say we have to go, not yet.'

His words came straight from the heart. Before Valérie could respond, Nathalie made the decision for them. 'All right, you stay here for now. I'll ask my Resistance contacts if they know where your wife and daughter are. They're based in the Jura Mountains north of us rather than where you came from, but they might have heard something.' She held out her hand. 'Do you have a photograph I can show them?'

He took a small, dog-eared photograph out of his jacket pocket slowly and handed it across to her. Valérie stood up and came closer to look. He had described them to her, but he hadn't shown her a photograph before, and she could see in how tightly he clutched it between his thumb and forefinger just how precious it was to him. They were all smiling at the camera, Pierre looking happy and proud, his stunning wife with her arm around Jules and a blonde girl, younger than Jules. Valérie glanced down at Jules and smiled. He might have his father's darker colouring, but he had his mother's features, the same sloping eyebrows and shy smile.

'It's the only photo I have of us all.'

'I'll take care of it, I promise.'

Nathalie put it into her bag and rummaged around before she took out a thick wad of Swiss francs and handed them across to him. 'You might need this.'

He looked down at the notes in his hand but could only croak his thanks.

Nathalie touched Valérie's arm. 'I'd better go.'

Valérie hugged Pierre and Jules and followed Nathalie. They were silent as they walked downstairs into the cramped hall, lingering at the door before Valérie opened it.

'Thank you so much for that. They need all the help they can get.'

Nathalie's eyes were bright with unshed tears. 'It makes all the difference, meeting the people you're actually helping, talking with them and understanding what they really need.' She looked away. 'Christophe said I should tell you when I was handing over the money to the Resistance. He doesn't like me going up into the forest on my own and no one knowing. He always worries that someone will stop me, or something will go wrong. The next one is Friday evening. That's why I was so relieved you came to see me today, because I won't be at work tomorrow.'

'How do you arrange it?'

'I put a small sign at the back of the jewellery shop window at the weekend advertising a sale of second-hand jewellery in Martigny. That tells them I'll drop off the money the following Friday at the agreed time. Monsieur Savarin likes me to arrange the window designs, so I can include that whenever I want to. And when I'm not using the sign, I just hide it underneath the velvet cloth.'

Valérie was impressed. It was a simple arrangement, but

nevertheless effective. She tried to think of some way she could help Nathalie. 'You never know who picks up the message?'

Nathalie shook her head. 'And I usually don't see anyone in the Risoux Forest either. There is a particular place I leave the package, by a low wall that marks the border with France. But this time, I'll wait and speak to them. I'll show them the photograph and see if they know where Anne-Marie and Madeleine could be.'

Valérie tried not to let her concern show. Nathalie knew the risks of wandering round the border area unprotected, but she couldn't just leave her to face the danger alone. A familiar prickling sensation down her spine told her danger was coming, but she didn't know who for. 'Let me come with you, just this once. I have a bad feeling about it. I don't think you should go alone.'

Nathalie shook her head. 'No, I'll be fine, I've done this before. You need to stay and look after Pierre and Jules.' Her voice was decisive. 'I'll try my Resistance contacts to see if they know where Anne-Marie and Madeleine are. If they don't know anything, you can then go to that address in France and see if they're there.'

Valérie was torn, still filled with anxiety at the thought of Nathalie going into the forest without her. 'Have you never seen any of the Nazi guards up there? I thought they patrolled that part of the forest very tightly.'

She crossed her arms and shivered. 'I try not to think about that. I avoid the main checkpoints and the busy roads. I try to stay in Switzerland, though it depends where the guards are. Sometimes I have to go further into the forest than I'd like because I don't want to be seen. The forest is very thick, so I make sure I keep out of sight. There are plenty of places to hide if I hear someone coming.' She squared her shoulders. 'I need to go now.'

They embraced when they got outside, Valérie reluctant to

let go of her friend, but buoyed by the fierce determination in her eyes.

'Just be careful,' said Valérie.

'I will.'

'I'll call into the shop on Saturday to see you.'

Nathalie nodded. 'I'd like that.'

As she watched Nathalie walk along the narrow lane down the hill and disappear into the dusk, Valérie felt her stomach clench. While she knew her fears were driven by the Resistance friends she'd already lost in recent months, she could not help feeling terrified about the dangers Nathalie might encounter alone in the forest. She couldn't get out of her mind the Resistance fighters who were brutally beaten and murdered in Annemasse. Glancing up at the shuttered window above the bookshop, she shook herself, willing herself to be as brave as Nathalie and Pierre.

FIFTEEN

VALÉRIE

Valérie knocked on the door to the grocer's shop. It was late now, well after closing time, so the shop was dark inside, with no barbs of light escaping from behind the shuttered windows, and the heavy door was firmly locked. She tried the door handle and knocked again, more loudly this time, wondering if Bernard had given up on her. It was only a few minutes after the time they'd agreed, so he must be in there. He was probably still in a bad mood after the scene with Geraldine and she looked behind her across the square, impatient to be inside and out of sight of curious neighbours. She clutched her basket in front of her like a talisman, as if it would ward off any unwelcome questions.

Just as she was about to give up on him, she heard the rattle of the key in the lock and the door finally opened. Valérie slipped inside and Bernard bolted the door behind her. 'Is everything all right? I was worried about you. I thought you weren't coming,' he said, looking at her in concern.

'I'm sorry I'm late, there's a lot going on at the moment.'

'You weren't followed?'

'I checked. It's very quiet out there.'

He nodded, then led her to the back of the shop, behind the

counter, where he picked up some packages and placed them in her basket. He gave her some potato bread, some butter wrapped in paper and a lump of cheese.

'There's enough for you too. I thought you might have missed supper.'

Touched, Valérie smiled. 'Thanks.'

He handed her a key. 'You'll need this to get into Henry's apartment.'

He took her through the passageway behind the old wooden counter and opened the back door. She paused, wondering how best to start, then just decided to plunge in. 'Can I ask you something?'

'I suppose so.'

'You must be still working for Henry.'

He hesitated for a few seconds, then nodded.

'Has he told you he's looking for a traitor in the Resistance? Someone leaking information to the Germans.'

'He mentioned it.'

'Did Emile ever tell you he thought someone was feeding information about the Resistance to the Germans?'

Bernard shook his head. 'We never talked about anything like that.' He held her gaze. 'Emile never knew I worked for the SOE. No one knows even now, apart from you.' He shrugged. 'I don't do much. I pass information on to Henry about the smugglers I know, people who source supplies I can't get anywhere else. I know some of them take refugees across the border because I hear snippets of information they share with one another, but they never talk to me about it. It isn't exactly something they want to broadcast.'

Valérie had always put Bernard down as one of the people profiting from the war, buying and selling goods to make money for themselves. But then she'd witnessed his shock when Emile had died and had found out that he was involved with the SOE, another person working for Henry.

She didn't want to contemplate who else he might be working for.

'You thought the smugglers had killed Emile, didn't you? That he'd got in their way once too often and they decided to get rid of him, before he took away more of their money.'

He sighed. 'I thought that, yes. But I was wrong. I know they resented what he was doing, but one person couldn't damage their business enough to take such drastic action. They tried to frighten him off the night he was beaten up, but I think that's as far as they took it.' He laughed bitterly. 'And I pay them a premium for the stuff they get for me. They don't need the money, I make sure of that.'

'I think Emile discovered someone in the Resistance was a traitor, and they wanted to stop him from giving their identity away.'

Bernard shook his head. 'I don't know anything about that. I can't help you.'

She grasped his arm. 'Emile may not have been murdered by one of the passeurs, but someone wanted him silenced. I just don't know who it is.'

He sighed. 'I'm sorry about what happened to Emile. I liked him; he was a good person. But I don't know anything about a traitor.' He looked around them and lowered his voice. 'And I think you need to be careful, Valérie. If Emile died because he wouldn't keep his suspicions to himself, then you'll be next in line if you keep asking all these questions.'

Valérie shook her head. 'You know I have to find out the truth, I'm hiding a family whose lives depend on it.'

'And that's your problem. You can never leave things alone or accept you can't change things. You'll get yourself killed one of these days because you've meddled in something you don't understand.'

He nodded as if he'd done all that could be expected of him, then closed the shop door behind him. Valérie walked down the lane, glancing up at the bookshop, glad to see that it looked dark and deserted. No one would suspect anyone was in there, and they had to keep it that way. She carried on and crossed the Place de Bel-Air to the north bank of the river, passing the elegant apartment blocks in the Place De-Grenus, and let herself into Henry's building.

She ran up the stairs and opened the door to the apartment, closing it quickly behind her. Taking a deep breath to calm herself, she went towards the parlour. As she pushed the door, it slipped out of her fingers and banged against the wall.

A man half lying on the sofa jerked his head round to face her and pulled out a pistol.

Valérie's heart skipped a beat. It was him, sitting in front of her, the bearded man from the square, the one who'd pushed Emile.

Bernard had led her into a trap.

'It's you!' she gasped. 'What are you doing here?'

She dropped the basket and groped for the knife in her belt, knowing that it was a poor defence against his pistol. She'd left behind the gun Jean had given her and cursed her stupidity.

The man got to his feet, staggering as he stood up, his pistol pointing at her in a shaking hand. 'I'm Tom,' he said slowly. 'Who are you?'

She couldn't answer, couldn't seem to get any words to take shape. Deep from within her, the question burst out, her voice sounding unlike her own, as if a stranger was speaking. 'Why did you kill my friend?'

He looked just as shocked as she felt. 'What are you talking about? Who's your friend?'

'You're lying.' She stepped forward. 'You pushed him in front of a tram in the Place de Bel-Air. Just before Christmas. I've been looking for you for months.'

'Valérie.'

She spun around when she heard Henry's voice behind her.

He ran past her into the room and caught the man as he stag-gered, helping him to sit down.

'Come and help me. He's hurt.' He took some bandages out of his pocket, supporting the man with his other arm.

She was trying to take in what was happening. The man who'd killed Emile was sitting in front of her and Henry was asking her to help him. He didn't understand who this man was.

'Henry, what are you doing? Don't you know what he did?'

'What the hell is she talking about?' the man gasped in English. 'You said you'd briefed your people here, promised they would bring me some food. I didn't expect some mad woman trying to kill me.'

Valérie gazed at him, rocked by the sudden switch of language.

Henry stood up and came towards Valérie, grasping her hand and forcing her arm down. She struggled to pull away from his grip, her feet sliding on the carpet, but he was too strong. The knife dropped to the floor, and she looked around wildly for something else she could use as a weapon, but he grasped her chin in his other hand, forcing her to look up at him.

'Let me go,' she hissed. Blind rage boiled up inside her and she tried to break away. 'Get away from me. You don't know what you're doing.'

'Calm down. Tom had nothing to do with Emile's death. He's one of ours, the English agent I told you about, the one we had to get out of France. You can't have seen him in the square the day Emile died. He's been working undercover for months.'

Valérie tried to pull away, but he was too strong. Her words came out in a sob. 'I'm telling you he was there, he's the one who killed Emile. I don't care what his name is, or what he's done. I know what I saw.'

She watched as Henry's expression changed and his dark eyes softened in sympathy, responding to her desperation. She tried to pull away, needing to keep hold of her anger. 'You're wrong, Valérie,' he said gently. 'Tom isn't the person who pushed Emile. This man was nowhere near Emile when he died.'

She looked up at him, the only sound in the room her rapid breathing.

'That's not quite true, Henry.'

They both stared at the injured man, frozen into silence by his statement, waiting for him to explain. He'd pulled himself upright and looked straight at Valérie. 'I remember that day, and yes. I was near your friend when he fell in front of the tram. I swear that I had nothing to do with his death, but I saw what happened.'

He stopped and took a few breaths before he could carry on. 'I was behind the person who pushed him in front of that tram.'

The effort was too much for him. He'd scarcely got the last word out when he groaned and clutched his side, before crumpling on to the floor with a dull thud.

'No.'

Henry ran across to lift him up, fresh blood seeping from the man's wound and staining Henry's hands a deep red. His words seemed to echo round the room, long after he'd spoken.

The realisation filled Valérie's mind: she was right. This man could tell her who had killed Emile and who was behind the deaths of so many people fleeing across the border. The person who was still betraying the Resistance, and who right now was endangering the lives of Pierre and Jules.

SIXTEEN

VALÉRIE

Valérie took a step towards Tom, excitement flooding though her body. 'Who did it? Please, you must tell me.'

'Someone in front of me... I saw the hand on his back.'

He breathed out the words before he fainted and fell back into Henry's arms.

Henry felt his pulse.

'Will he be all right? He has to wake up, he has to tell me what else he saw.'

She couldn't bear to be so close and then to have the source of her information snatched away.

'Hand me those cushions.' Henry's order brought her sharply to her senses. 'He's in no fit state to answer your questions.'

He glanced down at the sickly grey face. 'If we don't get a doctor to him, I'm not sure you'll ever get the answers you're looking for.'

'What can I do?'

He gestured to the pile of blankets and cushions stacked on a chair in the corner. 'We need to make him comfortable.'

She ran to pick up a couple of the cushions and they

propped the man up into a half-sitting position. He groaned and his head lolled forward, dark hair flopping over his clammy forehead.

'Water...' he whispered.

Henry put a water bottle to his lips, and he took a few sips before falling back into a swoon.

'We need to get a doctor. He's lost too much blood already.'

Valérie stood up, eager to do anything to help. 'I'll go. Our local doctor lives near here, I can go and fetch him.' She went to leave but Henry reached across and grasped her arm to stop her.

'No. Not him. I don't trust him.'

She tried to pull away.

'What do you mean? He's been our doctor for years. He's looked after us since we were small. Why don't you trust him?'

'Nazi sympathiser,' he snapped. 'Wouldn't hesitate to tell his German friends about treating the English spy they're so eager to find.'

'No, surely not him. I can't believe it.'

'You'll have to take my word for it,' he said harshly. 'The doctor I need lives in the next block, on the first floor. He's helped me out before and knows when to keep quiet.' He stood up and they faced one another across the prone figure.

'You stay here. I'll go and get him. It'll be quicker. He knows me and will come immediately.'

She glanced down at the unconscious man. 'All right, but don't take too long.'

Despite their situation, his features relaxed into a smile. 'I'll try not to. Believe me, I want him to survive just as much as you do. Just promise me you won't bombard him with questions if he wakes up.'

'What do you mean?' she protested, feeling herself flush. 'I'm not that selfish.'

'Selfish isn't the word I'd use. I would say single-minded, determined, won't take no for an answer. I know you're desperate to find out who killed Emile, but it won't help you if he dies before he's able to tell you what he knows.'

His grin faded and he held her gaze before finally saying the words she'd waited for months to hear. 'I owe you an apology. I should have done more to help you. If our friend here survives and can tell us more, we might just have found our traitor.' He glanced down again. 'But he won't be able to tell us anything until that bullet has come out. He probably won't wake up again, but if he does there's water in the bottle if he's thirsty.'

The injured man moved, and his face clenched in pain, even though his eyes didn't open. Valérie felt a stab of pity for him, this man who had fought for his country in the shadows and had barely escaped with his life.

'What's his real name?'

'I don't know. I only know him as Tom.'

She nodded. She could tell without looking at Henry's grim expression that their problems were far from over. He'd never get Tom out of Geneva if the man didn't recover quickly. They were hiding him under the nose of the Gestapo who had followed him across the border. They would know he was wounded and would be waiting, searching everywhere.

Before he left, Henry delivered a final warning. 'The only other person who knows we're here is Bernard. If anyone else tries to come in, they're the enemy. Keep your knife out.'

After Henry had left, the room seemed much smaller. It was also colder, so Valérie picked up one of the blankets and wrapped it round her shoulders, before dragging one of the armchairs next to the sofa. Even though she argued with Henry and resented his single-minded approach, at least he had the grace to admit when he was wrong.

She studied the man lying in front of her. He was slightly built, only a few years older than her, but Henry had said he'd been working with the French Resistance for months. He had one of those bearded faces that could disappear in a crowd, the same as thousands of young French workers, perfect for a spy working undercover. She sat watching him, wondering where he came from and what he'd left behind in England. He was unnaturally pale and seemed to be hardly breathing. She bent down to listen more closely, relieved to feel his shallow breath on her cheek, and she pulled the blanket over him to keep him warm.

The minutes dragged past. Valérie closed her eyes and tried to doze, but she was too uncomfortable. She checked Tom every few minutes to assure herself he was still breathing and then fixed her gaze on to the door, all her senses alert for a noise outside.

It was only when she got up to fetch another blanket to put over her patient, stretching to ease her stiff muscles, that she heard a noise outside the door and froze. She dropped the blanket and felt for her knife, staring at the door opening slowly in front of her. She could hardly breathe, the skin at the back of her neck prickling with fear.

Bernard's dark head appeared round the door and Valérie let out her breath in a sigh and lowered the knife. She felt weak with relief. She picked up the blanket from the floor and wrapped it round her shoulders.

'What are you doing here?' she hissed. 'You gave me such a fright.'

He slipped inside the door, checking behind him before he closed it. He was looking as scared as she felt.

He gestured towards the prone figure on the sofa. 'The Swiss police are looking for him everywhere. They came to the shop, asking all kinds of questions. The Germans have given them some story about him being a dangerous criminal, said he was being shielded by people in this area. They know he's here somewhere, so I thought I'd better warn Henry.'

Valérie went back to her chair and Bernard looked around the room. 'Where is Henry?'

'Gone to get a doctor.'

She checked him again. His hands felt icy cold to the touch, and she pulled the blanket up to his chin, worried that he was so still, hardly breathing.

'He's been unconscious for ages and hasn't been able to eat the food you gave me for him, or drink any of the water.'

'I wondered why you were still here. I saw your bike at the café and thought something must have gone wrong.'

Valérie checked her watch. 'Henry shouldn't be much longer.'

As if in response to her words, the door opened in front of them and Henry came in, followed by an older man carrying a bag. He glanced at Valérie and Bernard, but all his attention was focused on the figure lying on the sofa.

'Do what you can. He's in bad shape.'

Valérie stood up to let the doctor get closer to his patient, and Henry handed her the basket.

'You'd better go now; the police are everywhere. It won't be safe if you wait here for much longer.'

'I'll come back tomorrow and see how he is.'

Henry wasn't watching her, concentrating on the doctor as he examined his patient. She grasped his sleeve. 'Please Henry, keep him here until I come back. I want to speak to him again, find out if he saw who we're looking for. I need to hear it for myself.'

Henry nodded, and Valérie led Bernard downstairs without a backward glance. She stopped at the bottom of the stairs and opened the door carefully, looking up and down the street before venturing outside. They went through the Place de Bel-Air and, once safely over the Rhône, climbed up the alley into the old town leading through Bernard's shop.

'If someone asks you, you've been visiting my mother.'

She nodded, then followed Bernard through the shop, and

he let her out of the front door after checking the square was clear.

She crossed the cobbled square to pick up her bike and paused behind the café until two policemen walked past, then headed for home. Adrenaline was pulsing through her body; she was so thrilled by the knowledge that Tom had seen the person who had pushed Emile. For the first time in months, she might be close to getting justice for her friend. And if she or the Resistance could find Anne-Marie and Madeleine, then she could finally reunite them with Pierre and Jules.

But her positive mood faded away at the thought of crossing the border into France, and Nathalie heading into the forest. Both alone, both in grave danger.

All actions for the Resistance carried risks, she knew that, but straying into Nazi territory felt like tempting certain death.

SEVENTEEN

ANNE-MARIE

Annemasse, France

As darkness fell, Anne-Marie heard the shouting from inside the house. She glanced at Madeleine, who was curled up asleep on the blankets on the ground, then crept to the door of the shed and opened it a few inches, a cool breeze coming in through the narrow opening.

She looked across the ill-kempt garden at the back of the house and jerked her head back when she heard a man's voice, loud and angry. There was a pause before she heard the raised voice of a woman, then hysterical sobs. Then to her horror, she heard a gunshot, the noise loud and violent in the quiet evening.

A figure hit the back door, grey hair pushed against the glass and fingers scrabbling on the surface. Swallowing the nausea that threatened to overcome her, Anne-Marie looked on in horror as the woman's body jerked away from the door.

Fear gripped her body, and she felt frozen to the spot. But she would have to act, now. They needed to get out right away.

She couldn't bear to think about the kind elderly couple who had tried to help them, brutally killed just a few metres away. This was their payment for supporting the Resistance. Murdered in their own home for their bravery and humanity.

Anne-Marie bent her head and tears filled her eyes when she realised that she didn't even know their names.

Another gunshot shocked her into movement, and she tried to keep her voice under control. 'Come on, Madeleine. We must leave.'

She pulled her weakly protesting daughter up and clutched her to her side as she peered out of the shed and stepped into the garden. She looked around but no one had come outside the house, though she could hear a man's voice shouting from inside.

Anne-Marie dragged Madeleine to the back gate and ran out of the garden. She took Madeleine's hand and walked more slowly to the end of the street, knowing that if they were running, they would be instantly suspicious and could be shot on sight. Head down, she walked with Madeleine, hearing shouts in the streets behind her.

Nobody accosted them or asked what they were doing, but she felt horribly visible and sighed with relief when they reached the forest at the edge of town and could hide under cover of trees. This was the opposite way from the border with Switzerland, she knew that, but they had to get somewhere safer.

Clinging to Madeleine's hand, Anne-Marie ran through the forest and stumbled in the dark. Soon, behind her she heard more angry shouts in German and shots rang through the trees, so she picked up Madeleine and ran as fast as her legs would go.

Her heart in her mouth, she prayed desperately that Pierre and Jules were safe, and that somehow Madeleine would make it out of this alive.

'You're going too fast, Maman. This game isn't fun anymore.'

'I'm sorry, my love. We're here now. Let's hide.'

She breathed a sigh of relief as they came up towards a farmhouse, the sound of shouts far behind them, but in the window she could see the farmer and his wife entertaining a German soldier. She pulled back into the trees when she saw a driver in the black car outside the house and hoped desperately that they hadn't been seen.

'Where are we going, Maman?' whispered Madeleine. 'It's dark, and I'm tired after all our running.'

'I know, ma fille. We just need to get inside. It will be better than the shed. There will be more room, and it will be warmer.'

She led them into a nearby barn. It was empty but retained the strong smell of the cows who'd been kept there. In the corner of the barn there was still a bundle of straw, and she sank down on it with Madeleine, her body shaking uncontrollably after their narrow escape, breathing deeply to calm her shudders. Then she heard a car door open and close, before the engine started and the car drove away. Now she only had to fear the farmer and his wife, Nazi sympathisers who would probably hand them over as soon as they found them.

Suddenly she heard the barn door open, and she clutched Madeleine closer. A torch light shone round the opposite corner of the barn, and she held her breath, her heart beating so loudly in her chest that she thought it could be heard. She pressed a hand over Madeleine's mouth, terrified she'd give them away...

EIGHTEEN

PHILIPPE

Saint-Maurice, Valais, Switzerland

Christophe's warning about Stefano was still ringing in Philippe's ears when his unit left the Fort for their next exercise, walking at first, with their skis strapped across their backs until they got to higher ground and better snow. As they climbed, the patches of white grew larger until they started to merge on the higher slopes into a deeper covering. The Spring snow was icy this early in the morning but would soften through the day.

Light snow had started falling and the cloud was low in the sky. Philippe frowned at the conditions, as everyone strapped on their skis. The exercise had only just begun, and the weather already looked like it might close in.

Every unit took their turn in strict rotation to check that the explosives planted underneath the mountain roads and bridges on the cliff faces above the Rhône Valley could be detonated in the event of an invasion. His job today was to check the roads and passes above the Col de la Croix near Villars, a part of the mountain he knew well. He usually liked these regular exercises in the mountains because it was an opportunity to spend the day outside, but today he felt tense and watchful, more inclined to look over his shoulder for a sudden attack than relax into the familiar tasks.

'Avalanche weather,' sniffed one of his soldiers who came from the Valais area. 'We had fresh snow last night, which will melt when the temperatures rise in the afternoon. We'd better get back before we have to walk all the way home through the slush.'

Philippe nodded. He'd skied in these mountains since he was small. Although he'd never been caught in an avalanche, he knew all the signs: the large cracks in the surface snow high up in the valley and, at the foot of the slopes, new blocks of ice that had rolled down gulleys and crevasses to lie drunkenly on their side.

'All right men, we need to get the job done as quickly as possible. Keep to the usual roads and tracks. No diversions into the deep powder, however solid it looks. We'll stop at each location and decide on the next stage.'

His men nodded, wise to the risks of triggering an avalanche.

In one way it was a tedious job, marching along the mountain roads checking each bridge and stretches of road overhanging sheer drops, only able to ski on the stretches at the higher passes where some spring snow remained. But as Philippe checked the gear of each man and gave his instructions, he knew it was vital to prevent anyone tampering with the explosives, which would protect the Alps from invasion. He expected a thoroughly professional job to be done.

They'd done this patrol regularly in their old unit and they might get some good ski runs if they were lucky. He looked up at the sky. The weather was getting worse, a blustery wind blowing the snow off the tops of the mountains and funnelling through the trees on their route. Philippe glanced up at the higher peaks breaking through the low grey cloud that had settled along the top of the ridge. 'Make sure you stick together and don't lose sight of the man in front. Stefano, you lead the way.'

The young soldier nodded without looking up at Philippe and trudged away as if he was carrying the weight of the world on his shoulders. The others fell into line behind him. Philippe could have sworn that Stefano was avoiding him and seemed reluctant to initiate any conversation, unlike on the previous exercise. He turned his face to the strong breeze to try to clear his thoughts, over-sensitive to the least signal. He'd feel better when he could concentrate on the job without his mind buzzing with needless suspicions.

They met hardly anyone on the way. The few chalets scattered along the hillside all seemed deserted, the only sign of life a thin plume of smoke coming from one of the chimneys. It was still early in the year so most of the cattle remained on the lower slopes or in the barns where they'd been kept over the winter. They passed one farmer feeding his cattle in a barn from hay loaded in a horse-drawn cart.

The men made good progress, the first few hours uneventful as they checked the sites on the outward route and slowly climbed up to the highest bridge on their list, covering more ground by skiing on the stretches where the snow was still deep. This last bridge spanned a deep crevasse where melting snow streamed down the sheer rock face to the valley hundreds of metres below. They stopped at the bridge and one of his men went to carry out the check. After a few minutes, they heard a shout from underneath the bridge, then his head and shoulders appeared and the other men pulled him up the last few feet to the road.

'All in place and operational.'

Philippe nodded. They'd been going without a break for several hours and he glanced around him, wondering if they should stop here. The bridge was surrounded by deep drifts and they were exposed to the wind, which had grown even stronger, flicking snow off the trees in clouds of white mist. Despite being in the middle of the day, they were surrounded by the low cloud and Philippe shivered in the biting cold. He made his decision rapidly. It was better to get his men lower down and out of the wind than to stay in such an exposed spot.

'We'll ski down to the next bridge, stop for a longer break. Then it's downhill back to the Fort.'

He spoke to the man nearest to him. 'You lead the way. Stop at the next bridge on the route and wait for the rest of us to catch up with you.'

He nodded and Philippe watched them ski off in line and disappear round the bend in the track one by one, before tying on his skis and bending down to tighten the strap on his ski boots.

Then some sixth sense warned him he wasn't alone. He looked up to the slope above the bridge and saw a group of men in white ski suits staring down at him. Before he could move, three of the group peeled off from the rest and raced down the slope, surrounding him in seconds. He grabbed his poles in a futile attempt to defend himself, but the lead skier, a tall, powerful man, simply flicked them away to the edge of the road then slid to a halt next to him, blocking his escape route. It had all happened so quickly.

Taller than average, Philippe usually looked down at other people, but he had to look up at this man. Could it be the German spy Max had warned him about? He was older than Philippe and his manner supremely confident, as he took complete control of the situation. He glanced at the other two men, faces hidden by their ski goggles, but there was no escape there. They had the same determined air about them as their leader, who pulled off his goggles.

He cursed his carelessness. He had been warned by Max and then by Christophe. And he hadn't even taken the precaution of staying with the others. He'd sent them away. The Germans must have been following them all morning, waiting for him to be split off from his men. He kept his features expressionless, trying not to show his fear.

'I have wanted to meet you for some time,' said the tall man speaking in a strong German accent, his hard eyes staring at Philippe. 'My sources tell me you have the information I need.'

Philippe didn't reply. This was it – the approach Max had said to expect. He clenched his fists unconsciously and felt himself flush when the man smirked at the powerless gesture.

'You are the man who knows where the Swiss have laid their defensive charges, not just here but in the whole area. It would be better for you to share that information with us.'

'I don't know what you're talking about,' hissed Philippe. 'I lead this unit, that's all. You've mistaken me for someone else.'

The man leaned so close to Philippe that he could feel warm breath on his cheek, the clipped German accent growing more pronounced.

'I don't think so. You are Philippe Cherix, you worked for Roger Favre on the maps of this area and are continuing with his work.'

Philippe felt the men crowd closer on his other side, unsteadying him on his skis, watching him in case he tried to fight his way out.

'I'm telling you that you've got the wrong person.'

The German smirked again, as if the conversation was going just as he'd expected.

'If not for your sake, you might like to think about your unit. An accident could happen to your men out here on one of these exercises. It would be so easy to arrange. And nobody would ever know what had happened.'

He gestured to his men high on the slope watching them. Philippe knew they could ski down to where his unit was waiting for him and surprise them with a sudden attack. It would be so easy. The German turned back to him.

'Or consider your friends. Christophe, for example, with his futile attempts to steal German property. I wonder whether his superior officers know what he's really doing when he's picking up their supplies at the station.'

Philippe bit his lip, knowing any denial would be a waste of breath. Maybe they'd already questioned the German who'd caught Christophe. But no one could prove he'd been there. The German's next words punctured any ragged composure he had left.

'And your friend Valérie, left behind in Geneva. It would be such a shame to see her lovely features damaged, but it could be done so easily...'

'No!' he roared, and tried to raise his fists, but the other Germans pulled his arms roughly behind his back and twisted him round to face the steep drop at the edge of the bridge. He heard the man's low voice close to his ear.

'Or we could just throw you over the bridge now, get rid of you in an unfortunate accident. It's very tempting. We'll find another way to get what we want. There are plenty of people who are happy to work with us for the right price.'

Philippe used all his strength and anger to free his arms and punched one of his captors, who fell back clutching his nose. At a signal from their leader, the men on the slope started to ski down to join them. Philippe struggled against the arms holding him in an iron grip. He'd never be able to fight six of them. They pushed him inexorably towards the edge of the precipice, only a low wall between the road and the sheer drop. That must have been their plan all along: kill him and replace him with someone more amenable. Or maybe they wanted to show how easily they could destroy his friends. He looked over the precipice and felt dizzy, his heart pounding in his chest. He could see no way out, no way of escaping.

A deafening crack echoed down the mountain, followed by a deep rumbling noise. The grip on his arms loosened and he pulled free, grasping the rail at the end of the bridge like a drowning man. He pulled himself upright against the structure and away from the cliff edge.

The ground was shaking. He launched himself off the barrier and pushed past the tall German, who was staring in horror as his men were swallowed up in the wall of snow crashing over them. He skied away as fast as he could, bending low to gain speed, not daring to look behind him at the avalanche destroying all in its path.

The roaring noise followed him and grew louder as he tried to outrun it. He heard nothing but the deafening noise until finally snow engulfed him, and he fell over in a tangle of skis. He tried to claw his way to the surface as he'd been taught.

He was trapped in silent darkness, not sure which way was up, an icy coffin all around him, heavy snow pinning him down. *Don't panic*, he told himself, *remember your training*. He blinked a couple of times and managed to move his head to breathe out the snow from his nose and mouth. He didn't know how far under the snow he was trapped. When he tried to move his arms and legs, he could only move one arm.

He clawed at the snow where it looked lighter than the rest, feeling the breath constrict in his throat, not knowing which way he was facing. The small air pocket around him was disappearing and he knew he had very little time left.

He tried to move his limbs again. He would not give up, not after surviving the onslaught of the avalanche. He'd heard stories about people being buried only a few centimetres under the surface and dying because they had thought they were past saving. He knew he had to keep going, for as long as he still had breath. He thought of Valérie and how she had never given up on him before. He wouldn't give up either.

He scrabbled at the snow with renewed vigour and

suddenly felt his arm break out from the covering and into the freezing air. He tried to move closer to the light, but the snow was too heavy. It hurt him to breathe. He was so close, but there was no one there to see him. No one to dig him out.

His body went limp, and he closed his eyes, his mind clutching hold of Valérie before everything went dark.

NINETEEN

VALÉRIE

Geneva, Switzerland

Throughout the next day, Valérie couldn't get her fears about Nathalie out of her mind. When she wasn't thinking about Nathalie, she fretted about whether Tom was recovering and if he could identify the traitor. She packed and delivered watch mechanisms robotically, trying to blot out her worries by hard work, before she stood at Henry's door on the Place De-Grenus.

She let herself into Henry's block and ran up the stairs to his apartment, her heart beating with excitement. All she needed was for Tom to be conscious and she could show him Marianne's photograph. If he recognised one of the group as the man who'd pushed Emile, then she'd have the truth at last.

Valérie pushed open the door leading into the parlour and looked inside. Tom was lying on the sofa, his white face pointed towards the door, eyes closed. It was totally silent in the room. For a second, she thought he was dead, that she'd come back too late. Her heart dropped like a stone. She took a step forward and gasped when his eyes opened suddenly, and he smiled.

'I hope you aren't going to pull out your knife this time.'

She smiled in relief. 'I thought for a minute you were...'

'Dead? No, they haven't got rid of me yet. Henry's doctor patched me up.' He pulled himself up. 'Do you have any food in that basket? I'm starving.'

She laughed and walked across to him, unpacking her basket. 'Bernard gave me something for you.'

He grasped the bread with his good hand and started to eat. She glanced round at the door as if someone had followed her inside. 'The Germans are still looking for you.'

'Henry's going to get me away tonight, after dark. He thinks it's too dangerous to stay here. And I wouldn't mind sleeping in a proper bed.'

'Where will you go?'

'To the nearest place where I can be picked up. He's trying to organise it now.'

'The airport here in Geneva?'

'Possibly, though it's watched all the time. It might be better from one of the smaller military airports further up the valley. Less obvious.'

'But surely, you're safer now you're in Switzerland and out of occupied France?'

He grimaced. 'Safer certainly, but if they can catch me before I leave Geneva, the Germans could whisk me back over the border. Assisted by the ever so friendly Swiss police.'

They had so little time. Valérie bent down and took out from her satchel the photograph of the Resistance unit and handed it to him. 'Do you recognise any of these people? Is one of them the person who pushed Emile?'

She waited for his reply, holding her breath, hands clasped tightly in her lap. She watched for any spark of recognition, any sign that he saw in the photograph the answer to her question. He shook his head and handed her back the photograph.

'I'm sorry Valérie, I don't recognise anyone.'

She let out her breath in a deep sigh. If it wasn't someone in the Resistance cell at Annemasse, it could be anyone. She was right back at the beginning.

'I keeled over before I got the chance to tell you last night, but I didn't see his whole face. The person who pushed your friend was turned away from me and all I saw was the side of his cheek. What I did see very clearly was his hand on your friend's back and his foot in front of him, so that he toppled over on to the line. When everyone screamed, the man ran away from me, so I never saw his face.'

Valérie's heart sank. 'You didn't see his face? You wouldn't be able to recognise him again? Not even his height or hair colour?'

He shook his head. 'I'm sorry. I've been thinking about it all night, once I began to feel more myself, trying to remember everything I saw that day.' He paused. 'The cheek I saw was very smooth, like a woman's face. It certainly wasn't an older man's face.'

Her mind was racing through the possibilities, and she twisted her hair around her fingers, trying to see some way forward, but it seemed hopeless. Tom had seen someone push Emile, but it could have been anyone under the age of thirty.

They both turned as the door opened behind Valérie and Henry came into the room. He glanced from one to the other. 'What's the matter?'

'He didn't recognise the person who pushed Emile.' said Valérie. She stood up and handed him the photograph. 'I thought it might be someone in this photo.'

'I didn't see the whole face, Henry. It could have been anybody.' Tom sounded apologetic, but definite.

Henry put his hand on her shoulder. 'I'm sorry, I really hoped you'd find the answer.'

Without thinking, Valérie buried her face into his shoulder, unable to stop the tears. She felt him dry her cheeks with his handkerchief and his soft breath on her face. 'We'll find another way. Now we can describe who pushed Emile a little more, I can go back to the police and get them to check their records.'

She looked up into his eyes. 'You said the police tried their best already. What else can they do?'

'I might have ways of persuading them to look again, try a bit harder. I've done a few favours for Nicolas Cherix in the last few years. He's going to start paying me back by helping us get Tom out of Geneva tonight. I might tug his conscience about Emile and get him to reopen the case. I think he sees more than his superiors are prepared to admit.'

Valérie sank down on to the chair again. She might be going to marry his son, but she knew Nicolas Cherix didn't openly approve of Swiss citizens helping the French Resistance.

Henry noticed her expression. 'You know his heart is in the right place. He sincerely believes everything he does is to protect Switzerland and keep the people of Geneva safe. He just might not always do it in the way you think he should.'

She watched Tom hobbling around the cellar, his strength much improved but the beads of sweat on his forehead showing the effort it was taking to take a few steps.

Sighing, Valérie stood up and took her leave. Tom made a small bow from the other side of the room and leaned heavily on the back of a chair. 'Thank you for all you've done. I'm sorry I couldn't give you what you wanted in return. I hope you find out who killed your friend.'

Valérie left the apartment with her heart heavy, despite Henry's attempts to keep her hopes alive.

TWENTY

VALÉRIE

After a restless night punctuated by dreams of Nathalie, Anne-Marie and Madeleine running from danger, and Pierre and Jules being roughly pulled out of the bookshop and pushed into cars to be taken back over the border, Valérie was exhausted before the day had even begun. She left the house just before nine, intent on visiting Nathalie in the jewellery shop as soon as it opened, to make sure she was safe.

Under the warming sun, surrounded by people going about their normal business, she wondered how they could lead such normal lives, when right in their midst innocent people were hiding, afraid of being sent back into the living nightmare of occupied France.

As she cycled down to Monsieur Savarin's shop, her fears for Nathalie grew and she pedalled as hard as she could. Leaving her bike outside, she pushed open the heavy door of the jewellery shop, hesitating for a moment when she saw Maurice behind the counter and a woman bending over a tray of glittering rings. Maurice looked up and frowned when he saw her, leaving her in no doubt that he saw her as a nuisance rather than a real customer. Piqued by his reaction, she let the door close behind her and took a few steps inside. He could at least pretend that she was a customer, she thought resentfully, rather than try to make her feel she didn't belong in his hallowed territory.

Maurice murmured something to the woman, who stared at Valérie. It was Elsa Bauer, the woman she'd seen with Henry at the Hotel d'Angleterre. Elsa was wearing a blue dress and matching jacket of fine wool and could have walked out of the pages of a fashion magazine. She nodded at Valérie, her features expressionless, and then turned back to the counter. Maurice came out from behind the counter and spoke in a fierce whisper. 'What do you want?'

'I came to see Nathalie, is she here?'

'No. She hasn't come in today.'

Her heart jumped in her chest and her skin prickled as she looked around the shop for her friend, desperate for him to be wrong.

'Why hasn't she come in? Do you know?'

'No. She hasn't even sent a message. She won't keep her job if she carries on like this.'

'Is your father here?'

'He can't see you. He isn't well today.'

'But I need to speak to him.'

They weren't whispering any longer. Maurice looked around to check that Elsa was still occupied at the counter. 'You can't speak to him. I told you he isn't well.'

Seriously worried now, Valérie took a step towards the door at the back of the shop that led through to their office. She had to see Monsieur Savarin, in case he knew why Nathalie hadn't come in to work. Nathalie was more likely to have confided in him if she expected to be late.

'Where do you think you're going?' Maurice caught her arm in a painful grip.

'I need to speak to him.' She stopped herself from blurting

out that Nathalie might be in danger, could be hurt; he was the last person she could trust.

'Maurice, I need some help over here.' Elsa's sharp voice made him loosen his grip and move away from Valérie.

'Of course, Madame. Let me deal with this young person first and I'll be right with you.'

'But I was here first, Maurice. I think you should serve me before your other customer. I'm sure she won't mind waiting a few more minutes.'

'Of course not,' Valérie replied, giving Maurice no choice but to go back to Elsa.

'Could you show me the tray of rings up there, in the case behind you?'

When Maurice turned his back to them and reached up to unlock the glass case, Elsa looked across and smiled at Valérie. It was only for a split second and Valérie blinked at her in surprise. Then Elsa nodded at the door at the back of the shop, which was slowly opening, and Monsieur Savarin came out. He was moving more hesitantly than the last time she'd been there, but he lifted his eyes to Valérie's face and shuffled forward eagerly. 'Mademoiselle, you have news of Nathalie? She is ill perhaps. Is that why she is not at work today?'

Valérie shook her head. 'I'm afraid I don't know, Monsieur. I thought she would be with you.'

His wrinkled face fell. 'It is not like her to miss her work. I hope nothing has happened to her.'

'So do I.'

Valérie's words came out in a whisper. She hardly knew what she was saying, her mind swimming in fear. The door to the shop opened again and Valérie looked round to see Nicolas Cherix come inside. She could feel the blood drain away from her face as the policeman approached Monsieur Savarin.

'Could I have a word please, Monsieur?'

Elsa smiled sweetly at Maurice. 'I can't decide what I'd like. I'll come back later when it's a little quieter.'

The door closed behind her before Nicolas Cherix turned to Valérie. 'Hello, Valérie. I'm afraid I need to speak to Monsieur Savarin about a private matter.'

'If it's about Nathalie, then she's my friend... please let me stay.'

Before he could answer, the old jeweller came to her rescue. 'This young lady is as worried about Nathalie as we are.' He glanced at Maurice, who was putting away the trays of rings. 'You can say what you have come to say to all of us, Monsieur Cherix.'

He nodded. 'Very well. The police chief in Nyon contacted me early this morning to say that Nathalie Masson has been reported missing. Can you confirm that she works here?'

Monsieur Savarin nodded.

'And how long has she worked here?'

'Less than a year, probably nine months or so. Her aunt is a long-standing customer and when I told her we needed more help in the shop on one of her visits, she suggested her niece.'

'We didn't need any help, Father,' interrupted Maurice. 'I keep telling you that we can manage perfectly well on our own.'

Monsieur Savarin ignored his son. 'She did a lot of the work in the office, dealt with our suppliers and did our books, which freed up Maurice to deal with our customers.'

'And when did you last see her?'

'Thursday night, when she left work. She had yesterday off and was due back this morning, but she hasn't come in.'

'I met her on Thursday night after work,' added Valérie. 'We went to the Café de Paris for an hour and then she went home.'

'And that was the last time you saw her?'

'Yes. I arranged to call by the shop today. We thought we might meet up after work.'

Valérie knew he had to go through all his questions, but she was desperate to find out what he knew. Monsieur Savarin had sat down on a chair next to the counter as if his legs couldn't carry him any longer. His voice sounded weak and very old. 'What can have happened to Nathalie?'

'I'm afraid we don't know, Monsieur. Her aunt said she went out yesterday evening. She told her aunt she was meeting someone and left in a rush because she was late. She didn't come back last night, and it's the first time she's ever stayed out all night. Were you the person Nathalie went out to meet?' he asked Valérie.

'No.'

'And did she tell you who she was going to meet?'

'No.'

Valérie looked unblinkingly at him. Something had happened to Nathalie in the Risoux Forest. She felt a cold weight in the pit of her stomach as her mind played over the awful possibilities. She should have gone with her, but it was too late now.

'Are you sure, Valérie? If there is anything you know that might explain her disappearance, you need to tell me.'

She held his gaze and saw the genuine appeal in his eyes. She realised in that moment that Henry was right, that all Philippe's father wanted was to protect the people of Geneva. There was a girl missing and it was his duty to find her. She might have to trust him and tell him what she knew before long, but not here, not now. Nathalie might be in hiding, she might be okay, and the last thing she would want was her cover to be blown to the Swiss police.

'I knew that girl was trouble,' burst out Maurice. 'Looked down her nose at our best customers, refused to serve them.'

'Maurice, please...' begged his father.

His outburst sealed Valérie's silence. She would go and look for Nathalie herself and if she failed to find her, then she would go to the police. 'I'm sorry I can't help you.'

She could tell Nicolas Cherix didn't believe her, but for some reason he decided to accept her statement for now. He looked at Maurice and his father.

'Do either of you know where Nathalie could have been yesterday?'

They shook their heads.

'If any of you remember any other information that will help to find Nathalie, you know where I am.'

With that parting shot, he left. Valérie waited until she heard his car start up and then followed him out of the door without another word. She grabbed her bike and rode off in the opposite direction towards Cornavin station, glancing behind her every few minutes to check that the police car hadn't changed direction to follow her.

All her worst fears seemed to have come true. As she cycled, she could not stop thinking about what had happened to the Resistance fighters who were murdered so horribly near Annemasse. And then she remembered: Nathalie knew where Pierre and Jules were hiding, and she had been carrying the photograph of the whole family. If the Nazis found it, they would surely torture her, and she could tell the Nazis everything they wanted to know. Valérie cycled even faster to the station, swerving past pedestrians, terror about what could have happened to Nathalie filling her mind. Could she still save her?

TWENTY-ONE

VALÉRIE

Valérie cycled past the grand frontage of the post office without slowing down. She'd have to explain to her father why she'd failed to send off his packages, but all she could think of right now was looking for Nathalie. It would take her the best part of the day to cycle from Nyon to the edge of the forest and get the train back to Geneva, and she pushed through the pain in her legs, willing herself forward. She couldn't afford to waste any time.

Nyon was one of the first stops on the main line round the lakeside and Valérie waited impatiently for the twenty minutes to pass. The train was busy, as always, but she hardly noticed her fellow passengers, totally focused on her search. Every time the train slowed down to go through a station she held her breath, hoping it wouldn't stop and lose precious time. The second it stopped at Nyon, she pushed the door open. She looked straight ahead, avoiding the curious looks of the people on the platform, and cycled as fast as she could through the centre of town away from the lakeside and through the villages, towards the steep hill rising in front of her.

She had to go west from the main road, in the direction of

La Dôle, the highest peak looking over Lac Léman, then strike out into the forest at the start of the climb, making sure she avoided the border guards who patrolled this part of the Vaud region. She and Philippe had gone for walks in the forest before the war and she thought she knew the various spots where the road touched the border, but it had been a few years since then and it might take her some time to find the right spot. Flashes of memory from those trips came back to her as she recognised the bends in the road and the hedgerows snaking into the distance.

The insistent voice that said she should have told the police where Nathalie was going and left it up to them to find her was suppressed. If Nathalie was okay and the Swiss police knew what she was up to, her work for the Resistance could be all over. And Valérie had no doubt that Maurice Savarin was just waiting for an excuse to get rid of Nathalie. She also didn't want rumours of deserted train carriages and stolen art treasures spread around Geneva or Saint-Maurice. Christophe's task was dangerous enough without attracting attention from the German spies operating in the area.

She didn't meet anyone after she left the main town, cycling past farms and barns. People were working in the fields, but no one took any interest in her. It was a fine day, with only a few clouds in the sky, exactly the type of weather that might entice someone to go for a bike ride in the country. After an hour, she turned on to the narrow lane that led into the forest and stopped to catch her breath and take a sip of water from the bottle in her basket. She scanned the fields and the road ahead to check for any patrols, but saw no one. Her eyes fixed on an old barn at the edge of the trees and she glanced down at her bike. She would leave it there out of sight and go the rest of the way on foot.

The vast barn was completely empty, but the pungent smell of the cattle that had been kept there all winter hung around her until she left the open fields. She stepped carefully over the

rough grass and walked slowly into the forest, looking all around
and listening for the slightest noise.

She felt very alone and wished she had Philippe with her.
She realised suddenly that no one knew where she was. She
pushed away the thought that she could disappear just like
Nathalie had, and Philippe wouldn't even know where to look
for her.

The ground underfoot was damp from the recent rain and
the tree stumps sticking up through the ground forced her to
pick her way carefully through the undergrowth. Staring
through the trees rather than at her feet, she almost tripped on
the uneven ground and glanced down, clutching a branch to
stop her fall. She would break her leg if she wasn't careful. She
went forward even more cautiously, trying to concentrate on
what was around her rather than on the fear sapping her
resolve.

Through the trees she glimpsed a clearing and headed in
that direction. After walking for a few minutes, she came to a
low wall. Nathalie had said she'd leave her package next to the
wall, which marked the border. This could be the place. Valérie
brushed her foot along the grass next to the wall and bent down
to search alongside it for any kind of clue that someone had
been there, but there was nothing in the undergrowth. She
walked all around the stone wall, but there was nothing to find.

She scanned the clearing up ahead. A flock of birds flut-
tered over the space in the trees, their chirping loud in the
silence. She walked up the shallow incline towards the clearing,
her heart beating faster as she went further into France and left
the safety of Switzerland behind. Dark shapes marked the grass
at the opposite edge of the clearing, and she hesitated, heart
thumping in her chest, knowing she should probably just turn
back. She hadn't planned on going this far into France but
couldn't stop herself now.

She skirted round the trees, ready to jump into the forest if someone came. Just as she swivelled around at the distant sound of a twig snapping, she almost trod on a man's shoulder and recoiled from his body, which was twisted in death, but not before she saw his hands tied behind his back.

This had been an execution.

She took a couple of deep breaths to push back the wave of nausea threatening to overpower her. Forcing herself to look beyond him, she saw two other bodies, all shot.

One of them was a woman, her blonde hair glinting in a shaft of sunlight piercing through the gathering clouds.

'No, please God, it can't be...' she moaned as she went closer to the woman's body, feeling suddenly cold all over. Her boot caught a patch of wet grass and she slid forward, unwittingly nudging the woman with her foot. The body twisted round, and Valérie jumped back, her hand over her mouth as she saw the beautiful familiar face covered in blood and purple bruises, eyes open in death.

'Nathalie... oh my poor Nathalie. What have they done?'

She fell to her knees in front of Nathalie, blinded by tears, her heart thumping in her chest. Wiping her face, Valérie leaned over and closed Nathalie's eyes with a shaking hand. This was her friend and she refused to be frightened of her body.

She stared through her tears at Nathalie's bruised face again, at her blood-stained jacket and at the hands tied painfully behind her back.

Steeling herself, Valérie felt in Nathalie's pockets, but there was no photograph. Had she told them what she knew to try to save her life? Whatever she'd said, it hadn't made any difference and they'd shot her anyway.

Valérie felt a deep anger bursting through her grief and shock. Nathalie's precious life shouldn't have ended like this, hunted like an animal and shot in the forest.

Overcome by her emotions, she looked away from

Nathalie's face and down in front of her. Something was glinting in the grass and Valérie stretched over and picked up Nathalie's edelweiss necklace, the glittering diamond at the centre and the white enamel over the fine silverwork on the flower sprays unmistakeable. She would give it to Christophe and tell him what had happened here.

A faint shout echoed through the trees and Valérie scrambled to her feet and sprinted back towards the deeper bushes across the low wall at the Swiss border, squeezing through the wet leaves, her mind still trying to take in what she'd seen.

She felt sick as she imagined what Nathalie had been through, the horror of discovery and the terror of impending death.

Someone had betrayed them. And the Nazis had the photo Nathalie had brought, of Anne-Marie and Madeleine.

A cold prickling feeling slid down her neck when she looked back through the thick leaves and saw the man Henry identified as Schneider, marching into the far side of the clearing. He was dressed this time in the black uniform of the Gestapo. No casual clothes to hide his true identity any longer. She watched him order two of the soldiers to dig a shallow pit, the noise of their shovels loud in the quiet clearing, and the third one to haul the bodies closer. So, whoever had betrayed the Resistance was working with Schneider and he'd come back to clear up what he'd done, to remove the evidence that he'd killed a Swiss citizen. Valérie bent her head, unable to watch the men throw the bodies into the shallow grave like sacks of rubbish.

When she looked up again her heart jumped when she saw Schneider at the border, only a few metres away from her, staring at the ground around the wall as if he was searching for something. She could hear him muttering under his breath as he kicked the tufts of grass. He scanned the area and then looked straight at the bushes she was hiding behind. She closed her eyes, too terrified to move or to breathe.

A shout from one of the soldiers made her open her eyes. Schneider had turned to look back to the clearing and he waved in acknowledgement, stamping his heavy boots on the wet grass. Valérie bent her head and felt the trickles of sweat running down her back, swallowing to keep down the nausea. She stood immobile for what seemed like hours until the Germans had thrown their shovels into the back of a truck and had driven away, terrified it was some trick and they would pounce on her when she finally came out of her hiding place.

She pushed her way out of the bushes and walked on trembling legs over to the newly dug mound of earth. It might be in France, but Nicolas Cherix would surely get Nathalie's body back for a proper burial. She turned away from the clearing, desperate to leave the horror behind her, but as she stumbled away, she heard a rumble of thunder and looked up, the outside world intruding on her own personal nightmare. It was cooler, the sun had disappeared behind the clouds, and she could feel rain in the air. She glanced at her watch and was shocked to discover that she'd been in the forest for hours. Casting caution aside, she ran back to the edge of the forest, stumbling and slipping over the uneven ground.

By the time she reached the barn where she'd left her bike, it was raining heavily. She stood under the high doorway waiting for the shower to pass, but the cloud was hanging low over the hills and the rain looked set to continue. She gazed at the wide fields and clutched her wet coat more tightly around her, tears clouding her vision.

Nathalie was dead and she would never see her again. She swallowed, tasting salty tears, willing herself to be strong. Desperate to blot out what she'd seen, her mind raced ahead to what she had to do. After Nicolas, she had to tell Henry what Schneider had done. He was the only person she knew who could do something about it. She'd have to get Pierre and Jules out of Geneva. Pierre could no longer object, it was too dangerous. Then she had to go into France herself for Anne-Marie and Madeleine. They couldn't die like Nathalie had. She wouldn't let that happen.

When the rain slackened, she left the shelter, pulling her collar up and cycling through the damp air. She watched for any vehicle coming towards her in case the Germans decided to double back to the Swiss side of the border, but they had disappeared back into the French Jura region and she didn't see any further sign of them.

It was already early evening and Nyon station was busy, with crowds of people walking on to the platforms past the small station building. Valérie sat in her wet clothes on a platform bench surrounded by the other passengers waiting for the first train to arrive for Geneva. She stuck her hands into her pockets to try to stop them from shaking, but her whole body felt chilled. She glanced at the people around her, businessmen with briefcases, schoolchildren giggling together, and housewives with baskets of shopping. She wanted to shout at them all to wake up, to understand what was going on under their noses.

'Are you all right?' The plump middle-aged woman sitting next to her spoke in a low voice. 'You look as if you've had a shock.'

'Thank you, I'm just cold. I got caught in the rain...'

Valérie smoothed down her hair with a shaking hand and the woman took a cloth from the top of her basket. 'Here, you can use this to dry your hair.'

'Thank you,' she repeated, her voice trembling.

They watched a group of local gendarmes standing on the platform.

'They're saying a girl from the town has gone missing. The police are asking everyone if they've seen her.'

Valérie nodded, unable to speak anymore.

The woman shook her head. 'It doesn't look good.'

She scrutinised the gendarmes. Valérie followed her gaze, wondering if she should go up to the police and tell them where they could find Nathalie. Then she turned away. It was Philippe's father she needed to tell. He would know what to do.

She tried to give the woman back the cloth, but she shook her head. 'It's fine. You keep it. I've got lots of them.'

The small act of kindness unlocked the emotions Valérie was trying so hard to hide. She felt her eyes fill with tears and kept her head down.

When the train arrived in Cornavin station, Valérie lugged her bike down on to the platform and steered it outside. It was almost dark, and it felt like years since she'd left the station earlier that day.

Her heart beating fast, she rode to the bookshop on the way to the police station, terrified that Nathalie had been forced to tell the Germans about Pierre and Jules' hiding place and that she would find the building broken in. She stopped and examined the door and then the windows upstairs, breathing a sigh of relief that everything was as it should be. She knew she'd need to move Pierre and Jules as soon as she could, but it would look so suspicious to take a small child on a late train or move them around the town in the dark; it could be just as dangerous as leaving them for one more night. She would have to wait until first thing in the morning.

Valérie ran up the steps into the police station and she approached the desk, breathless and clutching the pain in her side. 'Could I speak to Monsieur Cherix, please?'

At that moment, Philippe's father walked in and took one look at Valérie. 'You'd better come into my office.'

Valérie could hardly speak when she sat down, shaking violently and dripping water onto the floor.

'You look frozen.' He took one of his spare overcoats from the cupboard. She took her coat off and he hung it over the back of a chair while he wrapped the thicker one around her shoulders.

'I got soaked.'

'Where were you?'

'Nyon.'

'Where Nathalie went missing? We haven't found her anywhere. Do you have something to tell me?'

She closed her eyes for a second, but then looked up at him. 'Nathalie's dead. I found her just across the border with some members of the French Resistance.'

'My God, what happened?' He leaned forward, white with shock.

'They were all shot. Their hands had been tied and then they were all shot.' Her voice was shaking so that she could barely get the words out, and she took a deep breath before carrying on. 'And when I was there, the Germans came and buried their bodies. A man called Schneider was in charge.'

Nicolas Cherix rocked back in his chair. 'The man who's always asking questions over here? He goes drinking with some of my men.'

'He was in an SS uniform. Henry Grant told me he was a senior Nazi who infiltrated the Resistance years before the war. He comes over here as part of his intelligence gathering.'

Nicolas stood up suddenly and walked up and down the room, before turning back to Valérie. 'How dare he? He must have known she was Swiss, or he wouldn't have bothered to bury her.'

She swallowed, the terror of hiding so close to the German soldiers coming flooding back, the narrowness of her own escape fresh in her mind. 'I can tell you exactly where they are.' She grasped his arm. 'You have to go and get her, so her family can bury her properly.' Her voice ended on a sob, and he took her hand in both of his.

'I'm so sorry you had to see this, Valérie. I'll go and find her, get her back. I'll ask the local police to help me.'

He frowned and ran a hand across his tired face. 'I can make a formal complaint about Schneider killing a Swiss citizen, but if she was in France, there's little I can do, as it's outside my jurisdiction.'

'I know. I'm going to see Henry Grant. He'll do something about Schneider. Nathalie was killed helping the Resistance and they must all have been betrayed by someone they trusted. We have a traitor who is betraying the Resistance from Annemasse right up to the Jura Mountains and if we don't find him and stop him, more people will die.'

'You think this is the same traitor who killed Emile.'

'Yes, I think so.'

'I'll go and get a map so you can show me exactly where she is.'

Valérie waited impatiently for him to come back. The SOE's purpose was to support the Resistance and fight for the Allies. They didn't heed geographical borders and she was confident they would want Schneider dead as much as she did.

TWENTY-TWO
VALÉRIE

It was almost dark when she rode along the Rue des Etuves, turned into the Place De-Grenus and rang the bell to Henry's apartment. He let her in, and she ran up the marble stairs and into the apartment. She sat down heavily on the sofa, her legs tired and suddenly wobbly, and as he sat next to her she tried to speak, but only gasped and lifted her head.

'What's happened?' he said quietly.

'It's Nathalie, my friend. She was meeting the Resistance last night in the Risoux Forest.' The shock of what had happened hit her again and her voice shook. 'They were all shot by the SS. They're all dead. It was Schneider. He's behind it. I want you to kill him.'

Valérie felt Henry's steady eyes on her. 'You need a drink.'

She shook her head. 'I couldn't swallow anything. Henry, I should have been there. I should have been with Nathalie.'

He sat down next to her on the sofa. 'You mustn't blame yourself. You couldn't have known what would happen up there. They had no idea they were walking into a trap.'

'No, it was my fault. She was my friend, and I had a feeling something bad was going to happen. I should have insisted I went with her.'

She felt sick when she thought about how terrified Nathalie must have felt in that moment when she knew it was all over. Had she told them about Pierre and Jules in the bookshop? She knew Nathalie would never want to betray anyone, but the cruelty of the Nazis knew no bounds, and nobody could know how they would react if they thought they were going to be shot. But if she had told them, surely the bookshop would already have been broken into?

'Then they would have killed you too.'

'Maybe not. If there had been two of us, it might have made a difference. We could have got away.'

His expression hardened. 'You can't prevent the worst happening, whatever you do. We're up against an enemy prepared to use any means to win.'

'I need to tell Christophe and Philippe what happened. The German authorities probably know about the stolen goods now. It will be too dangerous for them to raid the trains in Saint-Maurice station.'

'Okay, I can drive you there.'

She studied his face. 'The traitor must be working for Schneider, and everyone's at risk until they're stopped. Tell me what you're planning. I need to know what you're doing to stop them.'

After a few moments, he nodded. 'I have an idea for how we could trap our traitor and pay Schneider back, but I'll need help to bring it off.'

'Tell me.'

'My sources tell me that Jean is struggling to get the Maquis up to strength on the Glières Plateau. Several of his best fighters have been captured around Annecy. And they're running out of weapons. I've been getting messages that he needs more arms and equipment. If I made it known through the Resistance that we plan to hand them over to Jean, I think the Germans would try to stop us.'

'So, we set a trap? In Switzerland?'

'If I'm right, we could also catch the person who killed Emile.'

She bit the inside of her lip.

'Also, if the Resistance can find the mother and daughter of your French family, Jean can take them across the border. It can't be Annemasse, as the border guards are looking for them there. It'll have to be from the Jura, through the Risoux Forest.'

'That's where I'm going to take Pierre and Jules. I need to get them out of Geneva. We could unite them in Nyon.'

'Yes. We can get the whole family to safety from there.'

'But isn't it too dangerous? The Germans are looking for Pierre and Anne-Marie.'

'That's why I want us to be there to help. We'll make sure the meeting to hand over the arms is timed for later, after the family are safely together and taken further into Switzerland.' His mouth smiled but his eyes were as hard as flint. 'I'll have reinforcements they won't expect.'

'You'll be waiting for them.'

'Yes, we'll be waiting.'

'I don't know how Christophe will react, what he might do when he hears about Nathalie.'

'He mustn't do anything. That's very important. We have to act carefully if we want to trap the traitor and stop Schneider.'

She nodded, knowing he was right, but not at all sure Christophe would see it that way.

'He'll come after Schneider. The moment he knows who was responsible for Nathalie's death, he'll want revenge.'

'That's why I'm going to involve Christophe,' Henry said. 'It's the best way to stop him from taking his own revenge and dying in the process. I'll let you know when I've arranged the meeting in Saint-Maurice.'

He kissed her on the cheek, his dark eyes full of understanding. 'If you feel responsible for everything that goes wrong, you won't be able to do the work we need you to do.'

'I know you're right in here...' She pointed at her forehead, then she laid her fist on the blanket over her heart. 'But not in here.'

He took her hand and unfolded her fingers, clasping it in his own. 'Your hands are cold.'

His eyes darkened as he looked down at her, sympathy replaced by something deeper and she stared at him, breathing more quickly. The air around them stood still, a spell binding them together. She was drowning in his gaze, and it seemed the most natural thing in the world to lean towards him.

'You need to get warm,' he breathed before his lips came down on to hers and he kissed her, his arm pulling her closer. She closed her eyes, the feel of his cheek against hers and the faint smell of his aftershave mixed with tobacco filling her nostrils. But then she came to her senses and pulled away.

'I'm sorry. I don't know what I was thinking.' She reached a hand up to wipe her mouth, as if she could take away the feeling of his lips on hers, feeling sick at her betrayal of Philippe.

Her words seemed to bring him to his senses, and he placed her hands back on her lap and stood up to put some distance between them. Despite her guilt, a thrill of excitement flooded through her when she saw him trying to get himself under control, the cool, calculating Englishman not so cool anymore.

He cleared his throat. 'It was my fault. I have a job to do and if I let my feelings get in the way it will put us all at risk.'

She nodded and he came back to sit beside her, as if drawn to her side. 'My God Valérie, you feel responsible for what happened to Nathalie. What do you think I feel thinking about your work for the Resistance? But if I dwell on that I won't be able to do my job.' He clenched his hands together. 'If something happens to you because I let my feelings get in the way, then I couldn't live with myself.'

Despite his words, she felt him lean towards her again, felt his warm breath on her cheek, but this time she didn't respond to him. She was beginning to think that Henry was prepared to do anything to win the war. That included using any tactics, including charm, to get others to do what he wanted.

She bent down to pick up her coat and he helped her put it on at the door to the apartment. Valérie ran down the stairs, picked up her bike and let herself out of the block. She cycled down the Rue des Etuves and across the Place de Bel-Air, her emotions aflame, feeling terribly guilty that she'd kissed another man. But she ruthlessly suppressed her confused feelings. She knew without doubt that Henry could get justice for her friend. She had to keep it together, for Nathalie, and for the family who were depending on her.

She was certain now that the Germans had the photo of Pierre and his family and would be searching for them all with renewed vigour. Once Pierre and Jules were safe, she would go to the address in Annemasse to look for Anne-Marie and Madeleine, and find a way to get them to Jean.

She'd failed to save Nathalie; she wasn't about to make the same mistake again.

TWENTY-THREE

VALÉRIE

Early the next morning, desperate not to waste any valuable time, Valérie rode her bike through the old town, pushed it through the alley and leaned it against the wall next to the book-shop. She let herself inside and ran up the stairs to the apartment, straining to hear piano music, but all was silent. She took a deep breath, bracing herself to tell them what had happened to Nathalie and what it meant for them.

'Pierre,' she called quietly and heard a response from one of the bedrooms. She went in and saw Jules lying on the bed and Pierre sitting next to him.

'What's the matter?'

'He didn't sleep very well last night. Sometimes he gets so scared. And he doesn't like it here. He can't go outside and play.'

She sat down and took a deep breath.

'I have some terrible news.' When he gazed at her with stricken eyes, she stretched out her hand. 'No, it's not Anne-Marie or Madeleine. It's Nathalie.' She swallowed the lump in her throat. Talking about what had happened didn't get any easier.

'What's happened?' He looked down to check Jules was still asleep and then back up at Valérie. He saw the truth in her face. 'She's dead, isn't she? Your friend. I could feel it. It isn't safe, even here in Switzerland.'

She glanced at Jules, who was still asleep, his mouth curved into a smile, dark lashes fanning over his cheeks. 'When she was meeting the Resistance, they were betrayed, and the Germans shot them all. I don't know exactly what happened, whether she told them anything about the Resistance, why she was meeting them...'

'And whether she said anything about us.'

'Yes, you're no longer safe here. You'll have to leave Geneva right away.'

'Now?'

'Yes, you'll need to come with me right now. We'll go to Nathalie's aunt's house. Where she suggested you could stay.'

'Will we be safe there?'

'I don't know. It's still close to France, just next to the Risoux Forest, but Nathalie believed you would still be in Geneva, so the Germans will think that too. We'll bring Anne-Marie and Madeleine to you there as soon as we've found them.' She sighed. 'It's the best I can do.'

'Okay, I understand. I'll get my bag ready.' He caressed Jules' cheek. 'At least he'll be pleased to move.'

Valérie clapped her hand to her forehead. 'I should have thought. There's the remains of a whole bookshop downstairs. There must be a book he'd like, I'll get him something you can take with you.'

She ran downstairs and paused at the doorway to the bookshop, breathing in the musty air. She studied the piles of books in the corner and the broken shelves and then the front window, checking that no one could see inside. It was so grubby it dimmed the bright sunlight, and she could only make out blurred figures when they walked past the front of the shop.

Trying to remember where the children's books had been kept, she went towards one of the sets of shelves where she remembered the larger, more colourful covers. She'd picked the right place and pulled out a few that Jules might like, one of wild animals, another about steam engines.

A rustling sound came from the pile of books at the far side of the shop, and she shuddered. Despite the cat, the rats were still there. She saw the place her mother used to sit, sorting out books at a small desk behind a decorated silk screen. Under one of the shelving units, she saw pieces of the screen, the frame broken, and silk torn, and some desk drawers tossed to one side, books and papers strewn over the floor. She stepped over the rubbish on the floor and pulled across one of the solid wooden drawers, and crouching low, she picked up some of the papers. There were pages from an English novel, bills for books and, at the bottom of the pile, a small notebook.

With shaking fingers, Valérie opened the notebook and saw her mother's handwriting. Inside the front cover, she'd written her name, Thérèse Hallez, and the date August 1937 – a few months before her death. Valérie looked around her, wondering again why the place had been left in such a mess, as if someone had been searching for something.

Valérie turned the pages of the notebook. It was a diary, with dates at the top of each page and notes of what had happened on that day, names of people who must have come into the shop. There were references to Monsieur Steinberg, to books being delivered, pages full of book titles. Her mother's neat handwriting peppered here and there with Jacob Steinberg's distinctive, sloping script.

She didn't realise she was crying until a large tear dropped on to her knee. She sniffed loudly and wiped her eyes, desperate to protect the precious pages. She flipped through another few pages and saw that the end of the notebook was blank. Turning back to the last entries, they were the same as before, lists of people who had come into the shop and titles of books. She longed to talk to her mother again, to share her sorrow about Nathalie, her worries about Pierre and his family, and to confide in her how she'd betrayed Philippe, kissing Henry in a moment of weakness.

Someone rattled the front door and Valérie looked up to see two figures outside. She ducked down behind the shelving unit in case they could see her. She would wait until they went away. No one could get in without a key. She looked down again at the final few entries and closed the notebook carefully, putting it into her pocket with shaking fingers and crossing her arms in front of her as if she could ward off the memories evoked by a few notes.

The door rattled again, and Valérie looked into the hall leading to the stairs, wondering if she could distract them and let Pierre and Jules escape. She listened for the sounds of the door being tried again and shrank back when she heard a low voice only a few metres away from her hiding place.

'Who has the key to this place?'

Her heart sank. She recognised the voice of the policeman who had a reputation for finding escaped refugees and sending them back to France. She saw his bulky figure through the glass. Then she heard the calmer, clipped tones of Nicolas Cherix. 'There isn't a key. This shop is abandoned, there's no one inside.'

The younger man paused a moment, clearly considering how far to push his superior officer. 'There must be a key. Who owns this building now?'

'It's private property and it's closed. We're wasting our time here.'

The sound of voices grew fainter, and Valérie waited for several minutes until she was sure they had gone. Taking her chance, she ran to the stairs and up into the parlour.

'You were ages,' said Jules, before seeing the books in her

arms. She handed them over and he sat on the floor under the shaft of sunlight shining through the cracked shutter, totally absorbed in the new books.

'Thank you,' said Pierre. He glanced his son. 'We're ready.' He held up a small knapsack, all they possessed in the world, and Valérie swallowed the lump in her throat.

They left the bookshop and walked down the lane out of the old town, each holding one of Jules' hands, pretending to be a family once again. He skipped between them, glad to be in the fresh air and looking with interest all around him. The spring sun was warm, and Pierre lifted his face. 'I know it's dangerous, but it's good to be outside again.'

Feeling more confident in their anonymity among the crowds, they crossed the Place de Bel-Air. Valérie's stride faltered when she heard a police siren come towards them, but the car rushed past them without stopping. She glanced across at Pierre and they kept on walking. They reached the Place de Cornavin and walked through the entrance hall into the station, across the geometric tiles on the floor under the rays of sunlight streaming through the tall windows.

Not wanting to split up, they queued together for tickets and headed for the platform to catch the first train going round Lac Léman. The compartment was busy, and Valérie sat next to Jules and opposite Pierre. She glanced across at a woman who was watching them and returned her smile. She felt for a moment that she was with her own future family, Philippe sitting opposite her and their son next to her, and she closed her eyes, wishing with all her heart that it would come true.

They passed the outskirts of Geneva next to fields where crops were starting to grow. More men were working in the fields now that the army was focused on guarding the Alps. Everyone knew that the National Redoubt strategy left much of Switzerland exposed to a German invasion, but they trusted General Guisan to protect the country's heart.

After twenty minutes they reached Nyon and Valérie led the way off the train, just before a group of border police got onto the train to check everyone's papers. Valérie breathed a sigh of relief. She remembered the last time she'd taken this journey, the border police had taken away a mother and children because their papers were suspicious. If the police had got on a few minutes earlier, that could have been it for Pierre and Jules.

They walked through the town towards Nathalie's aunt's house, past shops in the centre near the station and then along quieter streets. Finally, they reached the front door of the small villa in a street at the very edge of the town and Valérie rang the bell, suddenly filled with doubt about their welcome. Did her aunt even know what had happened to Nathalie?

The door opened and a short, round woman stood in front of them. Her hair was more grey than blonde, but she must have been very pretty when she was younger. Her resemblance to Nathalie was striking and Valérie took a step backwards, wincing inwardly at the thought of her friend.

'I'm Brigitte Masson. Can I help you?' Her voice was soft and slow.

'My name is Valérie. I'm a friend of Nathalie's.'

The woman took a step forward. 'Do you have news of her? The police have been in touch.' Her eyes filled with tears. 'They asked for my brother's name and address, said they needed to see them first.'

'I'm sorry, Madame, but we should go.'

'No, don't go.' Brigitte Masson turned to Pierre and Jules. 'Is this the French family she talked to me about? The one she wanted to come here?'

'Yes, this is the family. Pierre and Jules Weil, this is Nathalie's aunt.'

They shook hands and Brigitte ruffled Jules' hair.

'It was getting too dangerous in Geneva for them.'

'Of course. I will help, it's the least I can do.'

When she led them inside, a small dog excitedly rushed at them and jumped up at Jules' legs. Jules crouched down and patted the twisting ball of fur, looking excitedly up at his father, who nodded before Jules raced inside after the dog.

They followed Jules into a simply furnished living room, with a door opening out into the back garden. The dog led Jules to the door and Brigitte smiled and nodded. 'Go outside my dear, the garden's perfectly safe. No one can get in or out.'

Jules and his new friend ran outside, and the sound of his laughter filled the room.

'Will I tell him to be quieter?' Pierre took a step towards the door, but Brigitte held out her hand. 'Leave him. I can tell my neighbours that my nephew and his family are here to stay for a few days. No one will ask any questions.'

Valérie's gaze rested on the photographs on the small table at the side of the room. The one of Nathalie smiling with her aunt brought tears to Valérie's eyes and she dragged her gaze away from it.

'I need to go now, Madame.'

Brigitte reached out and held her hand.

'We just have to trust in God, my dear. There are some things we cannot prevent.'

Valérie knew she would never accept that she couldn't change things, but she couldn't argue with Brigitte when she saw the pain in her eyes. 'I'll send you a message before we come and fetch Pierre and Jules. It won't be long.'

Jules came running back inside, followed by the dog. Brigitte stood up. 'Would you like something to drink?'

He nodded enthusiastically.

'I'd better go and leave you to rest.' Valérie hugged Pierre and Jules and watched as Jules followed Brigitte into the kitchen. 'I'm going to look for Anne-Marie and Madeleine now.'

'I know, and I'm so grateful. But please take care, Valérie. After what happened to your friend, I couldn't bear it if you were hurt. You're taking such a risk, going over there.'

'There's no other way, Pierre. You know that.'

Brigitte came back and they went to the front door together, followed by the sounds of the dog barking and Jules' laughter, and Valérie embraced Brigitte.

'Thank you so much, I hope I'll be back soon with Pierre's wife and daughter.'

She left the house and headed for the station, almost running in her eagerness. She tapped her foot impatiently as the train seemed to inch its way to Geneva, stopping for minutes at a time before it went slowly on its way.

Please be there, please be safe, she whispered over and over again in her head, as if the mantra could keep Anne-Marie and Madeleine alive.

TWENTY-FOUR

VALÉRIE

Annemasse, France

Valérie went straight from the Gare Cornavin in Geneva to the streets heading south out of the city after picking up her bike at the back of the bookshop. She rode along the Route de Malagnou towards the border with France, passing workers bent over in the fields sowing seeds. It was a cloudy day, mist still settling on the trees next to the River Arve near Vessy. She looked across at Philippe's grandfather's farmhouse, its white stone walls visible through the green foliage, trying to remember the last time they'd been there together, but then turned her head away as she looked ahead towards the border crossing.

The road was quiet, and she only passed one lorry heading to the city and a horse and cart moving between the nearby farms. It was lunchtime, so everyone had gone inside to have their midday meal.

The closer she got to France, the more tense she felt, and she trembled, knowing she was about to do exactly what Philippe had warned her against, knowing that she might never come back again. But she would never forgive herself for not accompanying Nathalie when she could have helped her, and now she couldn't just leave Anne-Marie and Madeleine to their fate. She might be risking her future with Philippe, but she knew that any minute now, they could be captured too.

People were milling around the Chêne-Thônex border crossing, tradesmen patiently waiting to come into Switzerland, a couple of Swiss soldiers chatting across the fence with Nazi guards and a group of railway workers smoking together on the Swiss side.

'Papers, Mademoiselle?' asked one of the Swiss Guards, holding his hand out. 'Why are you going into France?'

'I'm making some deliveries.' She'd decided to keep close to the truth, some inexpensive watch parts in the bottom of her basket and the address of an old French supplier safely in her pocket.

He nodded, without listening to her answer and handed the papers back.

'Better not stay too long. There might be trouble later.'

'What kind of trouble?'

He shrugged as if to say that what happened in France was out of his hands.

'Just the usual, rounding up Resistance sympathisers. You don't want to get caught up in it.' He nodded at the German guards a few metres away, watching them closely. 'These characters tend to act first and ask questions later. I don't know where you're going but you'd better avoid the area around the Place de l'Hôtel de Ville.'

'Thank you, Monsieur.'

He waved her through, and she handed her papers to the German guard. He checked them thoroughly before giving them back.

'How long are you planning to stay in France?'

'Only a few hours.'

He nodded. She rode her bike into the outskirts of

Annemasse and skirted the centre of town before cycling towards the address Pierre had given her. Along the streets leading to the centre, she saw rows of Nazi flags hanging from the buildings and caught sight of units of soldiers marching along the main thoroughfares.

The people she passed didn't look at her and hardly spoke to one another. The atmosphere was much quieter than in Switzerland, everyone looking down rather than ahead. She could taste the fear in the air.

Valérie kept to the back streets and jumped off her bike in front of the address she was given by Pierre, the faint sound of marching feet still audible across the town. She looked at the numbers on the houses and stopped when she saw number twenty-seven, an ordinary, small, detached house in its own garden.

This was it, but she felt her heart lurch when she looked more closely. The gate was open, swinging on its hinges and the house looked deserted. She took a few steps along the front path and stopped when she saw spots of blood on the gravel, then looked around to see if anyone was watching her. She swallowed the lump in her throat and could feel the prickle of fear slide down her back. Veering off the path, she pushed her bike around the back of the house and breathed a sigh of relief, feeling immediately less exposed.

Forcing her feet forward, she stretched out her hand towards the back door and pushed it open, then stepped back with a gasp when she saw the blood stains on the wooden floor a few metres inside the door and the long scratches along the length of the hall. Someone had been dragged outside, but who? There was no sound from the house. No one was left inside. She wondered if Anne-Marie and Madeleine had ever been there. Was this their blood?

She backed away from the door and turned reluctantly to the shed at the side. She would have to look inside, even though she feared what she might find, her heart beating painfully fast. Suddenly, a beam of sunlight pierced the thick cloud and shone directly on the door of the shed. The light shone on some blonde hairs that lifted in the slight wind blowing through the unkempt garden, unmistakeable against the darkness of the old wooden door.

Valérie went closer and stretched out her hand to touch the long blonde hairs and saw that they were wound around a rusty nail sticking out of the door. Had Anne-Marie left it as a sign that they had been there, or had they been dragged out of the shed by force? She rattled the door and it opened outwards. Taking a deep breath, Valérie peered into the darkness, but there was no one inside. She pulled the strands of hair off the nail and put them into her coat pocket.

As she felt the first spots of rain on her face, Valérie looked up at the grey sky, wondering how long she'd been there. She had to get away from this place. She steered her bike to the front of the house and onto the street. Glancing up and down the street, her heart sank when she saw a unit of German soldiers appear round the corner and point towards her.

She almost fled in the opposite direction, but it was too late.

'Halt.'

She stood and waited for them to come closer. Her knees were shaking, and she tried to keep her breathing steady. She might be Swiss and had every right to be here, but France was a strange and dangerous place, where anyone could disappear. And if they discovered she was working in the Resistance, she might never see another dawn.

'Heil Hitler.' She almost choked on the words.

'Heil Hitler,' said the first soldier, then immediately challenged her. 'What are you doing here?'

She didn't know what to reply. What could she say? Her mind went blank with fear, and she couldn't think of any reason to explain why she was at that house.

One of the men reached out to grasp the handlebars of her bike and she pulled it closer to try to create a barrier between them. She looked around in desperation, her options for escape all gone.

'Messieurs, messieurs. Let me through. My friend has made a mistake, she was coming to my bar and must have got lost.'

A tall, shapely woman wearing bright red lipstick pushed through the group of soldiers and took Valérie's arm in a warm grip. She wasn't young but her vigour belied the lines on her face. She turned to face the soldiers, who almost backed away from the confident burst of energy thrust into their midst.

'I can vouch for this girl.'

'Madame, two Resistance sympathisers were arrested here yesterday. We've been told to watch this place for further activity.'

She didn't flinch and her voice hardened.

'Then I suggest you do just that, Heinrich. I would be reluctant to exclude your unit from my bar, and from the pleasures of my girls.'

Valérie could hear the muttering of a couple of the men and the shuffling of their feet as they backed away. Their spokesman hesitated, then made a final attempt.

'You know this girl?'

'Of course I do.' The woman put her arm round Valérie's shoulder and answered while steering her away from the group of soldiers. 'She's one of my new girls, so you'll have the pleasure of meeting her when you next come to visit.'

They heard shouting from the next street and one of the other soldiers nudged Heinrich. 'It's the Gestapo.'

'Move!' the woman hissed in Valérie's ear, then led her across the street and down a small lane of terraced houses, going into the first one. 'Take your bike inside, quickly now.'

She locked the door behind them and went over to a small window next to the door, watching the street from behind a grubby net curtain. She pulled a chair across the narrow, dim hall and pushed Valérie into it. 'Sit down. You look like you're going to faint.' She turned her attention back to the window. 'You're lucky the Gestapo weren't with them. I wouldn't have stood a chance if they'd got their claws into you.'

Valérie stared at her, hardly able to believe they'd escaped, due wholly to the woman's confidence and bravery.

'They haven't followed us.' The woman looked down at Valérie. 'Why were you in that house, didn't you know that they were killed yesterday? Poor Edith. I warned her the Germans had started to watch the house, but she wouldn't listen.'

'I was looking for a woman and her daughter. I think they were there, but they've gone now.' Her narrow escape overcame her, and she covered her face with shaking hands, before looking up at the woman, her voice coming out in a whisper. 'Thank you. You saved my life.'

'You're very welcome. My name's Cécile.'

'Valérie.'

'You aren't from around here, are you?'

'I'm from Geneva. I came across this morning.'

'Well, the Gestapo wouldn't be interested where you were from, if they thought you were helping Jews escape.' She paused and then carried on. 'I suppose that's what you are doing.'

'Yes.'

'Come into the lounge. You'll have to stay here until they've gone, and we can decide which is the best way for you to go back.'

Valérie followed her into the room and glanced through another door opening into the hall, a bar in the corner and a few round tables and chairs set out before it. Although the lounge wasn't large, it had three velveteen sofas, all brightly coloured and set against the walls. With the old-fashioned, patterned wallpaper and ornaments set on antique tables, it looked exotic rather than tawdry.

The woman settled herself on one of the sofas. 'You can't afford to get caught here, even if you are Swiss.'

Valérie smoothed the material on the arm of the sofa and sighed. 'I know. I was warned it would be dangerous to come over here.'

'Mmm...' was the woman's only response. She glanced at the carriage clock on the mantelpiece. 'Are you hungry?'

Valérie nodded, realising suddenly that it must be well into the afternoon. She was ravenous. Cécile jumped up from the sofa and Valérie heard the clatter of plates from the kitchen. In response to the noise, girls drifted into the lounge, yawning and rubbing their eyes, some fully dressed and others still wearing nightclothes under their robes. Cécile came back, carrying large plates of sliced baguette, cheese and cold meats.

'This is Valérie, everyone. I'd like one of you to go with her to the border once we've eaten and make sure she gets safely back to Geneva.'

'I can go with her,' said a dark-haired girl. 'Karl said he'd be at the border crossing at Ambilly today. I could take her there.' She smiled at Valérie. 'My name's Delphine. I can distract them until you get across.'

Cécile nodded and they all started to eat.

A short while later, Cécile hugged Valérie at the front door, her amber perfume filling the narrow hall.

'I'll ask around about your missing friends. Find out where they're hiding and try to get them across the border, if I can.'

'Thank you. The Resistance unit I work with is led by Jean Bouvier, he will help.'

'I know Jean but he's still on the Glières Plateau, so if I need to get a message to you, where do I send it?'

'The Café de Paris on the Place du Bourg-de-Four.'

'The place George Lacroix owns? I know it.'

'Send your message there or get it to the SOE. They'll pass it to me.'

Cécile raised her curved eyebrows. 'We'd better get you out of France as soon as we can if you're connected to the SOE.'

Valérie held the woman's steady gaze. 'Please be quick. They don't have much time.'

'I know. I'll find them and send a message to Jean. He can certainly get them across the border easier than I can.'

Valérie and Delphine rode together north through Annemasse, avoiding the main streets. No one stopped them or even seemed to notice as they steadily cycled past German soldiers, French police and local townspeople going about their daily business. There was no eye contact with anyone, the sense of unease damping down any natural conversations between the people they passed.

The border at Ambilly was quieter than the road Valérie had followed to enter Annemasse but there were a few German soldiers, who watched them approach. Valérie didn't dare to lift her eyes towards the Swiss border guards a few metres away behind the barrier in case her fear transmitted itself to them.

Delphine kept a tight grip on Valérie's arm and walked right up to one of the younger guards, who looked little more than a schoolboy. 'Karl, how are you today? I wanted to see you, so I thought I'd take my Swiss friend home this way. She's late for work, so let her through, would you?'

Valérie looked at him, but he had no interest in her, smiling down at Delphine, who had dropped her bike to get closer to him, effectively blocking them from the other guards. He stuck out his hand mechanically. 'Papers please.' Valérie handed them over and he glanced at them briefly, all his attention still on Delphine, who was muttering into his ear.

He handed her back the papers and, not relinquishing her hold on him, Delphine virtually pushed her across the border. 'A bientôt, chérie,' she said gaily.

Valérie looked straight ahead and walked across the few metres to Switzerland, her back prickling with tension, expecting to be called back at any moment. But all she heard were muttered comments and snatches of laughter.

She showed her papers to the Swiss border police and then pedalled furiously away from the border, her heart racing. As she cycled, a heavy weight fell round her shoulders. She'd been too late to find Anne-Marie and Madeleine, and they were still in terrible danger. She hadn't managed to reunite the family. All her hopes were now on Cécile and Jean.

TWENTY-FIVE

PHILIPPE

Saint-Maurice, Valais, Switzerland

'Philippe, can you hear me?'

Someone shook his arm and he blinked open his eyes to see Stefano's worried face staring down at him. Philippe coughed and choked on the snow as Stefano pulled him up to a sitting position, and he looked around at the changed landscape. The snow that had cascaded down gave everything a new shape and he glanced back to the bridge where the road was completely submerged by the huge mound of fresh snow. There was no one there. He swallowed and turned towards Stefano. 'Did you see what happened?'

He nodded. 'They were swept away. All of them.'

Philippe struggled to take it in. Everything had happened so quickly. They were going to kill him and the next moment they were all dead. He looked at the slope above the bridge, a deep gouge in the hillside where the smooth snow had been.

'They set off the avalanche when they skied down. You were right about the conditions. If we'd gone up there, it would have been our unit at the bottom of the valley.'

Philippe studied Stefano. There was something he was missing. He couldn't work out what it was, what was bothering him. It must be shock. He took some deep breaths, trying to steady himself.

'You saved my life, I couldn't breathe under there.' He brushed the snow off his face with shaking fingers.

'When I saw them threatening to push you over the edge, I couldn't just leave.'

He realised what was puzzling him. Stefano had pulled him out of the snow, but he shouldn't have been there. He shouldn't have seen what had happened. Philippe shook his head and tried to focus. The chill felt like it had gone deep into his bones, making his hands shake and his teeth chatter, but he had to piece together what had happened and satisfy himself that the danger was over.

'You went against my orders and stayed behind. Why didn't you go with the rest of the unit?'

Stefano didn't reply, just shook his head and flushed a deep red. Philippe looked up at where the Germans had been standing on the bridge and then back at the guilty face turned away from him, everything suddenly clicking into place. Christophe's warning came back to him.

'It was you. You told them where we were?'

He hesitated, then nodded.

'Why, Stefano? Why would you do that?'

He didn't reply, just covered his face with his hands. Philippe could hardly make out the mumbled words. 'They knew some of my family are Fascists and thought I would help them. They must have followed me for months, watching me when we went down to Saint-Maurice. When I said I wouldn't help them, they started threatening me, saying they'd tell everyone I was a Nazi sympathiser. I'd be shot.'

Philippe struggled to get to his feet. He couldn't stay in the snow any longer or he'd freeze to death. He also needed time to think, to recover from the shock that one of his men had betrayed him. The first thing he had to do was to find the rest of his men and check they were all right, as he might not be the only one they had attacked. And then he had to warn Valérie, as she had been threatened too. He took a couple of deep breaths, refusing to give in to the panic that threatened to burst through, then spoke through clenched teeth.

'We need to get back, check the others are all right.'

He staggered over the deep snow and Stefano took his arm. He'd have liked to have shaken it off, but his legs were wobbling, and Philippe knew he couldn't manage to get there on his own. As they walked down together in silence, Philippe began to feel more in control. He glanced down at Stefano, who looked totally downcast as he plodded along, and his anger turned to pity. 'Don't look so miserable.'

Stefano looked up at Philippe, his haunted eyes more telling than his words, his face that of a frightened boy. 'You don't know what it's like on the border with Italy, with the Fascists on one side and the Partisans on the other. Everybody must take sides. And even though we live in Switzerland, the pressure is still there, causing trouble and splitting up families.'

'And which side are you on?'

'I'm not a Fascist, if that's what you mean.'

'But you gave them my name?'

'I'm so sorry, Philippe. They threatened me and they said they'd kill my uncle too. I didn't know what to do.'

'Why did you stay behind when you saw what was happening?'

'I was frightened they would kill you. When I saw you fighting with them, trying to escape, I couldn't just leave you to die. I never thought that's what they planned to do.'

Philippe looked behind him as they turned the corner, the avalanche that nearly killed him disappearing. His body would have been sent back to his family. He would never have seen

Valérie again. He glanced at Stefano's downcast face, trudging along clutching Philippe's broken skis.

Stefano looked up at him. 'I'll be tried for treason, won't I? They'll shoot me.'

His words ended on a sob and Philippe made his decision. 'You saved my life. If you hadn't come back and dug me out of the snow, no one would have known what you'd done.'

'What will you tell them?'

'I'll say what happened, that the Germans followed us and surprised us. That you saw the avalanche and came back to rescue me.'

'You won't tell them it was my fault?'

'No. So long as you never do it again and you promise to tell me if you're ever approached again.'

Philippe focused on Stefano, saying each word slowly and deliberately. If he was going to cover this up, he had to be sure it wouldn't lead to an even worse security risk. They'd escaped this time, but they might not be so lucky again.

'These Germans may not come back, but there will be others. I need to trust you not to give them any more information.'

Stefano shuddered. 'I won't do it again.'

'They might threaten you.'

'You can trust me. I know I won't get a second chance.'

He smiled tremulously, hope shining through the despair. Philippe knew he was taking a risk, but Stefano had saved his life even when he knew that by doing so, he would be condemning himself. Philippe couldn't repay him by turning him in. Everyone deserved a second chance.

A few hundred metres ahead they saw the rest of his unit. It had begun to snow again, and they were huddled below a tree at the side of the road. Philippe had never been so thankful to see them all safe. They'd have a long trek back to the Fort but at least they'd survived.

When they heard what had happened, his unit insisted on strapping together their skis to carry Philippe back. He was grateful, as his whole body was aching from the fall. Lying on the hard platform, Philippe knew there would be no more train carriages full of valuables in the railway siding. That German officer might be dead, but he wouldn't be the only one to know what was going on in Saint-Maurice station.

He heard a shout ahead of them and a few moments later, Christophe's face appeared at his side.

'Where did you spring from?' Philippe pulled himself up on one elbow to stare at his friend, who took over from one of the men holding Philippe's makeshift stretcher.

'Thank God you're all right. What happened up there?'

'Got hit by an avalanche. Stefano pulled me out.'

Christophe's eyebrows shot up. 'You were lucky! I've got a truck waiting round the next bend to take you to the Fort.'

'How did you know to come and get me?'

'It was Max. He appeared at the Fort, said you were in danger, and someone had to go and find you.'

'Who told him?'

'He didn't say. But you know Max, got a finger in every pie. I'll say this for him, he wasn't going to be put off. Wherever he got his information from, he was worried enough that he came up to check you were okay. The minute he heard you were out on the mountain he insisted we go and find you.'

Max might trade in information, but his real loyalties remained true. Philippe looked back at his men, who were all listening intently. 'Just get me out of this freezing wind.'

They insisted on taking Philippe directly to the hospital ward in the Fort, despite his protests. Although he felt like he was aching all over, he knew he hadn't broken any bones. He wanted to make a full report to Major Toussaint. Christophe had gone to alert the major to the accident so someone could inform the Germans in Saint-Gingolph what had happened to their countrymen, but Philippe was more concerned about the threats the German had made before he died, wondering how many others knew as much as he did. He only managed a snatched conversation with Christophe.

'They weren't just after the maps. They knew you've been taking stuff from the carriages in the siding.'

Christophe looked positively shocked.

'You aren't going to tell the major anything about that, are you?'

'Of course not, but I'm afraid it has to stop now.'

Left alone, Philippe looked around the small hospital ward. It was equipped like any other, with four beds, lockers next to each of them and chairs for visitors. This ward had no windows and was only lit by electric light, with the sunlight and outside world beyond metres of rock.

The doctor, an abrupt but kindly man, gave a satisfied nod when he was finished with his thorough check. He surveyed Philippe wearily from under his bushy eyebrows. 'You were lucky to escape with a few aches and pains. Unlike those other poor devils who were caught in the middle of it.'

'When I heard the noise, I just tried to get as far away as possible.'

'Best thing to do. Lucky you didn't lose any of your own men.'

Philippe just nodded. No point telling the good doctor that the Germans had been waiting to get him on his own.

'Do you know what they were doing up there?'

Philippe shrugged, then winced as his bruised muscles protested. 'I don't know. Spying on our exercise, I suppose.'

The doctor looked as if he was about to say something else before he was interrupted.

'Thank you, Doctor. I'll speak to him now.'

The doctor nodded and left them alone, closing the door behind him. Major Toussaint came across and studied Philippe, then nodded as if he was satisfied with what he saw and sat down on the chair next to the bed. Up close, the major looked older than he remembered, his sandy hair dull in the glow of the lamp and his thin face pale from too long spent inside. They were all feeling the effects of the strain, constantly on the alert for an attack. 'Tell me everything that happened.'

'The Germans must have been following us all morning. We got to the highest point in the route, and I sent the men on ahead to the next bridge, so they could shelter from the freezing wind. I was just about to follow them, when they came out of nowhere.'

'Had you ever seen the leader before?'

'No, but he was tall, very confident. Could have been an athlete. He was the only one who took off his goggles so I didn't see any of the other faces.'

'We received reports that German spies are active in Saint-Maurice, gathering information about our defences. A new man appeared at the French border in Saint-Gingolph, based in the Hotel de France with the Wehrmacht. This man was a spy sent to document the Redoubt defences to prepare for a German invasion. We think that is the man who threatened you.'

'He said he'd harm my friends if I didn't agree to give him the information he wanted.'

A shiver went down Philippe's spine as he remembered the Germans pushing him towards the sheer drop, the scraping of his ski boots on the icy bridge.

'Did he say anything else?'

'No. He signalled for the others to come down and that's when the avalanche started.' Philippe cleared his throat. 'I thought he was going to kill me.'

The major shook his head. 'If I'm right about him, he was just trying to frighten you. He thought he had plenty of time to increase the pressure.'

'But how many others will know the information he had? '

'We have to assume some do.'

'I need to warn Valérie.'

The major stood up and looked down at him. 'Yes, they must know about your friend Valérie's activities with the resistance, as well as her involvement with us earlier this year.' He held up his hand as Philippe started to speak. 'However, we hardly think the Germans will threaten an innocent civilian in a neutral country.'

Philippe almost blurted out that Valérie might go into occupied France. She certainly wouldn't be safe there. 'I still need to warn her. If I write her a letter, would you get someone to deliver it?'

'Of course.'

When he'd gone, Philippe looked around the ward, feeling caged in the small space, his mind whirling. He clenched his fists at his sides, his anger slow to ignite but now pumping through his veins.

The Nazis thought they could blackmail him and use threats to Valérie to force him into handing over information recorded in the maps. They were wrong.

He'd risked his life before to prove his innocence. He would certainly risk it to protect the woman he loved.

TWENTY-SIX

VALÉRIE

Geneva, Switzerland

The next morning, Valérie left the house early. She had to do all the deliveries from the previous week when she'd fallen behind and knew it would take hours. She felt her father's worried glance rest on her a few times as she filled her basket, but she avoided his gaze.

'You'll be back for the opening party?' he asked.

It was the last thing she wanted to do, but his hesitant question filled her with remorse. She looked up at him, his spectacles perched on his nose above the grey moustache, his dapper figure looking once again like the prosperous businessman he used to be. Reopening the workshop had given him back some of his old purpose and she couldn't spoil it for him.

'As if I'd miss your grand opening,' she teased, hugging him before she left.

The dullness of the morning matched her mood as she cycled through the old town, deep in her thoughts. Even Geraldine's friendly wave and smile failed to lift her spirits: nothing could lift the dark clouds that seemed to be massing around her.

The morning passed in a blur of activity, and she crossed over to the north bank of the lake by mid-afternoon, turning instinctively towards the favourite bench on the Quai du Mont-Blanc, where she and Philippe used to meet. She gazed out at the lake, sparkling in the afternoon sunshine that had chased away the morning cloud and devoured the piece of bread and cheese Agathe packed for her, trying to feel Philippe's presence and wondering, with a sinking heart, if he would ever forgive her for what happened with Henry.

She watched the people passing by, a group of giggling schoolgirls being tormented by a couple of older boys, the laughter turning to indignant shouts when a boy snatched a book one of the girls was carrying and ran off with it. Everyone turned to look as the girls gave chase, a group of older matrons exchanging disapproving glances as the exuberant shrieks still echoed round the corner.

'May I join you?'

Valérie looked up to see Elsa standing next to the bench, the woman's tailored dress and matching jacket making her sorry she hadn't taken more care of her appearance that morning, when she'd thrown on her oldest skirt and jacket. Not really wanting to have to talk to anyone, but knowing it would be rude to refuse, Valérie moved along the bench to give Elsa some room.

'Of course...'

Elsa ran her perfectly manicured fingers through her wavy blonde hair and looked out at the lake.

'I'm glad I saw you. I wanted to speak to you.'

She turned to Valérie, her even features and high cheek-bones unchanged but in the sunlight her face seemed older, fine wrinkles highlighted in the unforgiving sunlight. Her blue eyes reflected the deep hue of the lake in front of them. 'I heard about your friend. I was devastated when I heard what happened to her. She was such a sweet girl... so helpful and kind.'

Valérie felt a lump in her throat. 'Who told you?' she mumbled.

'Henry. I'm so sorry, such a waste of life.' Elsa shuddered and her fingers gasped the strap of her bag so tightly that the knuckles turned white.

'Are you all right? I'm sorry, I didn't realise you knew Nathalie well.'

'Not really, I met her a few times in Monsieur Savarin's shop. She was always so helpful. It's just the pointlessness of it all, even Switzerland isn't free from such violence...' She smiled sadly. 'Wherever you are, it seems that violence isn't very far behind you.'

'Did you leave Austria before the war?'

Elsa was gazing across the lake. 'Yes, my husband was making his name as an artist in Vienna. The kind of artist the Nazis detest, not only because he was Jewish but because he painted in the abstract style they hate. We came to Switzerland because we could see how things were changing in Germany and we were worried Austria was going to go the same way.'

'Which it has.'

'Yes, as has all of Europe. So many artists and writers have had to leave their homes to try to build a new life. We used to meet our friends in Monsieur Steinberg's bookshop in the old town. I remember seeing you there once, sitting in a corner reading a book.'

'So, you must have known my mother?'

'Yes, I knew her. Everybody did. Jacob created a real community, made us coffee that was as good as the coffee we had in Vienna.' She smiled at the memory, then the smile faded. 'He was too trusting for his own good.'

'What do you mean?'

'My husband thought the bookshop was being watched.

Certainly, Henry's predecessor in the SOE thought so.' Elsa stood up suddenly. 'I'm sorry, I didn't mean to bore you about the past. I just wanted to say how sorry I am about Nathalie.' She shook Valérie's hand in a formal farewell and walked away.

Valérie stared out at the lake, thinking again about Nathalie, still struggling to believe she'd never see her shy smile again. Even though it was wartime and death was all around them, it was hard to process the fact that life could be over so quickly, that a soul could just vanish into thin air.

She got up and pushed her bike along the Rue du Mont-Blanc, trying to drum up some enthusiasm to make her last deliveries. Over the sound of car engines and the blaring of horns, she could hear the unmistakeable sound of choir music and turned towards it. The sound was coming from the Anglican Church along the street from the post office building. She strained to hear the pure notes above the noise of the street and went closer, captivated by its beauty.

Any time she accompanied her father to church, it was to the grand Cathédrale St-Pierre. And while she wasn't sure exactly what she believed in nowadays (with so much evil in the world, how could there be a God?) she had always found the cool, centuries-old building to be something of a refuge, a place where time seemed to stand still, and she felt somehow connected to the people she had loved and lost. Her mother, Emile and now Nathalie. The refugees she had built brief connections with, whose faces were imprinted on her memory before they fled further into the mountains. Pierre and Jules, who she'd now got to know and love. Now, this smaller, more simple building drew her in too. She sat down on one of the benches under the trees and let the music wash over her, chasing away her anxiety and her fears. To whatever or whoever was out there, she prayed that Anne-Marie and Madeleine, Pierre and Jules, would survive the war, and would have a future together under a brighter sky. Finally, filled with new energy, she got up and went to make the rest of her deliveries.

At the end of the afternoon, Valérie cycled towards the Place du Bourg-de-Four. The Café de Paris was quiet, with only a few customers sitting outside drinking coffee. Before she could cross the street, she heard her name being called.

'Valérie, over here.'

Marianne ran to her and Valérie hugged her friend. It was months since Marianne had ventured into the old town and she felt a rush of relief that she'd finally made it. Marianne felt thinner than before, the pain of the last few months still visible in her pale features and hesitant manner.

'I'm so pleased to see you. I wasn't sure when you'd come back to the café.'

'I thought it was time. And I wanted to tell you about some calls I've put through in the past couple of days at the telephone exchange. The conversations I heard might mean something to you.'

'Do you have any news about the French family? Does anyone know where the mother and daughter are?' asked Valérie urgently.

Marianne shook her head. 'Nothing definite. All we know is that they haven't been arrested.' She took a closer look at Valérie. 'Are you all right? You look like you've had a shock.'

'Yes, I'm okay.'

Valérie avoided Marianne's worried gaze and linked arms with her, steering her across the road. At the door to the café, they met Geraldine.

'Marianne, I'm so glad to see you back. I've missed you so much.' She held out her hands to them, but her smile faded when she looked at Valérie's face. 'What's happened?'

Valérie hadn't wanted to talk about it, but she couldn't help herself from crumbling at Geraldine's concern, tears springing into her eyes. 'Oh, Geraldine, Nathalie's dead. The Resistance fighters she went to meet were all killed too. And I let her go there alone.'

Geraldine didn't say anything, just hugged Valérie. Her arm still on her shoulders, she led them inside to their usual table at the back of the café.

'I'm so sorry, Valérie,' she said, trying to ignore her father who was gesticulating at a group of new customers. By the time he'd ordered her to get on with her work, Valérie had regained her composure and could meet Marianne's gaze.

'I'm so sorry about your friend, Valérie. But I'm glad I've come back. I missed seeing you all,' said Marianne.

'We missed you too.'

Valérie paused, then prompted her friend gently. 'So what did you hear on the calls? What did you want to tell me?'

'There was one between two men, made last night. They didn't identify themselves and spoke in French. One of them said that the information had been acted upon. He talked about the Risoux Forest, on the French Swiss border. Did your friend Nathalie meet the Resistance there? Was that what they were talking about?'

'Yes, I think it must have been.'

'I didn't hear any names mentioned, but he did say that their source was reliable.' Marianne looked into the distance, trying to remember everything she heard. 'You told me that there was a traitor in the Resistance. Is that who he was talking about?'

'It could be. He didn't say anything else? Any clue to identify who they were talking about?'

'No, nothing else.'

The sound of laughter rang through the café. François and Sébastien were sitting at one of the tables outside and François had his arm round Geraldine, who was trying to take his order through the giggles.

Marianne flushed and smiled shyly. 'Sébastien said he'd come and meet me. He's been very kind.'

Valérie watched them lounging casually over the table, totally at ease. François waved at her and then turned back to Sébastien, the fading sun glancing off their faces. Either of them could be the traitor. The two men got up and came inside, and Sébastien put his hand on Marianne's shoulder.

'Valérie?' François was smiling, with his attractive smile that invited a response, but Valérie was terrified that her doubts would show in her expression.

François bent down and kissed Marianne on both cheeks. 'I'm glad to see you're back.'

As François and Sébastien chatted lightly about work, Valérie listened to their conversation, her brain seething with suspicion. Geraldine came back into the café and looked at her, as if suddenly aware of the tense atmosphere. 'What's the matter?'

'Nothing. I need to go now,' she replied, standing up. 'It's my father's workshop opening party tonight and I need to be there.'

Despite the warm breeze blowing across the square, she hunched her shoulders and trudged to the other side of the square on her way home.

Her thoughts were fixed on Pierre and Jules hiding in Nyon, and Anne-Marie and Madeleine, still being hunted, so vulnerable and scared.

Everyone was at risk until she discovered who was betraying the Resistance.

TWENTY-SEVEN

VALÉRIE

By that evening, it had got much cooler and when Valérie walked to the workshop, the cobbles were wet. Valérie glanced up at the cloudy sky, hoping she wasn't going to get soaked, but the air was clear and fresh. It seemed quieter than usual for early evening, the heavy rain keeping everyone indoors. She stopped when she heard the guttural noise of aircraft flying directly overhead and she looked up to the sky, wondering where they were going. She couldn't pick out the metal shapes through the cloud, and the noise faded away. The streets of Geneva were dark, with no light to guide the Allied aircraft.

Her father's workshop was on the corner of the Rue de la Tertasse, high on the old city wall, looking over the Rhône to the north-west. It was a squat building only two storeys high, nestled between terraces of tall town houses and ideal for a watch workshop. The ground floor was a spacious storage area and the workshop on the first floor had large windows designed to let in the maximum amount of natural daylight to fill the space. It had been the Hallez watch workshop for generations.

She sighed as she carried her bike into the storeroom, which was where she'd once hid refugees escaping from France. It was no longer musty and unused, but a well-ordered space, with long tables set up against the far wall and boxes of supplies neatly stacked up in the corner. She looked around the room, seeing again the frightened faces of the people she'd hidden there, all desperate to get as far into Switzerland as they could to avoid being sent home.

A party was the last thing she felt like attending, but she knew she couldn't let down her father. Albert was finally ready to launch his new workshop after months of ordering new equipment, recruiting the old workers he'd paid off in the past and restocking his supplies.

Upstairs, she stood at the door and surveyed the workroom, now fully equipped, the new benches facing the tall north-facing windows and equipment and tools for half a dozen operators set up at regular intervals along the benches. Stools on tall legs were tidily stored under the benches, waiting to be used.

Her father was carefully reorganising his best tools on his desk at the end of the room. Valérie went up to him and kissed his cheek. He looked over the top of his spectacles to study the packages she'd deposited on the table.

'When is everyone coming?' she asked, pulling out one of the stools and perching on top of it, watching her father's delicate fingers arrange the equipment.

'Ten minutes or so.'

He looked across at the side of the room, where glasses and bottles of the local white wine grown on the steep slopes on the side of Lac Léman had been laid out on a table next to plates of bread and cheese.

'I hope we have enough to drink and eat. It's just as well your Aunt Paulette sent down some of their local cheese. It's impossible to get enough of anything in the city.'

'It'll be fine.' Valérie tried to calm his worries. 'I'm sure people will bring something. You know what it's like these days.

Everyone knows they need to bring their own food if they want to get enough to eat.'

Albert shook his head and sighed.

'It used to be so different. When we held parties, no one expected to have to bring anything.' He stared gloomily across at her.

'Enough looking back, you need to look forward. You have your workshop back.'

She jumped off the stool and poured out a couple of glasses of wine, handing one to her father. 'To the business.'

'The business.'

They shared a smile and drank the smooth wine. As if emboldened by the sip of wine, Albert ventured into an area he usually avoided. 'I thought I'd better invite Henry Grant as he paid for all of this.'

'I don't think he'll be able to come tonight.'

Her father frowned. 'Despite all he's done for us, I still worry about you seeing him so much. Something about that man feels dangerous to me.'

He went over to the stairs and checked no one had arrived and could hear their conversation, then came back to hold her hand lightly. 'Everything he does is for one purpose and that's to win the war. If he had to sacrifice you to further his cause, I don't think he'd hesitate.'

Valérie dropped her gaze and bit back the sharp rebuttal. 'I can take care of myself, I've already proved that.'

He patted her hand. 'I know you have, but please don't let him talk you into anything your good sense tells you to avoid. This war isn't going to end anytime soon, and things will get a lot uglier before they get better. They were saying on the radio tonight that there's been fierce fighting in North Africa. The Allies will be invading Italy next.'

He paused, and then continued. 'I'm worried about you, Valérie. I don't know what's happened, but something's upset you. I thought we were supposed to have no secrets between us anymore, but you don't tell me anything. I can't help you if you don't talk to me.'

She laid her head on his shoulder. 'You do help me, Papa, every day, but I can't talk about what I'm doing, it's safer that way. I will take care, I promise, but you must believe that I'm only doing what I think is right.'

She knew it wasn't a full answer, but he'd worry too much if she told him the truth. Was life always like this? Parents protected their children when they were small and then, only a few years later, the children grew up and instinctively shielded their parents.

They heard footsteps on the stairs and Geraldine appeared, holding a box. 'More supplies for your party.'

Valérie jumped off the stool and went to hug her friend. 'You didn't say you were coming.'

'I have a message for you. Someone delivered it after you left this afternoon and I thought you should get it quickly.' She handed a piece of paper to Valérie and went to set out the food she'd brought. Valérie walked to the side of the workshop and ripped open the envelope. There was a short note inside.

Received news that our friends are still well and have been sighted. We're hoping to see them soon. They don't have much time left. Suggest you use your contacts to arrange a successful meeting

Cécile

Valérie reread the note to make sure she understood its meaning. She felt a mix of emotions, from relief that Anne-Marie and Madeleine were still safe to apprehension about the fragility of that safety. Whatever its risks, she had to accept that Henry's plan was their only hope.

'Is anybody up there?'

She looked round to see a group come into the workshop, led by Pascal Dumont, one of her father's closest associates. Her father went to greet them and the moment of quiet was over.

Half an hour later, the workshop was full of people. Valérie went round topping up glasses when she saw them empty. She stood at the side of the room and looked at each familiar face, her father beaming amid the chatter. She smiled when she looked at him and realised that this was his family, the people who created fine watch mechanisms from combining the individual parts each of them produced. There were customers there too, representatives from some of the larger manufacturers who came from Neuchâtel and Le Locle. She knew many of them had been trained by her father.

Pascal came over to speak to Valérie. The last time she'd seen him he'd looked old and worried, questioning Albert about how he could keep his business going when he had to compete with the larger watch manufacturers undercutting his prices. He looked better today.

'This is a happy occasion. It's wonderful your father has been able to reopen his workshop. I never liked him having to work so hard at home to keep the business going. Things must be looking up.'

'Yes, the business is better now. And he's been able to hire some of his old workers. Much more like it used to be.'

'All the best equipment too.' Pascal looked around at the benches. 'It must have cost him a lot.'

She slipped her hand through his arm.

'Let's not talk about business tonight. Tell me about your family.'

It didn't take much for Pascal to talk about his grandchildren in Neuchâtel, his son's business and his daughter-in-law's cooking. Valérie let him reminisce, laughing at his anecdotes while she kept an eye on the rest of the room. She knew that he had only asked the questions everyone else was thinking, speculation about the sudden rise in Albert's fortunes high in the group of people who believed the days of small specialist watch producers were numbered. Little did they know that the SOE had funded the new workshop, to maintain the supply of watch mechanisms and jewel bearings the Allies used in their weapon sighting systems. Throughout the evening, Valérie heard her father smoothly turn away the same questions with a smile.

'Excuse me.'

An older man was in front of her, holding out his glass in a hand that wasn't quite steady. He was standing on his own, a little apart from the groups talking loudly, their ripples of laughter flowing through the workshop. She filled up his glass and he inclined his head a fraction. Everything about him was controlled and precise.

'You must be Albert's daughter.'

'Yes, Monsieur.'

'I am Otto Hoffman, from the German consulate.' He spoke French hesitantly with a strong German accent and tried to frame another sentence before stopping mid-way through and taking a gulp of wine.

Despite her instinctive desire to turn and walk away from the German, she made herself smile and speak his language.

'Guten Abend, I'm pleased to meet you at last. My father is very grateful for your help with our export licenses.'

The expression of relief that greeted her words was almost comical and he instantly lost his awkwardness.

'I am pleased to be of service. Trading between our countries is very important during these difficult times. I'm sure you agree.'

'Yes, we don't want to disappoint our German customers. We've been doing business with several of them for many years.'

He shook his head mournfully. 'I'm afraid that's why I've had to visit your father so often. The records of his past export licenses have all been lost. I haven't been able to find any of his files in the consulate. There's nothing about him at all.'

Another gulp of wine and he became more animated, the affront to his sense of order clear to see. 'My predecessor left very detailed notes about everyone he dealt with, but there's nothing about your father.' He shrugged. His responsibility, he seemed to suggest, would only go so far, as a mere official.

She tried not to let her relief show. Confirmation that the German consulate didn't include them in the list of Swiss citizens they spied on not only helped her father's business but gave her more freedom to work for the Resistance and help refugees get to safety across the border.

When the group started to thin out, Valérie went up to Albert, to see if she could leave. He was talking to a man she didn't know, large and dressed in an expensive suit that camouflaged his bulk, probably in his forties and very self-assured. She looked questioningly at her father.

'This is Monsieur Blanchet, from the Schweizerische Kreditanstalt.'

'I am delighted to meet you, Mademoiselle. So like your mother too.'

His broad smile didn't reach his eyes and he held her hand in a surprisingly strong grasp until she pulled away.

She didn't think they'd ever met before. She remembered an older man, quieter and more refined, who was her father's main contact at the bank. His successor wasn't someone to let a silence last for long and he spread his arms wide to take in the room. 'The bank is delighted to have helped with this project. We look forward to supporting your father's business for many years to come.'

She opened her mouth to say that the bank hadn't been so keen on her father's business for the years he'd been struggling, but Albert could see the indignation close to the surface and smoothly intervened, steering him away from her.

'Monsieur Blanchet, let me introduce you to Pascal, an old associate.'

She looked away from the banker's self-satisfied smirk and waved at a group leaving at the top of the stairs, before Geraldine came up to her and put an arm round her shoulders. 'You okay?'

Valérie leaned on her. 'Yes, I'm all right now. Thanks for your help tonight and for the message.'

Geraldine studied her face. 'You look better now, like you know what you want to do next.'

Valérie nodded and hugged her friend, holding on to the spark of hope in her heart.

Later that evening, when they were home, her father handed her another letter, smiling across at her. 'From Philippe. It was delivered by hand.' She clutched it to her chest and ran upstairs, eager to read his news. But it wasn't news he wanted to give her. It was a warning.

Ma chère Valérie

I had to write to you. Our adventure in Lavey last year hasn't gone unnoticed. I was told today that I am being watched and that you and Christophe may also be under surveillance. You should be all right so long as you stay in Switzerland, but please don't go into France because they have your name and might harm you. If they capture you, then they'll use you to blackmail me.

Do please take care and talk to my father if you think you're being followed. I'm also writing to him to let him know

the situation. I love you and I miss you every day. Write to me
soon. Please take care of yourself.

Avec tout mon amour

Philippe

Valérie set down his letter, shocked not only by his words but by the fact that he was driven to write them at all. No wonder the letter had been hand-delivered. They always avoided talking about their work in their letters but here he was, setting it all down. The need to warn her must have come above everything else and she'd gone and done the very thing he was so worried about.

More than ever before, she felt Philippe's love coming through his words and guilt filled her heart. She stroked the thin paper as if she was holding his hand, wishing he was there with her so that she could confess what she'd done, not only by going into France, but with Henry. Would he understand why she'd taken such a risk? And would he forgive her for betraying his trust?

TWENTY-EIGHT

ANNE-MARIE

Annemasse, France

Madeleine pulled the remains of the stale bread towards her and started to eat. 'Where did you get this, Maman? It's hard.'

Anne-Marie smiled at her daughter. 'I know, chérie, but it's all I could find.' She wasn't going to tell Madeleine that the only food outside was the bread put out for the dogs. 'I'm not sure this barn is a good place for us, I think we should leave soon.'

'But why? We have some blankets to sleep on and it's warm here.'

She didn't want to frighten her daughter, but Anne-Marie didn't like anything about the current hiding place. Although no one had come into the old barn since that first night, they had no food. Above all, she couldn't forget the German car they saw, the Nazi soldiers eating in the kitchen and the torch light that narrowly missed their dark shapes hiding in the straw.

'Put on your scarf Madeleine.' Anne-Marie tied a scarf around her own blonde hair and helped her daughter. She knew that the Nazis were searching for a blonde mother and daughter, so if they could conceal their appearance, they might buy some time.

She went towards the back of the barn and checked the loose plank of wood she'd found that morning, then came back to stand next to Madeleine, who was beside the barn door, pulling her back from the wide opening. They heard the noise of a car outside. Madeleine pulled at her mother's sleeve. 'It's the men who were here before.'

Her heart thumping, Anne-Marie took her hand, pulled her from the doorway and they ran together to the back wall. 'We need to play hide and seek again, can you run with me through the trees?' she said quickly, holding Madeleine's arm.

'Yes, Maman, I can run fast.'

They squeezed through the narrow gap in the wall and ran into the trees. Behind them, they heard shouting and confused noises. Instinctively, Anne-Marie pulled Madeleine closer to her side and bent her head as they ran. She looked wildly around for a place to hide but the trees were thinning out and she came to the edge of a country road. She looked behind her, but there was no one there.

Then she heard the noise of a car on the road. They must have come round to see if they could cut them off. Trying to keep to the shelter of the trees she swung off to the right where the woodland seemed denser with some dead trees that had collapsed to the ground.

'This is a good hiding place, let's go in here.'

They scrambled over the roots and hid themselves between two large trees. To Anne-Marie's relief, Madeleine happily snuggled down in their cosy hiding place, seeming to fully believe that they were simply playing.

They stayed there until it was fully dark, and she could hear no sounds from the farm or the road.

'Maman, I'm hungry,' said Madeleine plaintively. 'Can we get up now? I don't want to play any longer.'

'Yes, we need to find somewhere better to sleep.'

They walked further into the wood and Anne-Marie saw what looked like a woodsman's cottage. There were no lights coming from the windows. Maybe they were in luck, and it was deserted. Anne-Marie walked towards the door, but it opened suddenly, and she saw an old woman holding a rifle pointed at them. She was small and looked frail, but she held the gun firmly and her eyes flashed in the moonlight.

'What do you want?' she said, keeping the rifle trained on them.

Anne-Marie didn't know what to say or do. She felt so tired, she couldn't run any further. 'We just need somewhere to stay, Madame, just a few days and then we'll go.'

'I'm hungry, Madame,' said Madeleine.

The old woman lowered the rifle to the ground. 'I'm sorry if I frightened you, you never know who might be outside. Come in.' She beckoned them to follow her. They walked into the cottage and the old woman lit an oil lamp, the dim light showing a simple wooden table and chairs and one comfortable chair, with a battered cushion at the headrest. There was a door leading out of the room that was open a few inches.

'Sit down, you look exhausted. I'll get you something to eat and drink.' The old woman went to a dresser on the other side of the room and started to put out plates.

Anne-Marie looked around the room to try to get a clue about whether they were safe or not, but there was nothing she could see that would tell her the sympathies of the old woman. She could see in a small glass cabinet on a high shelf in the dresser a small silver cup and what looked like medals. In the simplicity and plainness of the cottage, it was the only ornament she could see.

Her eye was caught by a slight movement of the door at the back of the room. It could have been a breath of wind or a draught, but she knew suddenly that there was someone else in the other room, listening to them. Anne-Marie looked around for some way to escape but the front door was shut, and the old woman was handing Madeleine a piece of bread. She glanced back at the door, hardly breathing. Who was there? Had she fallen into another trap?

TWENTY-NINE
VALÉRIE

Geneva, Switzerland

The next morning, Valérie did her tasks mechanically and tried to ignore the concerned glances cast in her direction by her father, terrified in case she blurted out the thoughts weighing her down. She looked out for Henry, hoping he would come and take her to Saint-Maurice soon. Anything would be better than this agony of uncertainty, not knowing whether delaying even a few days would lead to more deaths.

She even offered to dig over the yard leading into the new workshop, hoping that hard physical work would help to pass the time. She was there, spade in hand, when a shout made her look up.

'Come with me.'

She ran to the gate and Henry was leaning against a black saloon, a smile in his eyes, looking casual in an open-necked shirt. 'Your chauffeur awaits.'

She looked down at the faded floral dress she was wearing. 'I need to change. I only wear this when I'm working in the garden.'

'Looks all right to me. And we don't have time for you to go back and change. Are you coming or not?'

'Yes. I just need to lock up the workshop and get my cardigan.'

A few moments later Valérie climbed into the car, relieved that she was taking some action. They drove slowly out of the old town.

'I've arranged to meet up with Christophe and Philippe this afternoon,' said Henry.

She put her hand on his arm. 'Oh, I have to tell my father I'll be away. I can't leave him for a whole day without letting him know.'

'I've told him already.' He grinned, looking younger and more carefree than she'd ever seen him before. 'He seemed surprised.'

Despite herself, she responded to his mood, the black cloud lifting a fraction. 'What did you say to him?'

'That I'd promised to take you out of town for lunch and we'd be back sometime this evening.'

He chuckled and glanced at her to see she was sharing the joke. She tried to smile in response.

'What's the matter? Something's happened, hasn't it?'

It was useless to pretend.

'I went across to Annemasse to try to find Anne-Marie and Madeleine but they weren't at the address I had for them. I think they were there but there's no sign of them now.' She put up a shaking hand to her forehead. 'There were blood stains in the house. The Nazis had shot the people who were helping them.'

'The Resistance is looking for them,' Henry said quietly.

'I got a note saying they'd been spotted by someone I met in France, but that time is running out. I'm worried sick. If we can't get them across to Switzerland in the next few days, I'm sure they'll be caught. And even though I took Pierre and Jules to Nyon, they aren't safe yet. If they're found, they'll be sent back to France.'

'Valérie, calm down. The Resistance know how urgent this is and you must trust when they say they'll get them out.'

She looked up at Henry, who was concentrating on the road in front of him, the city centre streets busy as always. It made it easier to talk to his profile, to see the reaction from his expression and pick up the slightest inflexion in his voice.

'Every time I meet a member of the Resistance, I worry that they're the traitor. I can't help myself.'

'Whoever it is, we need proof.'

Valérie looked out of the window, catching glimpses of the wide expanse of Lac Léman between the buildings as they drove through the towns and villages circling the edge of the water. She knew he was right, that it was better to keep an open mind.

'There is another possibility we need to consider.'

His words came out slowly, as if he was reluctant to articulate his thoughts.

'I know you think that the person who killed Emile is our traitor, but what if it isn't the same person? We might be looking for two people.'

They didn't speak for some minutes, Valérie turning over in her mind what he'd said. Finally, she broke the silence.

'But that throws everything wide open. It could be anyone giving information to the Germans.'

'No, our traitor must be part of the Resistance to have hard information about their plans. Someone else might know snippets of information, but nothing about planned Resistance operations. No, I'm afraid it has to be someone in that world, someone we all trust.'

Sébastien's face came into her mind, laughing with François and walking away with Marianne. There were too many possibilities. And if they didn't identify the traitor, people would keep dying. She looked out of the window at the men working in the fields next to the road. They had no choice but to set the trap and flush him out.

She settled back into her seat and looked ahead towards the Alps looming above Villeneuve, the town at the east end of Lac Léman, and stretching into the distance at the end of the lake. They only had a few more kilometres drive up the valley to reach Saint-Maurice, following the Rhône as it flowed towards the lake.

Reaching into her pocket, she felt the edges of the edelweiss necklace. Nathalie's presence was so strong that Valérie could imagine her friend was there with them. She dreaded facing Christophe's pain and telling him about what she'd seen. But she knew he deserved to know everything; no matter how much it would hurt.

THIRTY

VALÉRIE

Saint-Maurice, Valais, Switzerland

They parked outside the Château de Saint-Maurice, on the road along the cliffside above the town, standing proudly above the narrow valley. The castle had been built in medieval times and was now being used by the Swiss military as part of the complex of fortresses guarding the western flank of the National Redoubt.

Valérie got out of the car and felt the afternoon sun warm her shoulders. She stretched her stiff limbs and gazed up at the cliffs that soared above the town, hiding the men and machinery defending their country. At the side of the car, small clumps of primroses were growing in the hostile environment, and she stepped round them to follow Henry to the main door past two soldiers guarding the entrance.

Inside, another soldier led them through a maze of corridors, before opening a door into a meeting room, with tables in the middle, surrounded by chairs, all arranged to face one direction. On the wall in front of the chairs was a map of the Alps. It looked like a training room. Narrow windows on the left-hand side let in natural daylight, though none of them were open to freshen the dusty room.

Christophe and Philippe were sitting at one of the tables and turned towards the door when they entered, together with another man Valérie didn't know. Henry walked up to him and shook his hand, grasping his shoulder with the other.

'Yves, I'm so sorry about Nathalie,' he said.

Turning her gaze from Nathalie's older brother, Valérie looked at Christophe and was shocked by his appearance. His face was pale and drawn and his eyes, usually brimming with laughter, were empty of expression. She walked up to him and hugged him, feeling him tense in her arms. Then she turned to Philippe, who was standing rigidly beside him, looking uncertainly at her. He held out his arms and she walked into his familiar embrace, feeling him sigh heavily.

'Thank God you're safe. I've been so worried about you.'

She avoided his eyes, knowing what his reaction would be once he'd found out what she'd done. 'Of course, I'm fine.'

'But why are you here?' He nodded to Henry. 'We were told someone from the SOE would tell us more about what happened to Nathalie. What do you have to do with all this?'

Christophe stared at Valérie. 'The police told us that she was dead, that she was caught up in a Resistance ambush, but that's all they said.'

'Let's all sit down,' said Henry quietly. 'Valérie is here because she has more information about what happened to Nathalie.'

She took a deep breath, feeling all their eyes upon her. They sat down opposite her, and she could feel the intensity of their gaze. She looked straight at Philippe, blinking back the heavy tears in her eyes.

'Nathalie was in the Risoux Forest on Friday night to hand over money to the Resistance. She planned to ask them about the French family I'm trying to get out of France. The Germans must have been waiting and they were attacked. Their hands were tied, they were beaten, and they were all shot.'

Valérie's voice cracked as she remembered Nathalie's body lying in the wet grass. She could still see her bruised and bloodied face, and was certain she would never forget it.

'I saw her body, and while I was there the Germans came back to bury them.' She swallowed and then carried on. 'I... I hid in the trees until they'd gone, and I found this next to her in the grass. Then I went straight back and told your father where she was, Philippe, so he could return her body to her family.'

Valérie pulled out the edelweiss necklace from her pocket and handed it to Christophe, who held it in the palm of his hand as if it was the most precious jewel in the world.

'Her necklace...' he breathed and bent his head.

She hunched her shoulders, unable to stop the tears brimming over onto her cheeks.

Christophe lifted his eyes slowly from the necklace. 'Who did it? Who killed her?'

'An SS officer called Schneider,' Henry replied. 'Young and keen. Willing to kill everyone in his path. He worked undercover in France before the fall of Vichy France and infiltrated the Resistance. Someone has been feeding him information for months and we think they told him about this handover.'

'Schneider was the man I saw in the forest, he was in charge,' said Valérie.

Christophe groaned and covered his face with his hands. 'It's my fault. I should never have let her do something so dangerous, go up into the forest all alone like that.'

'No,' Yves cut across him. 'You couldn't have stopped her. Nobody could. Nathalie wanted to do this, it was her decision. We heard last night that the SS came into Saint-Gingolph, the town on the border between Switzerland and France, and arrested the Germans who were stealing the valuables. It sounds like Schneider was behind it.'

He looked across at Philippe. 'Taking over from the German killed in the avalanche.'

'Avalanche. What avalanche?' Valérie demanded.

Philippe hesitated, then told her about his narrow escape. 'You know what it's like up there at this time of year?'

She nodded, stunned at his words. He'd warned her, but the Germans had targeted him instead.

It was as if he was talking about something that had happened to a stranger, and she wondered how he could stay so calm and controlled. She knew the mountains as well as he did and how lucky he was to be alive.

All of them were risking their lives in different ways.

Christophe slammed his fist on the table. 'What are we waiting for then? If Schneider is here, we could go and finish him off now.'

Philippe caught his arm and made his friend look at him. 'You won't get anywhere near him.'

'It isn't just Schneider we want,' said Henry calmly. 'It's the one who's giving him the information we have to catch as well, before he betrays anyone else.' He looked around them. 'Schneider and his informant operate in France across the border from Geneva. Our traitor is someone who knows the units around Annemasse and in the Jura Mountains and can move between them.'

'So do you have a plan?' asked Christophe impatiently.

'I do,' Henry replied grimly. He took out a map of Nyon from his pocket and spread it out on the table.

'I've told Jean to get Madeleine and Anne-Marie out of France on Thursday night if he's found them in time, and take them through the Risoux Forest, to reunite them with the father and son and get them further into Switzerland. They'll be safely away before we try to catch the traitor, and my men will be there in the forest to protect them. We've told a few carefully chosen people about a later meeting to hand over arms and explosives to Jean, who will take them into France. We've also said we have information about a traitor in the Resistance. I believe Schneider will want to intercept the arms and find out if we know who his traitor is. If we're lucky, our traitor will come along too to discover if we really know his identity. We'll be ready to attack.'

'We'll be the ones waiting?' asked Christophe.

Henry nodded. 'My men will be outside, and we'll be hiding in a separate section of the barn near the border. I need at least one expert marksmen inside the location.'

He looked at Philippe. 'That's your role. Valérie will meet Jean, Anne-Marie and Madeleine and take them to the barn. By then, we three will be in position. My men will get the French family away before the scheduled meeting. I'll have my men watching the barn and they'll alert us if something goes wrong. Schneider won't be keen to advertise his presence so I don't think he'll have a lot of men with him.'

Henry paused, his expression grim. 'If I have my way, they won't walk out of the place alive. They must be stopped, it's our chance to set the German efforts back for months. The refugees will come across at 9pm and the meeting to hand over the money is set for 11pm. We all meet in Place De-Grenus at 8pm and drive out to Noyer.'

'But what if Anne-Marie and Madeleine are late?' said Valérie. 'They could get mixed up in something even more dangerous.'

Henry's voice was as hard as flint. 'We've called in a lot of favours to get them out. People have risked their lives to find them. Your friend Cécile is one of them. We just have to trust that they reach Jean in time.'

Soon Valérie and Philippe were alone in the room. Christophe and Yves had walked out with Henry and closed the door firmly behind them.

Valérie looked at Philippe, trying to work out what he was thinking. Neither of them spoke. It was as if each were waiting for the other to say something first.

Finally, Philippe muttered in a low voice, 'You ignored my warning, didn't you? You went into France, despite what I said and after what had happened to Nathalie. I can see it in your face.'

Keeping all emotion out of her voice, knowing he had the right to be angry, she told him the truth. 'I didn't have any choice. I found where Anne-Marie and Madeleine had been hiding, but they'd gone by the time I got there.'

'So, you risked your life, our future, for nothing?'

She touched his arm, but he didn't take her hand. 'It wasn't for nothing, Philippe. I just got there too late, that's all.'

'Are you going to try again?'

'No, you were right. It's too dangerous for me to go back to France. Cécile promised to find them, and Jean will take them across.' She shrugged her shoulders. 'I just have to hope they will succeed.'

She watched him struggle to reply and she reached out and touched his face, but he looked away, unable to hide his anger, and started to pace the floor. Rather than calming down, he seemed to grow angrier the more he walked.

'And Henry Grant. He's just using you, Valérie. Why don't you realise that?'

She felt a sharp stab of guilt when she remembered Henry's kiss but pushed the memory away. 'You know why. We need him,' she insisted.

She grasped his hand when he came close, but he pulled away, as if unable to stop his pacing.

'Nathalie's death mustn't be for nothing. And this is our chance to get justice for Emile.'

Philippe said nothing for a few minutes then spoke grudgingly. 'I still don't like it... I don't trust that man.'

'But he's our only hope.' She felt her eyes fill with tears and dashed them away. 'I didn't have a choice, Philippe. I knew what I was risking, and that you had asked me not to go, but I had to do something.'

He shook his head and suddenly her temper flared up. He doubted her abilities and her choices, and his desire to protect her felt more like control.

The old frustration boiled over, and her words tumbled out in a rush. 'It wasn't me who almost got killed.'

'I didn't go looking for trouble, Valérie. They came after me, not the other way around...'

Their gaze locked, but before either of them could speak again, there was a knock at the door and a soldier came in. 'You're needed, Mademoiselle. Monsieur Grant says you must leave now.'

Valérie took a step towards Philippe, hit by the fact that she'd almost lost him and that she didn't know when she'd see him again, but he didn't move, his face still full of anger.

'Mademoiselle.'

The soldier's voice was insistent and with a sob she whirled round and brushed through the door. She walked along the corridors towards the main door of the chateau, breathing in with huge gulps and trying to hold back her emotion. By the time she got to the main door, she'd got herself under control, hugged Christophe and climbed into the front seat of the car.

Henry drove away and a few minutes later, they stopped across from Saint-Maurice station in front of the Café de la Gare. The broad road next to the station was full of vehicles, carts and horses, all picking up goods from the yard.

'One of the trains has come in. They'll need me,' Yves said

as he scrambled out of the car. He leaned into the driver's window and shook Henry's hand, looking from him to Valérie.

'Thank you for telling me what happened to my sister.'

He crossed the square, waving to one of the other railway workers loading boxes of supplies on to a cart, before running across to help him load up the last of the boxes. The noise of the train filled the station as it slowly started on its journey to Brig, along the Rhône valley. Once it had pulled out of the station, Valérie searched for Yves, but he'd merged into the scene of activity around the station, passengers leaving the platform and vehicles being driven away.

Henry started the car and waited until the horse-drawn cart Yves had helped to load drove past them before driving away. As they accelerated in front of the cart, the farmer nodded a greeting. It was all so ordinary and comforting and she glanced at Henry, concentrating on manoeuvring the car past an army lorry. At least he didn't question her choices.

She hunched her shoulders as they drove towards the lake, looking up at the snow-covered peaks towering over the Rhône valley. This was the place that Nathalie had loved, and Valérie felt a small degree of comfort that she would be brought back to Saint-Maurice.

Her thoughts went to Philippe and the avalanche that had almost taken him from her too. He hadn't wanted to talk about it, but she knew how lucky he'd been to survive. Her eyes filled with tears when she remembered how she and Philippe had parted in such anger and she twisted her engagement ring on the chain around her neck. Their relationship couldn't end like that, she wouldn't let it.

She sat up in her seat, determination chasing away the tears, and knew that just as she would fight for Pierre and Anne-Marie, she would fight for Philippe.

THIRTY-ONE

VALÉRIE

Henry drove fast along the main road up the Rhône valley and they didn't speak as the powerful car ate up the kilometres. It would take several hours to get back to Geneva and Valérie closed her eyes. It was certainly better than a cramped train ride, stopping at scheduled and unscheduled stops, not knowing when you would reach your destination. They reached Villeneuve, the town at the end of the lake and Henry turned left at the main junction rather than right. Valérie looked at him in surprise.

'Aren't we going back on the north side of the lake? Are you taking the road through France?' The border with France at Saint-Gingolph was only a few kilometres away. Philippe's warning about the dangers of going into France were fresh in her mind.

'I want to meet a man at Évian. I thought we should have something to eat there. I don't know about you, but I'm ravenous. I don't see why we shouldn't enjoy ourselves.'

'But Henry, the Nazis have my name. It's too dangerous for me to go into France.'

He touched her cheek with his hand in a fleeting gesture. 'Don't look so worried. You'll be perfectly safe with me.'

He smiled across at her, looking younger again and free from the worries that he seemed to carry around with him in Geneva. She tried to relax into her seat, biting back her doubts, wondering how he could be so confident. She just hoped he was right.

'Enjoy the drive. No one knows where we are or is watching what we're doing.'

Valérie didn't know this road as well as the one on the other side of the lake that remained within Switzerland. The border between Switzerland and France started at Saint-Gingolph and then struck out into the middle of Lac Léman, the south bank in occupied France and the north bank in Switzerland. The pleasure steamers that had criss-crossed the large expanse of water had been stopped at the start of the war to prevent refugees escaping from France and all she could see were a few small fishing boats bobbing up and down on the southern shore. There were more trees along this side, their heavy branches leaning into the water and fringing the view of the towns of Vevey and Montreux on the other side.

They drove into Saint-Gingolph and up ahead of them she saw the low buildings of the border post, with groups of German soldiers and border policemen stopping the vehicles in turn. The road had been quiet but ahead of them a German convoy was waiting at the checkpoint in France, the noise of their engines filling the air as they blocked the route across the border. Henry and Valérie wound their windows up to keep out the smell of the fumes, but the noxious air crept into the car despite their efforts.

After a few minutes sitting behind a goods lorry, Henry cursed. 'This is taking far too long. I'm going to take a shortcut.'

He wound down his window and shouted to the nearest

German soldier, who reluctantly came up to the car. Valérie looked at Henry in surprise as he spoke in perfect German. He'd only ever spoken to her in French and English. Her German wasn't perfect but she didn't need to understand much of the language to see that he was trying to skip the queue. When Henry showed the young Wehrmacht soldier his identity papers, the reaction was almost comical. The soldier inspected the papers, then handed them back and snapped to attention. By this time his senior officer had come to see what was going on. He took one look at the identity papers and responded to the barked order by shouting at the truck in front to move out of the way to let them through. This was achieved with much complaining, but Henry finally had enough space to ease the car out of the queue and drive across the border, leaving a row of soldiers making the Nazi salute behind them. No one had asked for her papers.

'I didn't know you could speak German,' was the first comment Valérie could come up with.

He grinned at her, a hint of apology in his smile. 'I can speak four languages, not all fluently but my French and German are pretty good.'

'And what identity papers do you have that make them do anything you ask?'

He looked so like a guilty schoolboy that she laughed.

'They thought you were a member of the SS, didn't they?'

He nodded. 'Identity papers stolen from some high-ranking party official. He looks like me. I hadn't tried to use them before, so it's good to know they work.'

He seemed to feel buoyed by his success rather than relieved, as Valérie felt, that they hadn't been arrested and thrown into a French prison, where they would be completely unable to help Pierre, Anne-Marie and the children.

She'd been frustrated by Philippe's attempts to protect her and had appreciated Henry's belief in her abilities, but she was beginning to realise that Henry's capable demeanour covered up a hunger to win and a willingness to take crazy risks to do it. Valérie could see how he used his charm to get people to do what he wanted and although she responded to his smile, she felt a note of warning. She would risk her life to reunite Anne-Marie and Madeleine with Jules and Pierre, but she knew instinctively that she didn't feel the same excitement in courting danger that she could see in Henry's eyes. It was the same thrill that she saw in Christophe. He didn't hide it as well as Henry, but there was only a paper-thin difference between them.

They drove into Évian, past large banners displaying the swastika sign on each side of the road. Valérie had seen the same Nazi placards on most of the larger houses since they'd crossed the border, the change from neutral Switzerland to occupied France stark and shocking. She saw the familiar dome of the spa building loom over the gardens stretching out to the edge of the lake. Despite the brooding presence of German soldiers, couples were strolling along the waterfront and the restaurants facing on to the lake were buzzing with people.

Henry drove past the spa building and stopped opposite a small, dimly lit restaurant. He switched off the car and watched the diners inside for a few moments. Valérie followed his gaze. 'Is everything all right?'

'I think so. All looks quiet to me.' He smiled across at her. 'Come on, let's go and eat.'

They waited until a military car passed in front of them and Henry put his arm around Valérie's shoulders as they crossed the road. They stopped abruptly at the door to the restaurant when a group of German officers came out in front of them. The Germans were talking loudly to one another and hardly noticed them, apart from the man bringing up the rear who nodded his thanks as he passed.

Once inside, Valérie glanced around and was relieved to see no other uniforms.

'Henri... mon ami.' The owner, a large man in a white

apron, came towards them and held out his hands. He shook Henry's hand and came closer to him, muttering in his ear.

'You have just missed our friendly local Gestapo... Not looking for you, I hope.'

Then he smiled at Valérie. 'But who is this beautiful young lady?' He bowed over her hand. 'Your servant, Mademoiselle.'

He nudged Henry. 'Where are your manners? You must introduce me, mon ami.'

Henry smiled. 'Valérie, meet my old friend Robert Delacroix. He's a charmer and a crook but he serves the best coq au vin I've tasted this side of Paris.'

'You flatter me Henri. Come and sit down and I will see if we have any left.'

He led them to a table in the far corner of the restaurant, away from the other diners and handed them some menus. Henry glanced round the room and spoke in a low voice. 'Do you have them?'

'But of course, mon ami. All as arranged. But you eat first, hein? You must not work all the time when you are accompanied by a lady.'

He wobbled away and Valérie watched as he made his way delicately between the tables, his large bulk avoiding all the obstacles on his way with unexpected grace.

'He's right,' said Henry. 'All we've done today is work and I promised you a day out.'

He picked up her hand lying on the table between them and kissed the inside of her wrist, before laying it back on the table and sighing. Valérie felt herself flush. She looked back down at the menu and shifted uncomfortably, when Robert came over to take their order.

Over the next hour Valérie tried to relax, feeling guilty that she was having a meal out when Pierre, Jules, Anne-Marie and Madeleine were still in such danger. She watched Henry, forcing herself to listen to him, trying to take her mind off her worries.

They were interrupted by Robert who had come up next to them without making a sound. They both jumped and Henry frowned. 'What is it?'

'The Germans are coming back. They're searching for someone, so I think it best if you're not here when they come.'

'Where can we get out?'

'There is a door at the side. Hurry now, you must go.'

Valérie grabbed her coat and they followed Robert through the kitchen and out of the side of the restaurant into a narrow street that led round to the front. Henry grasped his hand. 'Thank you.'

'We haven't paid,' Valérie started to say but stopped when she saw Henry hand over a wad of francs and receive a package in return, which he carefully stored in one of the inside pockets in his coat.

'It is all settled, my dear,' said Robert. 'Now go, I have someone watching your car and it is safe, but you must leave now before they come.'

Henry grabbed Valérie's hand and they ran to the street and jumped into the car. Henry started it smoothly and drove off, looking in his rear-view mirror. Valérie looked round to see unformed soldiers spill on to the street where they'd been parked. The soldiers were going into all the restaurants in that part of the street, and she saw them pull Robert outside before the car turned the corner.

'Will he be all right?' She looked away from Henry's forbidding expression.

'If I know Robert, he'll be fine.'

He took his hand off the wheel and checked his inside pocket, to make sure he had the envelope.

'What did he give you?'

He glanced at her. She felt that he didn't want to answer,

but then he spoke. 'False identity papers. Robert supplies some of the best. I need them for the SOE agents we're expecting over the next few months. Once we've captured our traitor, we'll be able to send more agents across the border. My superiors in London have been very reluctant to parachute in more men and women until they are sure they won't be betrayed.'

He paused and then carried on. 'Our operation to catch the traitor is what they're waiting for. If we don't succeed, then they won't send across any more agents. Our airdrops have been intercepted over the last few weeks and the Maquis are running short of weapons and ammunition. We need to do something to make sure we can resupply them.'

They didn't talk much on the rest of the way, and Valérie was sure that Henry looked in his rear-view mirror more times than usual. The conviction that someone was following them took hold of her mind and prevented any casual conversation. She was ashamed of losing her temper with Philippe, when all he wanted to do was to keep her safe.

Valérie sat up in her seat as they drove up to the border to get back into Switzerland, but this time only a single border guard checked their papers and waved them through. In the dim headlights of passing cars, Valérie thought that Henry looked tired, his confidence at the previous border post a faint memory.

'You can drop me at the bottom of the hill.'

He shook his head. 'I'll take you home.'

She didn't argue, too tired to protest. 'Thank you.'

He stopped the car in front of her house, and they looked at one another in the dull light.

'I'm sorry about what happened in Évian,' he said.

She put her hand on his arm. 'It wasn't your fault. I just hope your friend is all right.'

'Robert will be fine. He's a survivor.'

Valérie nodded. 'We all have to be. I'll see you on Thursday, Henry.'

She got out of the car and walked to her front door, seeing her father's relieved face appear at the window. If he knew what she was caught up in, it would tear him apart.

THIRTY-TWO

VALÉRIE

Thursday evening finally arrived. Valérie had been a bundle of nerves all day, unable to stop herself from thinking about Anne-Marie and Madeleine and whether Jean had got them safely out of Annemasse. Despite Henry's confidence, she had no idea if he'd even found them, or if they'd been captured. She'd sent a message to Pierre that they should be ready to leave that night, desperately hoping that she wouldn't dash his hopes again.

'I'm going now. I'll be back as soon as I can...'

Her father looked up from his newspaper. 'I suppose it won't do any good to ask you not to go?'

She shook her head. 'I'm sorry, Papa. I told you I must go out tonight.'

'But it's raining. You'll get wet.'

'It's only a shower...'

She went up to him and kissed his cheek. He caught her hand as she stood up to leave. 'Who are you going to meet so late?'

'You know I can't tell you that.'

He sighed. 'I worry about you. It isn't safe to go out alone at night. That girl was killed, and the police won't say who did it.

Whoever it was could still be out there, waiting for another victim.'

She sat down on the sofa next to him, still holding his hand. He was looking older and frail and she felt a pang of guilt when she realised that the worry he felt for her was visibly ageing him, the grey hair at his temples now silver.

'I'm not going alone, Papa.'

He still looked worried, so she went further.

'Papa, listen to me. The person who killed that girl wasn't some random criminal. There's more behind her death than the police are saying. It won't happen again.'

'How do you know that?' he said, his voice filled with worry.

She looked up at the clock on the mantelpiece, surrounded by photographs of her with shooting prizes, from the older ones when she was quite small to the most recent, taken just before the outbreak of war. Her gaze lingered on the one of her and Philippe, both proudly holding trophies to the camera.

'I just do. I need to go, or I'll be late.'

A quick squeeze of his hand and she turned to leave, hardening her heart. She had to hide from him that she was going so close to the French border, because he would make himself ill with worry. Over the last few months, she'd seen him become much more anxious about her, struggling to deal with the stresses of the war surrounding them, particularly when it spilled over into their lives. He seemed to accept the risks he was running supplying Henry Grant with watch mechanisms and jewel bearings, but even though he knew she was still hiding refugees he didn't like her talking about the details of what she was doing.

Valérie felt like everything she had ever done to help the Resistance had been leading up this moment, to this night. She was filled with adrenaline at the thought of avenging Nathalie and Emile's murders, and seeing Pierre and Jules reunited with the rest of their family. She went straight to Henry's apartment on the Place De-Grenus, pressed the bell and looked up at the first-floor window to see if anyone was there.

Just as she was about to ring the bell again, the door opened and she took a step back. Henry waved her inside and she saw Philippe behind him.

'He wanted to speak to you first,' said Henry.

Philippe walked towards her and gathered her hands in his.

'Come up when you're ready. Just don't be long.' Henry ran upstairs but neither of them looked at him.

Valérie walked into Philippe's arms and sighed as she felt the barriers between them crumble away.

'You were right to be angry that I went into France, but I had to try to find them and reunite the family. With everything going on around me I have no control over, it was one thing I could do.' She looked up at him, tears in her eyes. 'I hated leaving you like that in Saint-Maurice, so angry with me.'

He tightened his arm around her. 'I shouldn't have got angry. It doesn't help anything. I'm sorry.' He smiled down at her. 'It's one of the reasons I love you, the sense of never quite knowing what you might do next. Life with you is never dull.'

Valérie chuckled. 'It's my auburn hair.'

'Although it might not always seem like it, I wouldn't have it any other way.'

'But you were right about not trusting Henry,' she said quietly. 'I made a mistake...'

Philippe touched her lips with his fingers. 'I don't want to know, Valérie. We all make mistakes. All I want to know is that you love me.'

'Yes, I do, more than anything.' She held him close, the memory of Henry's kiss disappearing from their world, then she kissed him again. 'It's going to be dangerous for everyone tonight. Please be careful.'

'You too.' He glanced up the stairs. 'We'd better go up.'

When they entered the parlour, Yves nodded a greeting and

Christophe came and hugged her. The familiar grin of the co-conspirator was there, but he was a faint echo of his former self. They sat for a while, waiting for Henry to tell them it was time to go. The silence was heavy between them, tension written across all of their faces.

Finally, they crowded into the two cars parked on the street and drove out of Geneva to the north of the lake towards Nyon, Henry and his men in the first car and Valérie squeezed between Philippe and Christophe in the second. The sun was starting to fall in the sky, and they watched people trudging home along the city streets. Once they were out of the city, they drove along the side of the lake, the water shadowy in the gathering darkness. After a short time, they reached Nyon, the town quiet, and avoided the centre, taking the road past fields leading to the Risoux Forest, before turning off the main road into a dirt track. The car headlights were turned off and both cars slowed down as everyone's eyes grew accustomed to the darkness. The rain had stopped, and when Valérie looked up, she could see that the sky had cleared, some stars glinting through the darkness.

A large barn loomed out of the darkness and Valérie shivered when she saw the familiar shape, her mind filled with memories of Nathalie and the night she found her body. The cars stopped and they all got out. It was wet underfoot and Philippe clutched Valérie's hand as they watched the cars reverse back down the track. They didn't speak, afraid that their voices might be heard by any border patrols passing nearby, and Henry beckoned them to follow him into the barn. Inside, he bent down to whisper in her ear, 'You should go now. We'll hide. Yves will wait here for you to get back.'

She watched as Yves lit a torch and shone it against the side wall. She saw him move a couple of stools and sit down on one of them. Philippe squeezed her hand and then she was standing alone. She nodded at Yves and went outside. When she looked back, Yves had pulled the barn door shut and the barn looked deserted.

Valérie ran across the field to the edge of the Risoux Forest, her way lit by the stars. The trees around her swayed in the light wind blowing down off the Jura Mountains and she breathed in the forest smells of damp earth and pine trees, alert to the sounds all around her.

Before long she reached the meeting place at the side of the low wall on the border, and a few moments later she heard Jean's signal, the low call of a bird. Venturing out from the corner of a clump of trees, she stared through the gloom. She waited and watched, hardly breathing in case she missed them, but she could hear nothing except the sound of wind in the trees.

Panic flooded through her body. Had they been betrayed? Were Nazis closing in? She stamped her feet gently, which were getting numb and wet from the damp grass. The forest was silent again.

Then the swishing sound of the wind in the trees changed into the sound of boots tramping through the grass and she saw four figures coming towards them, one much smaller than the other three. Then she heard the first figure panting as it got closer and saw that two of them had light hair. She reached out her hand and grasped the wrist of the woman, pulling her across the wall, then reached for the small child beside her. They sat down heavily on the grass, panting and trying to catch their breath.

She heard Anne-Marie whisper and bent down to catch her words. 'Are we in Switzerland now?'

'You are. I'm so glad to see you, we've been looking for you desperately.'

'So we're safe?'

'Not just yet, but you will be soon. You must come with me, we need to get further away from the border.'

'Pierre and Jules...'

'They're safe. You'll see them very soon.'

A dark-haired young man came towards her with Jean. He was tall and thin, dressed in old clothes and wearing a battered beret clamped over his dark hair. She had never seen him before. For a moment, he reminded her of Emile, as he spoke in a low, urgent whisper. 'Cécile said to tell you that they're looking for the family all over Annemasse. They've asked the Swiss border police to watch out for them, so you need to get them away from here quickly.'

'Where did she find them?' asked Valérie.

'In a woodsman's cottage outside the town. One of our supporters was there after looking for them in the area, and they just walked in.'

The young man carried on, 'Cécile asked me to help Jean get them out.' He looked behind him. 'I don't think anyone followed us. They went after the other Resistance fighters who were acting as a decoy, but they laid a trap that almost caught us. Madeleine didn't see it and cut her leg before we realised it was there.' He indicated Madeleine's leg and she saw a dark line of blood running down her calf.

She squatted down and pulled a handkerchief from her pocket, tying it around Madeleine's leg. 'I'm so sorry you hurt your leg, Madeleine. That should make it feel better.'

'Thank you, Madame,' replied Madeleine in a small, scared voice.

Valérie stroked her hair and then stood up again. 'Thank Cécile for me.'

Her words were drowned out by more shouting, coming from behind, and then a gunshot rang through the air. 'I'll lead them away,' hissed the young man, who ran back into the forest.

Jean and Valérie helped Anne-Marie and Madeleine as they all scrambled to the edge of the forest in the direction of the barn. They heard another gunshot, further away, and

Valérie couldn't help herself from thinking about the brave young man who was taking their fire, but they kept on running.

They reached the barn and let themselves inside. Yves had been watching for them and he pulled the door shut when they were all inside. Valérie helped Madeleine to sit down on some blankets in the corner of the barn. She was limping now, having run too far with her injured leg.

'What happens now?' asked Jean.

'They have to go,' said Valérie. 'Yves will take them.' She walked towards Anne-Marie and Madeleine to help them to stand up, but she heard a noise behind her and spun around.

Her heart plummeted and she almost lost her footing when she saw the men at the door, the familiar features of Schneider in the dim light.

'Get some more light in here,' he snapped. One of his men placed a powerful torch on the ground that filled the space with a bright yellow light.

Anne-Marie and Madeleine backed away from the Germans, Anne-Marie trying to shield her daughter, but there was nowhere to go.

A hand gripped Valérie's shoulder and she felt the sharp point of a pistol stuck in her ribs. She looked up to see a large man behind her and then across at Yves, but his arms were twisted behind his back and a pistol was pointed at his head. She was held so tightly that she could hardly move, and icy dread filled the pit of her stomach. There were only three Germans inside the barn, but she knew there would be more outside.

She almost glanced behind her, then stopped herself in time, terrified she might give away that they were not alone. Philippe, Christophe and Henry were there somewhere, waiting in the darkness. But they couldn't afford to shoot. There would be too many innocent victims.

Schneider waved his gloved hand and the Germans dragged

them forward into the pool of light. Valérie staggered and gripped a wooden post to stop her legs from giving way. Yves looked as scared as she felt, his face white and eyes wide with shock.

Jean backed away from the men, looking wildly around the barn. 'There is no way out...' said Schneider as he walked forward. 'Guard the door, so we aren't disturbed,' he snapped at one of the men, who walked past them to stand with his back to the front door. 'And you,' he said to the other man, 'get that bag of weapons, and look outside, there must be more.' The second soldier picked up the bag at Yves' feet and went outside. They heard a brief conversation and then François walked in and stood next to Schneider. 'There's a car out there loaded with guns and ammunition,' he said.

Valérie gasped and he looked at her as if she was a stranger.

'What's going on? What are you doing here?' Jean's voice was shrill with disbelief and horror.

Valérie saw Schneider frown when his eyes rested on François and his hand went to his pistol.

Jean was staring at his young cousin and Valérie had to look away from the raw pain in his face. 'No, you can't be working for them. You wouldn't.' He took a step towards him. 'Not you, François. What have they done to you?'

François' handsome features twisted, and he pulled out his own gun. Jean recoiled from his blazing eyes as if he'd been struck.

'Don't say any more,' hissed François. 'You're wasting your breath. They're going to win this war, whatever we do.'

'And you expect them to keep their word?' Jean pointed a shaking finger at Schneider. 'You trust them rather than me? They'll use you and then they'll kill you. After all I've done, is that how you pay me back?'

Schneider turned towards Yves, pointing the pistol at his chest. 'We haven't time for this. Shoot them and then we'll get what we came for.' François looked at him for a long moment and then nodded. That one shared look told Valérie everything she needed to know. François didn't care that he'd revealed his true allegiance because he knew there would be no witnesses left alive to testify against him.

'No... François... you can't do this.' Jean leapt forward to seize the gun and François tried to shake him off. Valérie held her breath as they struggled together, then the sound of a gunshot in the enclosed space deafened her.

Jean staggered and then fell on to his knees, clutching his side. Valérie ran to help him, and she and Yves laid him gently down on the rough floor, before she looked up at François, who was staring down at Jean, his face like a mask. François showed no feeling at all, almost as if he was outside them all, watching a scene in which he had no role to play. Valérie's terror hardened into rage, and she stood up to face him.

'It was you all along. You lied to us. All this time you were giving the Nazis information...'

'Who are you to judge?' he spat out, lifting his gaze from Jean. 'You don't know what it's like in France, none of you Swiss understand.'

Valérie knew they had very little time left. She looked at Anne-Marie, who was shielding Madeleine's eyes. François probably never knew Nathalie or the other people he'd betrayed, but there was someone he did know.

'You killed Emile, didn't you? You were the one who pushed him in front of the tram, because he suspected you.'

François looked back at her, his eyes glinting. 'Yes, I pushed Emile. He was onto me.' He gave a humourless laugh. 'Don't any of you realise? It's only a matter of time before the Germans win the war. He picked the wrong side, just like you have.'

Valérie saw Schneider aim his pistol in her direction. She closed her eyes and waited for the shot. It was too late to stop him. She had failed to save Nathalie, and Anne-Marie and Madeleine were going to die now too.

The gun went off in the enclosed space and she staggered but didn't fall. She felt her body and knew she hadn't been hit.

Then she looked up and saw Schneider on the ground, arm stretched out, the pistol still in his hand and François clutching his chest as he fell backwards. A few seconds later, more shots punctured the air and the Germans at the door crumpled into a heap. Two shadowy figures ran into the light from the back of the barn. She looked up to see Philippe and Christophe race towards her, and relief flooded through her body as Philippe caught her in his arms and she clutched on to him.

'I'm so sorry Valérie, Henry told us to wait until François admitted his guilt, so we were sure we had the right man. But it was so close, I nearly lost you.'

His face was pale under the dirt, and he shuddered and pulled her even closer. Turning in his arms, she watched Christophe go up to François' body and nudge it with his foot, as if he had to check he was really dead.

Henry had run over to Jean, who was still lying in Yves' arms. Yves looked up. 'He's hurt, but I think he'll be all right.'

Getting up shakily, Valérie walked over to Anne-Marie and Madeleine, who were sitting on the ground still clutching one another, as if they couldn't believe they were still alive. She crouched down and stroked the little girl's hair.

'You'll be safe now. It's all over. Someone will take you to Pierre and Jules.'

Anne-Marie held her hand and kissed it. 'Thank you. Without you, we wouldn't have a future.'

Valérie gathered them into her arms and whispered, 'When you're far away from here, just write to me and let me know how you are, how the children are. That's all I ask.'

She was aware of someone behind her, and Henry bent

down to help up Anne-Marie and Madeleine. 'Come with me. One of my men will take you to your family.'

When they'd gone, Valérie went back into Philippe's warm embrace, her heart still pounding, exhaustion washing over her. The only one who didn't seem affected by their narrow escape was Henry, and, as he walked back into the barn, Valérie wondered at his control and his complete mastery of the situation. He'd been so determined to unmask the traitor that he'd almost killed them all in the process. The same excitement she'd seen in him when he'd pushed his way through the border at Saint-Gingolph rippled through his voice as he spoke. 'Well done everyone. We managed it, but there is a lot of tidying up to do before we can relax.'

They were all looking at him. 'I've told one of my men to drive into Nyon and find an ambulance for Jean. We also have a van that will take the Nazi bodies and dump them over the border. We need to get them out of Switzerland to stop too many questions being asked.'

'Maybe he suspected François all along,' said Yves, still holding Jean, who was beginning to stir. 'Has he ever said that to you?'

'No.' Henry shook his head. 'He loved François like a brother, he was as shocked as we all were.'

He raised his voice. 'Hurry up. Let's get out of here. We'll have to change the plan,' he said to Philippe. 'I wanted to get you and Christophe back to the Fort tonight, but it's too late now.'

'Look out...' Christophe launched himself across the barn, pointing to where Schneider had fallen, the front of his coat covered in blood. The German's pistol wavered towards Valérie as she stood alone, and she froze, her breath caught in her throat.

Suddenly Philippe lunged in front of her, just as the shot

exploded through the air. His body jerked and he crashed backwards on to the ground.

Crying out, she sank down next to him, only barely aware of the barrage of shots above her head.

'Philippe, what have you done?'

She sobbed bitterly, trying to find his wound and stem the flow of blood. Every nerve in her body was screaming, her brain refusing to process what was happening. 'Don't leave me, Philippe.'

'Came here to protect you.' He had to stop speaking as a wave of pain hit him and he groaned. 'Couldn't let you get shot... I love you, Valérie.'

Then his head lolled back, his eyes closing as he lay in her arms.

THIRTY-THREE

VALÉRIE

Christophe and Yves rushed to her side as Philippe opened his eyes again and tried to move. He groaned, his face a sickly grey colour.

Valérie wiped the tears from her face with a shaking hand and looked up at Henry who was staring down at them, his expression impossible to read. 'He needs to get to a hospital, now.'

'My men should have found an ambulance by now. I'll go and look.'

'Where was he shot?' asked Christophe, who crouched down beside her.

'In the back... I can't reach it.'

She looked down at her hand, covered in blood, as Christophe took off his jacket, turned Philippe gently over and pressed it into his wound. Tears flooded down her cheeks as she held his hand, speaking to him softly, telling him to stay awake, that they'd be in the hospital soon and everything was going to be okay.

'They've found an ambulance,' Henry shouted from the door. 'The driver will take Philippe to Geneva. We'll take Jean to hospital by car.' Two of Henry's men lifted Philippe on to a stretcher as gently as they could, but the movement made him groan in pain.

They drove slowly out of Nyon and towards Geneva through the deserted streets to the cantonal hospital, Philippe groaning every time they hit a bump on the road. Valérie kept her eyes fixed on his face, terrified that his breathing was so weak, and stroked his hair gently. She wished, more than anything, that it had been her who had taken the bullet, not him.

At the hospital, Philippe was rushed straight into the emergency rooms, and she stayed in the waiting area.

After a few hours, Nicolas Cherix came running into the room. 'Where is he?'

'They've taken him straight to the operating theatre,' said Valérie quietly. 'It looks very bad.' Her voice broke and she leaned on his shoulder.

Over the next few hours, they looked up every time someone came into the waiting room. Then they were the only ones left. Several times Philippe's father had tried to persuade Valérie to go home but she shook her head wearily.

The door opened and a young doctor came into the room.

'Monsieur Cherix?'

They moved to get up but he waved his hand and pulled up a chair. Valérie studied his tired face, trying to read the expression, the tension unbearable.

'How is my son?'

'He's resting. You won't be able to see him, I'm afraid. Tomorrow he can have visitors.'

'But is he going to be all right?'

'Yes, he'll live. But the bullet went very close to his spine, so we don't know how much damage has been caused. We decided not to dig it out because that can do just as much damage.'

Valérie let out her breath in a long sigh. He would live. That was all she cared about for the moment, that she wouldn't lose him.

'We'll have to wait to see how well he recovers.'

'Will he make a full recovery?' said Philippe's father.

The doctor shook his head sadly. 'I'm sorry, I don't think so. If his spine is damaged as I think it is, he won't walk again.'

They were both stunned into silence. Valérie shook her head, unable to accept his words. 'But there's a chance he'll recover?'

'If he's very lucky and the bullet missed his spine, then he'll make a full recovery. The extensive bruising makes it difficult to tell how much damage has been caused. He's young and fit, which is a plus, but from my experience of these injuries, if the spine is damaged then there's very little we can do to help him.'

Philippe's father bent his head.

'Does he know?' asked Valérie.

'Yes. He insisted we tell him everything.'

The doctor looked at Valérie and smiled.

'His reaction was exactly the same as yours, full of hope. If there's any chance of recovering from this, that's what he'll aim for.'

———

They stopped outside Valérie's house and she saw her father come up to the car and open the door to help her out.

'I'll send a police car tomorrow afternoon to take you to the hospital. You need to get some sleep,' said Nicolas.

Valérie went inside with her father, feeling comforted by the familiar smell of the house, a wave of fatigue sweeping over her so that she stumbled in the hall. She leaned her head on his shoulder, and as he held her in his arms she told him what had happened, her sentences broken and confused.

'They don't know whether the bullet hit Philippe's spine or

not. He might not be able to walk again.' She stopped, sobs choking in her throat.

'Don't try to explain. He's alive. Everything else can wait until tomorrow.'

He helped her upstairs and she sat on the side of her bed. He took her shoes off as if she was a little girl and kissed her forehead. 'Get into bed and rest.'

'Don't let me sleep too late. I need to go to hospital to see Philippe.'

He nodded and closed the door. Valérie undressed in front of the mirror, took off the chain round her neck and kissed her engagement ring. Suddenly overcome with relief, she smiled through her tears. Philippe was alive and they would still have a future together. Anne-Marie and Pierre were reunited at last. Valérie climbed into bed. She knew that whatever else happened, she and Philippe would face it together. She pulled up the covers and was asleep the moment her head touched the pillow.

THIRTY-FOUR

VALÉRIE

Valérie woke late the next morning and made her way downstairs to find her father in the kitchen with Marianne, who got up to hug her.

Her father put a cup of hot chocolate in front of her. 'I'll leave you two alone.'

Valérie held the warm cup between her hands, breathing in the sweet chocolate smell. Marianne glanced at the clock on the wall.

'I had to come and see you. Sébastien isn't home and I'm so worried about him. He isn't the traitor, is he? I don't think I could bear it.'

Valérie leaned forward and grasped Marianne's hand, staring into her dark eyes. 'Sébastien is totally in the clear, he isn't the traitor. It was François.' She told her about the events of the night, and when she broke down at her memory of Philippe getting shot, Marianne squeezed Valérie's hands. 'I'm so sorry.'

Valérie paused. 'There's something else you need to know,' she said. 'François admitted that he killed Emile. After all this time, I finally found out who did it.'

Marianne pulled her hands away and covered her face.

'I'm sorry, Marianne.'

'No. I need to know the truth.' She wiped her eyes as Valérie's father opened the door. 'The police car is here to take you to the hospital Valérie.'

Marianne and Valérie walked out together, and at the door Valérie gave her friend a hug before her father handed her a parcel.

'Agathe put together a few things to take to Philippe.'

At the hospital, she saw Christophe and Yves smoking at the side of the main door. She jumped out of the car and ran towards them, trying to read their expressions.

'Have you seen Philippe? What have the doctors said this morning?' asked Valérie.

'Nothing more than they told you last night,' answered Christophe. 'The doctors say they'll have to wait and see.' He pointed to the car park where Henry was watching the entrance to the hospital. 'He took us to see Philippe and he's now waiting for his men to come and take us back to Saint-Maurice. He told Major Toussaint what we'd done and he's promised I should get more time off to visit Philippe.'

Christophe seemed to have a weight lifted from his shoulders.

'You got justice for Nathalie,' said Valérie.

He sighed. 'Nothing will bring her back, I know, but it helps that the men who killed her paid the price.'

Yves stood up from the balustrade. 'We're very proud of what she did. When I go home, we'll talk about the plans for her funeral. At least we have her back.'

Christophe suddenly bent his head. 'I just can't believe she's gone. On a bright day like this, with the sun shining. She loved the mountains in the summer, the flowers and the meadows.' He took out of his top pocket the edelweiss necklace. 'And this is all I have left,' he said, his voice cracking.

'They're here', shouted Henry, throwing away his cigarette and pointing towards the approaching car.

'Come on Christophe, we can go home now,' said Yves.

Valérie watched the car approach.

'Get in,' said Henry. 'Thank you for all you've done.' They shook hands very formally with Henry, hugged Valérie and got into the car.

Valérie waved until the car had turned the corner and disappeared from sight, then looked up at Henry, suddenly aware he was watching her rather than the car.

'I'm sorry, Valérie. I should have noticed last night that Schneider was still alive. I was too confident. Philippe was quicker than the rest of us to see the danger.' He swallowed and looked much less like the man in control. 'He wanted to kill you and he could so easily have done it.'

Valérie still didn't know which was the real Henry, the one who was bold, detached and always in control of an operation or the empathetic one who cared about her. But right now, she couldn't bring herself to care. All she wanted to do was go in and see Philippe, who was always just her Philippe, the man she loved.

His eyes softened as he looked at her. 'I'm going away.'

'Where are you going?'

'They're transferring me to the office in Zurich. I asked for a move.'

'Why?'

'I think you know why, Valérie.'

He stretched out his hand and pushed back a curl of her hair from her forehead, as if he couldn't stop himself from touching her. She backed away.

'I knew last night that I couldn't stay here and do my job properly. Because I waited so long to make sure we caught the traitor, you could have died. If it hadn't been for Philippe, you would have.'

'Who'll take over from you?'

'They're sending someone else to work with the Resistance. His job will be much easier now François isn't feeding information to the Gestapo. More agents will be dropped into France and the Maquis still needs arms and funding.'

He pulled out a letter from his pocket and gave it to her.

'What's this?'

She looked at the lines of neat black handwriting across the page of yellow paper.

'I was tidying up my office and found this. It's a note from my predecessor about Jacob Steinberg and the bookshop your mother used to work in. I'd never seen it before. The Nazis were after him in the 1930s. They never found the information they were seeking, and Jacob thought they might come back. You must be careful if you're still using that place.'

He looked at the door to the hospital as a family came out.

'You'll be spending a lot of time here with Philippe, I guess. He'll need you now, while he's recovering.'

Valérie looked at Henry and his gaze dropped first. She had succeeded in saving Anne-Marie and Madeleine and in reuniting their family, but she knew that Henry's priorities had been different that night. For him, it was all about the traitor, and if there had been a choice, he would have sacrificed them all.

She walked away from him, knowing he was watching her until the door closed, and she pushed the letter into her satchel, looking for Philippe's ward. Taking a deep breath at the door, she pushed it open and walked in, smiling at him when he turned towards her. 'I hoped you'd come.'

'Of course. I'll be here every day until you get better.'

She sat down next to the bed, and he closed his fingers round her hand.

'I can't sit up, they don't know if I'll be able to walk again. You might not want to come and see an invalid every day.'

She bent down and kissed him.

'I'll come to see you as often as they'll let me. I love you Philippe. Do you think I'd leave you now?'

EPILOGUE

Two weeks later, Valérie stood outside the Saint-Maurice parish church in the late afternoon sun after Nathalie's simple funeral. Philippe was still in too much pain to come with her, but she watched as his father spoke to Nathalie's family. Nicolas had said he would drive her to Saint-Maurice, and she could see that it was important for him to be there. Nathalie's death and Philippe's accident had affected him profoundly.

Christophe came to stand next to her. He looked utterly bereft, as if his life's anchor had been swept away, his eyes red above dark shadows. 'How's Philippe? I miss him at the Fort.'

She smiled up at him. 'The doctors think the bullet may have missed his spine. It's early days yet, but they're hopeful he'll recover.' She didn't say how tentative the doctors were, but it was enough to see how her words lifted his spirits.

Nathalie's aunt came up and embraced her. 'I wanted to tell you how much happiness you brought to my house that awful night. When Anne-Marie and Madeleine came in, the joy blazing from all their faces was almost too blinding to witness. It was a wonderful moment. I hope they're all safe now.'

Valérie felt the familiar worry rise and she shook her head. 'I don't know, I've had no news from them yet.'

Before they left, they walked to Nathalie's graveside and placed their bunches of sweetly smelling edelweiss flowers on the fresh mound of earth. Valérie looked up into the sky, dappled blue and white, the sun bright and warm on her face.

Somewhere out there, she hoped Nathalie knew how loved she was. Without a doubt, the Germans had tried to get her to reveal the location of Pierre and Jules, and Nathalie had not betrayed them. She died a hero, and her sacrifice was not in vain. She would never be forgotten.

It was several months later when Valérie received the letter she'd been waiting for.

Ma chère Valérie

I am so glad to be able to write this letter to you. We are safe in the mountains and for the first time can be happy. We went to the address we were given, and the family there moved us further into Switzerland for our safety. The children have already made friends here and they're enjoying a normal child-hood once again.

I hope you and Philippe are safe now. There are no words to thank you for all that you have done. All I can say is that you have given us back our lives.

I have some joyful news for you. I have had a little girl. She came early and is small, but she is perfect. We're going to call her Valérie.

I was so sorry to hear about your friend Nathalie, Pierre told me how kind she'd been to them and how she'd tried to help find us.

When this war is over, I promise that we'll come and find you. Jules talks about you all the time.

In the meantime, please stay safe.

Thank you again,

Anne-Marie Weil

A LETTER FROM DIANNE

Thank you so much for reading *Under a Brighter Sky*.

If you enjoyed it, and want to keep up to date with all my latest releases, just sign up at the following link. Your email address will never be shared and you can unsubscribe at any time.

www.bookouture.com/dianne-haley

Before I wrote this book, I knew that Switzerland was neutral in WW2. What I didn't know was how many Swiss citizens helped Jewish refugees escape from occupied France. Despite the opposition of the Swiss authorities and often at great risk to themselves, they helped desperate people reach safety.

I also wasn't aware of the boom in the Swiss art market throughout the war because of art stolen from Jewish families across occupied Europe by the Nazi authorities. Even now, eighty years later, the discovery of hidden art works, and their rightful owners, shows the extent of the brutal theft that took place at that time.

If you enjoyed the story, it would be great if you could leave a short review. I appreciate all feedback from readers. It also helps to persuade other readers to pick up one of my books for the first time.

You can also get in touch through my Facebook page, Twitter, Goodreads or my website.

Thanks,

Dianne

diannehaley.com

 twitter.com/dhaley30

ACKNOWLEDGEMENTS

Thanks to Martin for his knowledge of Switzerland's geography, and his assistance with editing and developing my website. Thanks also to Alexander, Alice and Claire for proof-reading, editing support and social media guidance. I am grateful to Jean Weir and Norma Main for information on the 1940s, to Dr Winnie Weir and Dr Helen Macleod on medical matters, and to Kirsty, Katherine, Heather and Rachel Knott on French language and grammar. Thanks also to my writing buddies Jenny Harper, Jennifer Young and Lorna Fraser for their critiques and unfailing support, and to my outstanding editor Rhianna Louise, without whose ideas and encouragement I would not have realised the finished books.

Printed in Great Britain
by Amazon

42017331R00148